A FEAR OF DARK PLACES

A DI KIDSTON CRIME THRILLER
BOOK 2

JOHN HARKIN

BLOODHOUND
— BOOKS —

ALSO BY JOHN HARKIN

The DI Kidston Crime Thrillers

The Fear of Falling

———

Short Stories

Dancer. *Written in the Stars: An Anthology of Festive Short Stories*

For Ross

"Hope not ever to see Heaven. I have come to lead you to the other shore; into eternal darkness; into fire and into ice."

– Dante Alighieri, *Inferno*

CHAPTER ONE

WEDNESDAY, 25 JULY 1990

The seduction was following familiar lines. The boy had been happy to accept an invitation to do some landscaping work. For cash. The big houses in Pollokshields were a good source for casual work; painting and decorating, gardening, or landscaping. The job was laying fresh slabs for a new path in the back garden of a large, detached villa. It was a hot afternoon. On completing the paving job, the boy removed his T-shirt and dabbed the perspiration trickling down his impressively muscled abdomen as he slugged at a chilled bottle of Perrier.

That was the trigger.

'You can grab a quick shower through there, second on the right.' The man indicated a door into the main hallway. 'There's towels and a dressing gown in there you can use.'

'That would be great,' the boy said.

He returned ten minutes later dressed in a blue cotton monogrammed dressing gown, dabbing his still-wet hair with a towel and carrying his clothes in his other hand. 'That was a brilliant shower, thanks.'

'How about some extras?' the older man asked with a

recognisable look as he waved a brown envelope in one hand. With the other he folded two twenty-pound notes around the envelope. 'Forty above what we agreed?'

'For what?' The boy flashed his biggest smile. He knew how to play this game.

'For sex.' The man's soft brown eyes shone with desire. 'Let me start by helping you get dried off.' He reached for the towel, the boy pressing the damp cotton material into his hand. 'You're still very sweaty.' The man dabbed at the tanned, hard body.

'I don't take it up the arse, but for that you can give me a blow job.'

The man dropped to his knees and frantically pulled at the dressing-gown cord, opening the garment fully around the boy's torso and behind his hips. The boy towered over him. He was about twenty years younger but taller and in much better physical shape than his suitor. He was impressively hung, even when soft, and the man started to fellate him. Gently at first, his greedy mouth building up the speed of the thrusts as the boy grew harder. More frantic now.

'Easy, tiger.' The boy grabbed the man's hair to control the pace. 'Watch those teeth.'

The man looked up at the boy, imploringly. Wide-eyed and pleading. He caressed the edge of his hand along the cleft of the boy's firm buttocks, his forefinger hovering close to the sweet spot. Very close. Too close for comfort.

'No chance.' The boy stiffened and brought the movement to an abrupt stop, the man's head held tightly and immobile in his hands. He glared down at the man with cold dark eyes, something evil in his stare. 'I told you. I'm not some fucking homo. Is this what you want?' The boy pulled out and masturbated the final few strokes needed to ejaculate over the man's face.

'I'm sorry... I'm sorry.' The man was cowed now. 'Just take your money and go... please go.'

'You think I'm just some fucking rent boy you can dismiss with your money and your big fancy house.' The boy slipped the dressing-gown cord from its loops and twisted it around the man's neck. 'Is this what you fuckin' want?' He pulled tight on the cord and moved behind the still kneeling man. With his knee forced between the man's shoulder blades, the boy tugged and pulled. The man clawed frantically at the tightly wound fibres that were depriving him of speech. And oxygen. His wide brown eyes implored his assailant, *please no... please no.* But the boy pulled harder, twisted tighter until he saw the light go out in those sad frightened eyes. The man's face formed into a grotesque mask; eyes bulging, tongue purple and protruded. It was a familiar expression, and it stirred the boy's memory. When he released his grip on the cord, the man's limp, lifeless body collapsed to the floor.

The boy's pulse was racing now, his heart thumping in his chest. He slowed his breathing and surveyed the room. It was a large day room extended from an equally large kitchen with a long island unit with a double sink. Adjacent was a sizeable utility room with an old-fashioned clothesline pulley. His mind raced through the possibilities. He dragged the body the short distance to the utility room and lined it up below the pulley. Unhooking the rope from its bracket, he pulled it down and watched the empty clothesline rise to the high ceiling. Fully extended, it was long enough to do the job he needed. He ripped one of the furrowed wheel-track fixtures out of the ceiling, bringing down a cloud of plaster and dust. He fashioned a noose from the rope – seven turns would be enough – and slipped it over the man's neck. He pulled the noose tight, lifting the limp body from the floor. Right under the neck, in the same position as where the dressing-gown cord had cut off his life.

A kitchen footstool was added to the scene, forming a convincing tableau.

The boy leaned over the corpse and used the flap of the dressing gown to wipe a large glob of ejaculate from the man's forehead. He grabbed a damp tea towel from the kitchen counter and wiped all remaining traces of his spunk from the man's face and hair. As he dabbed at the dead man's face, he saw that the eyes were fixed wide open in that familiar grotesque stare. He patted around the unbreathing mouth, the swollen protruded tongue and placed the towel back in its original position.

He slipped the cord back through its loops and returned the dressing gown to the hook behind the shower-room door before changing back into his own clothes. He'd entered via the patio doors from the back garden and would leave by the same route. The rear garden was protected by tall hedges and was accessed from a high-walled back lane. There was a fair chance he wouldn't be seen. As he was leaving, the boy did a final survey of the room to reassure himself. He noticed a pale-wood-framed family picture of the man with what looked like his wife, son, and daughter. The entire scene looked like a tragic suicide.

He was never there.

CHAPTER TWO

TUESDAY, 14 AUGUST 1990

'Stay away from Kidston, I'm warning you.' Graeme Lindsay waved a finger at his client. 'You've got a two-year suspended jail sentence hanging over your head.'

Phil Canavan pulled on the metallic fingers of his prosthetic with his good left hand. He detested his fake limb – not much more than a mannequin's hand and a constant source of humiliation and a painful reminder of how he was bested by a madman the newspapers had named the Gorbals Samurai. He had just turned forty-one, tall and lean with close-cropped dark-brown hair, but the last three and a half years had required some difficult adjustments – physically and emotionally. Those who knew Canavan best would say he'd become withdrawn and lost much of his spark. They saw it in the haunted look in his eyes. 'But you agreed with me. Kidston could have done more to prevent this... this!' Canavan held the metal-and-rubber prosthetic limb up for the lawyer to inspect more closely.

'I did everything I could,' Lindsay said. 'I kept you out of jail and that was mostly down to your injury but I'm not a miracle worker, I can't get Kidston sacked. He was hailed as a hero after the trial.'

They were in Graeme Lindsay's plush offices in Carlton Place discussing recent correspondence regarding Canavan's case. Strathclyde Police had responded to the latest in a series of his lawyer's letters threatening to sue the force and alleging dereliction of duty by Detective Inspector Luc Kidston of the Gorbals CID, on the night Canavan's right hand had been severed by a samurai sword.

'Hero,' scoffed Canavan. 'He should have been sacked or at least demoted.'

Lindsay gave him a sour look. 'I warned you that a successful legal action against Strathclyde Police was unlikely, but you insisted, despite my advice to the contrary.'

'I wanted compensation.' Canavan glowered at his lawyer. 'I will have retribution.'

'You need to forget all that revenge stuff, Phil. You're respectable now, running Sarah's nightclub is a fresh start and a chance to put your criminal past behind you.'

Canavan's malevolent smile gave little away. He *was* respectable now, managing his little sister's nightclub. Sarah Canavan had acquired the spacious townhouse premises in Carlton Place on the south bank of the River Clyde. With its cobbled road surface and elegant Georgian townhouses formed by two long, neoclassical terraces of blonde sandstone, Carlton Place – the same location as Graeme Lindsay's office – was the premier showpiece address for the old Laurieston district. It connected to the north side of the river and Glasgow's city centre by the landmark South Portland Street suspension bridge. It was a brilliant location and a great venue for a nightclub with four floors including a basement. Sarah had worked with the builders, developers, designers, and marketing experts to create a buzz for her new venture. She'd named it Goodnights.

'You know I've transferred all my other business assets to Marty Sutherland.'

'Of course,' Lindsay said, 'and Goodnights should be more than enough for you to reinvent yourself as a legitimate businessman. Plenty of opportunities.'

Lindsay was right but the lawyer wasn't aware of the full picture. The club was proving adept at laundering money and evading tax, just like Sarah said it would. She was listed as the licensee and had asked her big brother to manage the place. It was his sister's way of drawing him out of his old life. And it had worked – up to a point. It was easy enough to transfer his heroin business to Sutherland, who was a trusted criminal associate. A substantial sum of money changed hands for an introduction to his Liverpool suppliers and his network of dealers. The changeover went efficiently; no blood was shed. Canavan still had enough muscle, clout and firepower to take on any rival, but his heart wasn't in it anymore. Canavan was out of the heroin business. But there was just one major snag. Goodnights presented a potentially new and lucrative market for cocaine, ecstasy, and poppers. Not the legitimate business opportunities that Graeme Lindsay was thinking about, but Phil Canavan couldn't resist it.

'So you'll drop all this vendetta nonsense with Kidston?' Lindsay asked.

'The man is fucking haunting me,' Canavan snapped back. 'He's determined I go back to jail.' Detective Inspector Kidston had thwarted Canavan's final big drugs deal when the Gorbals CID had picked up the buyer for his last ever consignment of heroin. After selling his heroin operation to Sutherland, the quality and price of a junkie's heroin fix varied until the new network settled down. Canavan had held on to some product by way of a pension plan. Two weeks ago, Canavan had brokered a deal to sell his last kilogram block of heroin for twenty thousand pounds to Marty Sutherland, who'd taken over the city's south-side trade. Sutherland had jumped at the deal and Canavan knew he would cut the heroin, adulterate it with all kinds of shit, and dilute the purity to a fifth or sixth of its original strength. The standard 'tenner bag' was a universal price point for street heroin but the dealer would decide the purity of a junkie's fix. Canavan was none the wiser as to what went wrong but the handover arranged for a late evening meeting in the quiet back streets of the Lawmoor industrial estate had been ambushed by the police. Kidston's plain-clothed detectives had jumped all over the cash and drugs with the couriers from both sides being arrested. His man, young Arthur Penman, was loyal and trusted. Both couriers were mid-level operatives, and it was highly unlikely that any fallout would reach as far as their bosses. One of Graeme Lindsay's legal associates would attempt to keep any custodial sentence for young Penman to a minimum, but both men would do their jail time and keep schtum.

Recalling his lost heroin reanimated Canavan's angst over his long-time nemesis. His lawyer had spent over two years on lawsuits and criminal injuries compensation claims, but now they'd run out of road. *How could Kidston be off the hook?* 'I had a gun, but I was only defending myself from a maniac rushing at me with a sword. That defence case you offered at the trial: that Kidston could have given me permission to shoot or commandeered my gun to stop me being attacked, that was a sound legal argument.'

'Hmm,' Lindsay pondered. 'I managed to persuade the judge and jury that you'd fired a warning shot. The fact that you were a victim, and the severity of your injury were the reasons the judge went easy on you.'

'Easy! Fucking easy?! What's so easy about going through the rest of my life with a tin hand?'

'Look, Phil. The police letter makes it crystal clear. There's no payout, no disciplinary action against Kidston. The letter quotes the judge's comments, "Detective Inspector Kidston, despite the twin threats against his life, remained calm and composed to ensure that this grave incident was resolved without loss of life". They've stonewalled it.'

'That's why I want to send Johnny Boy and the team to visit him with a couple of baseball bats. See how he likes spending three weeks in hospital.'

'Stay away from Kidston, I'm warning you.'

'And that prosecutor,' Canavan continued. 'He made it clear to the jury that I was not the victim that you portrayed. He could be doing with a visit from the boys to wipe that arrogant smile off his face.'

'Stay away from Ryan Ferrier and from Kidston,' Lindsay restated. 'You need to understand, if you harass either of them, it's straight to jail – do not pass go!'

CHAPTER THREE

W hen DI Luc Kidston and DS Gregor Stark entered the back door of Gorbals police office, their two uniformed community policing colleagues, constables Peter Costello and Chrissie McCartney, were standing at the uniform bar examining a stolen car radio cassette player for identification markings. With his massive height and build, the stereo looked like a toy in Costello's large hands. The big cop with the ruggedly handsome face and thick shock of white hair had been Kidston's tutor when the detective was a rookie fresh out of police college.

'Chrissie's just recovered this, Inspector,' Costello said. 'What do you think?'

'That looks like a Blaupunkt, Chrissie.' Kidston picked up the car stereo from the countertop and gave it the once-over. 'Nice bit of quality hi-fi, similar to mine but hopefully it's still in my BMW.' He handed the item to Stark.

The young detective sergeant scrutinised the item and placed it back on the counter. 'Managed to get that out without too much damage. Where's it from?'

'I caught Kevin Kelly screwing a black Ford Capri behind

the community centre.' The little policewoman was grinning from ear to ear. She pushed her shoulder-length blonde hair behind her ears. 'Tried to run away but I was too quick for him.'

'Good capture, Chrissie,' Kidston said. Stark nodded his approval.

The giant Costello beamed down at his diminutive colleague like a proud father. 'We think Kelly's been very active around the area of the community centre and the church but, of course, he's only putting his hands up for this one.'

'I think he's done more,' McCartney said. 'Peter's going to get a warrant to search his house.'

'We might not need a warrant,' Kidston informed her. 'Would Kelly know the "duty solicitor" sketch?' He directed his question at Costello.

'I doubt it,' Costello said. 'Kelly's just a young tearaway.'

Kidston had a quick look at the detainee through the detention-room window to confirm he'd never encountered Kelly before. He was a gawky nineteen-year-old, with a bad complexion and a nasty shell suit. 'Sergeant Baillie, duty solicitor to see Master Kelly.'

'Inspector.' Tam Baillie gave a knowing wink and pulled open the drawer under the bar counter. It contained dozens of unsolicited business cards from lawyers.

Kidston shuffled through the cards and selected one that he liked the look of. The card was printed in high gloss white paper with gold print and read *Fraser Kilpatrick Solicitors Limited*, and the lawyer's details were for a *Mr Gordon Fraser LLB (Hons)*.

Baillie opened the detention-room door. 'Somebody to see you, Kevin.'

Kidston stepped into the room and sat his lean six-foot-two frame down on the bench beside Kelly. 'Gordon Fraser, duty solicitor.' Kelly examined the card and seemed suitably impressed. With his taste for sober-coloured expensive suits, the handsome DI could easily pass for a lawyer. His unruly mop of raven-black hair was worn longer than regulation and was unlikely to identify him as a police detective. 'What have they charged you with, Kevin?'

'That wee poliswoman caught me screwing a Capri,' Kelly said sheepishly. 'I was away wi' the radio cassette.'

'Are they keeping you in for court, or letting you out?' Kidston's pale-green eyes fixed on an enormous plook on Kelly's forehead that looked close to erupting.

'They want me to admit all the other motors that I've screwed, and they'll let me go.'

'Just admit to the one they've arrested you for, Kevin. How many have you actually done?'

'I've done eight,' Kelly said with a sly smile, seemingly determined to impress his legal representative.

'You need to be careful, Kevin,' Kidston began. 'The police will want to search your flat and if they find eight stereos, you'll be in much bigger trouble. If you give me the name of a girlfriend or a pal, I can maybe get them shifted before the police put your door in. Unless you've sold them on?'

'Naw, naw, they're at my ma's.'

'Have you stashed them, or does she know that they're there?' Kidston asked. 'I can ask her to get them shifted in case the police come calling.'

'Naw, my ma knows where I've planked them. They're in the back of the hall cupboard, under an auld bedspread.'

'I can get word to her if you want, get them moved on before the police come knocking on her door?'

'Good man, my ma will know what to do, thanks.'

Kidston took a note of the address. 'Now, Kevin, remember just admit to the one you were caught for. Better give me back my business card, I'll get the desk sergeant to put it in your property bag.'

Kidston knocked on the glass of the detention-room door to signal that the interview was over and left the teenage criminal mastermind to reflect on how his lawyer had helped him get one over on the polis.

―――

Kidston scribbled down Mrs Kelly's address and handed it to McCartney. 'You'll find eight more car stereos in the hall cupboard, under an old bedspread. If his mammy admits to hiding them, you can threaten her with a reset charge but I'm sure she'll provide a statement that Kevin stashed them there.' Kidston grinned at the young policewoman. 'There you go, Chrissie, a nine-charge rollup; you're doing a brilliant job on my crime figures.'

McCartney beamed back at the DI, her smile a higher wattage than usual. 'Thanks, boss, that's brilliant. Every day's a school day.'

'Let me know if you need a hand to write up the case.' Stark flashed his brightest smile at his uniformed colleague, accentuating his boyish good looks. At thirty-two, Stark still looked like a young trainee detective, despite having over three years in the detective sergeant rank. 'A nine-charge rollup can be quite complex.'

'I think Chrissie's more than capable of writing up this case.' Costello bristled at the young DS. 'But thanks for the offer, Sergeant.'

Kidston tore the business card into tiny pieces and dropped them into the bin. 'Right, Sergeant Baillie, where do I collect my legal aid fees?'

CHAPTER FOUR

'Hey, tin haun, show us your claw.' The two young boys sped past him on their bikes.

Canavan had walked to the corner shop to buy himself an evening newspaper. On the way back he was scanning the sports headlines on the folded back page, the paper held one-handed. His prosthetic was tucked into his jerkin pocket.

'Fuck off!' Canavan gesticulated a 'get it right up you' with his folded *Evening Times*, but it didn't quite have the effect he was after. The two laughing boys were oblivious to his response as they accelerated off into the distance. Canavan had to admire their boldness but, once upon a time, he would have battered them or got Johnny Boy to give them a kicking. They might come again. Three years ago, he'd have used them as bike couriers to deliver tenner bags of heroin into the housing schemes.

Back in his own home, later that evening, Canavan reflected on his lawyer's words of warning. He'd tried and failed to take Kidston down through legal redress, and still, the detective loomed over him like a malignant shadow. His two-year suspended jail sentence had forced him out of the heroin trade, and he was living his life under the constant threat of imprisonment. He recalled Kidston's words after the trial: 'You're lucky, Phil, your operations and your tin hand have prevented you going to jail but that sentence means if you step one foot out of line, they'll be preparing a nice cell for you at Barlinnie, and I'll be watching you.' Canavan had retained his money lending business but was aware he couldn't afford any slip-ups. That bastard Kidston was determined to take him down.

Canavan's paranoia festered.

Even the ten-year-old Laphroaig he was sipping couldn't eliminate his sour disposition. A couple of lines of coke would see him right. He would do them later but was already savouring the prospect. In ten years of running the heroin trade in Glasgow's south side, Canavan had never once sampled the product. No way. He'd seen the effects of heroin on his clients. It never bothered him that the addicts had turned into an army of sub-human zombies. It never bothered him that young lives were destroyed. So long as his customers were able to rob, steal or borrow enough cash to buy their next tenner bag, Canavan was satisfied. But things were different now; the pace of his own cocaine dependency had surprised him. Two lines now, when one had been enough before. The intoxicating high of the drug lasting for a shorter time. That's how addiction worked – he knew that. Was he an addict? He would deny it; argue that he could walk away any time, but he chose not to.

Sometimes your drug chooses you.

Psychologically, he still had nightmares, recalling the terror of the attack, which had affected him more than he would ever admit. The euphoric high he got from cocaine eased his pain and erased the shameful memory of his humiliation. The trauma of the amputation left him with a constant ache in his stump. Full rehabilitation was never a possibility, and it was over three years since the attack. Chronic phantom limb syndrome, the doctors termed it. And as if the pain wasn't bad enough, there was the itching; an incessant angry itch he couldn't scratch on a hand that wasn't even there. And it drove him mad.

He poured himself another Laphroaig – a large one – and contemplated the detective that had dogged him most of his adult life. The whisky tiptoed on his palate; the smoky, peaty flavours, and the subtlest hint of seaweed that made the Islay malt so distinctive. It was Kidston, then a rookie detective constable, that put him in prison first time around at age twenty-six; a bad stabbing and the police had charged attempted murder. But he did the eighteen-month sentence easy. He was big Davie Canavan's boy; nobody was going to lay a finger on him. And he had the scar by then – his *Mars Bar*, as his loyal lieutenant, Johnny Boy referred to it; a two-inch scar that ran off the left side of his mouth. The deep, ragged gouge blighted his otherwise handsome features, but it helped forge his reputation as a hardman and a blade artist. He'd worn his battle scar with pride; it gave him the authenticity he craved and struck fear into his enemies. Now, wee boys in the street laughed at him.

He recalled a therapy workshop during his first incarceration in Barlinnie. A long-haired, hippie psychologist had asked if he was a naturally violent person. Canavan gave the man his answer: he never had any choice in the matter. From the time he stole a craft knife from his first-year high-school pottery class, Canavan lived by the blade. Stab or be stabbed. In the working-class housing schemes of Glasgow – the 'No Mean City' that spawned the razor gangs, the expectation of violence was all-pervasive. His late father was a violent man, who'd dished out terrible punishments to anyone who crossed him. When young Canavan stabbed his first victim, it wasn't about fear but survival. Back then, he'd been a victim just that one time – never again. He became the aggressor, enjoyed it and the reputation that went with it. The vicious cycle had begun and soon he was addicted to the adrenaline high of violence.

Sometimes your drug chooses you.

Sarah was very strict on her no drug dealing rule at Goodnights for fear of losing her liquor licence. 'If punters bring their own drugs with them, then it's not on us,' she had said. Phil had selected Billy Bannerman, the head steward, as his principal dealer for the club – and stressed that any deals were conducted without Sarah's knowledge. She had insisted that Thursday nights were gay nights. Following the success of Bennets nightclub in the nearby Merchant City, Glasgow had seen a massive expansion of the city's gay night-time economy. Ever the shrewd businesswoman, Sarah wanted to capitalise on what she called the pink pound. Knowing that Bennets ran a straight night on Thursdays, she hosted a gay night at Goodnights, and it was an instant success.

Bannerman, a veteran of all-nighters at Wigan Casino and Manchester's Hacienda Club in the heyday of Northern Soul, knew his way around pharmaceuticals. Eccies and poppers were very popular on a Thursday night. Phil Canavan hated gays; found them a strange and hysterical breed. But he was happy to take their money. He was pleasantly surprised by how much cash flowed through the nightclub. The mark-up on booze was astonishing, even more so for soft drinks. Sarah was able to sell off her chain of tanning salons and transition the business into the nightclub. She'd kept on some of her best girls to work as hostesses for the VIP lounge that she ran in the basement of Goodnights. There was cash money everywhere and Sarah did her own books, ensuring that the taxman took a minimum.

Canavan emptied a gram of coke from a small polythene bag and, using a credit card, piled it into two neat lines on his glass tabletop. He fished a little silver snuff spoon and straw set from his trouser pocket and set about the white powder. Canavan snorted the first line in a quick sweep, sniffing loudly, and shaking his head vigorously as the stimulant hit the spot. The second line followed immediately. The familiar dopamine high raced to his brain, his heart rate quickening as the drug coursed through his veins. *Satisfaction guaranteed.* This was great coke, high purity, undiluted. He should know; he'd been cutting his heroin with all kinds of shit to max out his profits. But this was the good stuff. Canavan thumbed some residual powder into his gums and rinsed it through with a mouthful of Laphroaig.

Feeling no pain.

The comedown would be brutal. But at least he was alone. He hated those coke users who got themselves overexcited, gibbering a lot of pish and yakking like weans. Not for him, if he couldn't get one of Sarah's girls to join him, he'd rather be alone, put a decent Western video on. You can keep your De Niro and your Pacino; they're both decent actors but not a patch on his big screen idols: James Stewart and John Wayne. The VHS tapes were piled up on the big TV unit: *The Man Who Shot Liberty Valance*, *The Searchers*, and his all-time favourite, *The Magnificent Seven*. He was in a *Liberty Valance* kind of mood and would watch it for the umpteenth time. He could recite the dialogue off by heart: *'This is the West, sir. When the legend becomes fact, print the legend'*.

Sated by his coke high, Canavan sipped his malt and let the Laphroaig linger on his palate, that hint of mossy peat satisfying his whisky yearnings. It was other hungers; a different thirst that tormented his unquiet soul. The craving for vengeance gnawed away at him. Kidston would pay for his missing hand. A sketchy plan was forming in his head; there may be a way to get his drugs money back. He stared into his glass. It wasn't a conversation; the whisky gave no answer. He swirled his vengeful thoughts in amber regrets.

He poured the last of the Laphroaig. He could taste the rich flavour now, savouring it. He stared at the ugly stump on his right arm. His *disability* – how he hated that word. Drinking with his left hand had never felt right. Such a simple, everyday matter but it still felt odd that the basic motor function of raising a glass was lost; it made his stump twitch. The challenge of doing everything left-handed had proven extremely difficult. Wearing a tie was an impossibility. He could hold a malt whisky wrong-handed, brush his teeth, and wipe his own arse. He had plenty of aides to drive him around in the Merc, but he couldn't give himself a decent wank.

He removed his prosthetic whenever he was at home; it was easier just to do without it and much less time rubbing ointment into his stump. There were two; the newest one was modern flesh-toned polycarbonate that looked reasonably lifelike – so long as you didn't look too closely. *Passive* or *cosmetic*, the therapist had described it, meaning that it was fucking useless to him. *A mannequin's hand.* The older one was heavier – a rubber-covered light metal, possibly a prototype, but the prosthetic socket had been a comfortable fit over his forearm. There had been drawers full of false limbs; leather, plastic and even wood. One of those drawers had contained his preferred hand. After use, the original prosthetic became damaged, the artificial skin covering peeling off in several places. Canavan had skinned all the rubber layer away to leave a menacing-looking metallic hand – a steel claw. He'd fashioned the tip of the metal forefinger into a sharp blade that could slice an apple. Or slash human flesh. Canavan dreamed of the day he could use it to rip Detective Inspector Luc Kidston's throat.

CHAPTER FIVE

THURSDAY, 16 AUGUST 1990

Chrissie McCartney almost spewed up her breakfast when she saw the bloody crime scene. The deceased was sprawled on an armchair, trousers around his ankles, his torso a seeping, bloody mess. There was so much blood that it was barely discernible that the deceased had been wearing a white shirt. His throat had been cut. A trail of crimson ran from his crotch, leaking into the upholstery, and pooled onto an expensive-looking rug. His genitalia had been mutilated, with the penis sliced off and stuffed into his mouth.

'That's definitely Ryan Ferrier, the procurator fiscal,' said Costello. 'Hard to identify him with the bloody mess on his face, but this is his home.' The house in Queen Mary Avenue, Crosshill was a large, detached sandstone villa, located in a small pocket of high value properties between Crosshill railway station and the Queen's Park recreation ground.

'With his family?' McCartney asked.

'Ferrier is gay... or was gay,' the big cop corrected himself. 'I don't think there was any other family staying here.'

McCartney returned to the outside front door of the house to attend Ferrier's cleaner who'd called 999 when she opened the house for her weekly cleaning and laundry duties. The poor woman was in a state of shock. McCartney gave her a seat in the rear of her panda car. When the cleaner had composed herself, McCartney noted a brief statement from her but asked her to wait until detectives could speak to her. Costello radioed for the duty casualty surgeon, police supervisors and for the CID to attend. He then went to the boot of the panda car and lifted out a roll of police barrier tape and cordoned off the area outside the large, detached house. The blue-and-white tape was looped around lampposts and metal gates to delineate and protect the initial crime scene.

'Chrissie,' Costello directed McCartney, 'can you note the registration number of every car in the street, two hundred yards either side of the murder house? One of them might be connected to the suspect and it might not be here tomorrow.' The young policewoman didn't argue with her much more experienced neighbour. Costello was the senior member of the community policing team with twenty-five years on the job and possessed the most natural policing instincts she'd ever seen. McCartney had been *'neighboured up'* with Costello for over four years and he was a first-class mentor. At twenty-seven, the former bank clerk from leafy, suburban Bearsden had just witnessed her grisliest crime scene in her eight years of police service.

By the time McCartney returned to the cordon, Costello was lifting the tape to allow a CID car to access the scene. At six feet five, the big cop afforded plenty of headroom for the blue, unmarked Ford Escort. It was DI Luc Kidston with DS Gregor Stark in attendance. They formed up at the entrance gate and Costello briefed the two detectives.

'It's pretty gruesome,' Costello said. 'A lot of blood. Dead overnight, by the look of it.'

'Straight in, straight out?' Kidston asked.

'Never touched anything,' Costello replied. 'Cleaning lady discovered him at 1000 hours, poor woman is in total shock. Chrissie managed to get a brief statement from her, and she'll drive her home when you gents are done with her.'

'You okay, Chrissie?' Kidston asked.

'I'm good thanks, boss. Nearly brought up my bacon roll. It's a hellish sight. Poor man's been butchered.'

'And it's definitely Ryan Ferrier?' Kidston asked.

'Very little doubt,' Costello replied. 'That white Cavalier in the driveway is registered to him. Chrissie's noted all the car registrations in the street. We'll add the list to our statements back at the station.'

'Good thinking, Peter,' Kidston said.

The two detectives donned white, hooded forensic suits and protective overshoes. Both men wore rubber gloves and cautiously entered the house. It was a grand, high-ceilinged lounge, tastefully decorated. Full height bay windows with long, heavy drapes in embroidered gold. A high gloss-black baby grand piano dominated the lounge, but the signature piece was a classic Le Corbusier chaise longue, upholstered in brown-and-white hide. It looked authentic. And very expensive. The deceased was slumped in a light-brown armchair of plush woollen fabric and positioned close to a stone fireplace. On a low side table sat a partially consumed meal, a three-quarters empty bottle of red wine and a half full wine glass. One wall was fully encased by a large display unit and bookcase stocked with books and objet d'art. The other walls contained oil paintings, watercolours and artworks including a giant framed vintage *Ballet Rambert* poster. Kidston recognised a large oil painting above the lounge fireplace as the work of Glasgow artist, Stephen Conroy. Another smaller painting, a still life in oil was definitely a Peploe. But it was the sprawled, bloodied body of the dead lawyer who demanded the detectives' attention.

Kidston surveyed the gruesome scene.

'Savage,' said Kidston. 'Why such a frenzied attack? What was behind it? Was it sexually motivated?' The detective squatted on his hunkers by the armchair for a closer inspection and meticulously lifted the blood-sodden shirt with a rubber-gloved forefinger. Much of the blood seemed to have originated from the gaping neck wound and what looked like multiple stab wounds to the chest. Those aspects would be confirmed or otherwise by a post-mortem. 'I know Ryan was gay. We'll need to have a close look at his personal relationships. As a fiscal, he'll have made some enemies with the cases he's prosecuted. We'll need to look at his conviction record.' Kidston remembered working very closely with Ferrier when he prosecuted the Gorbals Samurai case that resulted in convictions for Phil Canavan and Johnny Boy McManus.

'Nobody deserves to die like that,' Stark said. The baby-faced sergeant peered out from under the elasticated hood of his forensic suit and Kidston wondered if, for a moment, Stark was about to be sick.

'You okay, Gregor?'

'No murder weapon,' Stark said, ignoring the question and changing the subject.

'Only a fork without a matching knife. Looks like fillet steak.' Kidston examined the remnants on Ryan Ferrier's dinner plate. 'That missing knife could be our murder weapon. And a single wine glass.' Kidston leaned over the corpse, carefully checking either side of the body. 'Let's get the pathologist here with the SOCOs. Full fingerprinting, photography, and blood work. I'll contact Joe Sawyers and he'll probably want to bring Sam Brady to view the scene before the body's removed.' Detective Superintendent Joe

Sawyers was head of CID for the sprawling Southern Division, officially F-Division, but known colloquially as 'the South', and was Kidston's boss. Brady was the senior procurator fiscal for Glasgow. On call, duty fiscals were a key element of the force's response to serious crimes and featured on the lengthy 'call out' notification lists. Brady had lost one of his prosecutorial team and would want to attend and view Ryan Ferrier's remains for himself.

Kidston and Stark took a cautious cursory look around the remainder of the large four-bedroomed property. One of the ground-floor reception rooms had been converted to an office with a grand leather-topped double-pedestal desk and a plush Chesterfield-style swivel chair. Kidston could see that Ryan Ferrier was a man who liked to bring his work home with him. The desk was piled with manila case folders, from his work office.

'Ferrier's current and recent cases will all need to be looked into,' Kidston said, 'starting with these files.'

Stark made a note in his folder. 'Conviction record plus current and recent cases, noted. It'll be difficult to check if any files have been stolen from here.'

'I'm sure Sam Brady's staff will be able to help with that.'

Kidston took the stairs to check out the bedrooms. The smallest one was being used as a storeroom with an exercise bike, some old hi-fi equipment and a rowing machine taking up most of the floorspace. Two more were made out as well-equipped guest rooms. The master bedroom was huge and looked out over the back garden of the house. The large dark-wood sleigh-type bed hadn't been slept in – the Black Watch tartan coverlet undisturbed.

Kidston crossed to the bay window and stared out over the well-tended garden. He wasn't that high up but sensed that familiar giddy lurch of vertigo; so slight now, that there was no panic and no fear of a full-blown acrophobia attack. Kidston's phobia was a legacy of being thrown out a third-floor tenement window by a deranged old woman when he was seven years old. Following successful therapy, Kidston's fear of heights had, for the moment, been cured.

Satisfied that there was nothing untoward in any of the other rooms the two detectives returned to the murder scene. 'I've got a bad feeling about this one.' Kidston's detective instincts were kicking in. He was proud of his unblemished record as a senior investigating offer or SIO. All his murder enquiries had resulted in arrests and convictions – no senior detective wanted an unsolved murder on their personal file, but that fear of failure was ever present. Experience and intuition were telling him that this would be a challenging case. 'It's not looking like a slam dunk, Gregor.'

'A whodunnit, boss, and a high profile one.'

CHAPTER SIX

W hen the detectives emerged out into the midday sunshine, Costello and McCartney had been joined by more uniformed colleagues to protect the cordon. A traffic diversion had been set up to keep vehicles clear of the scene. A young, uniformed sergeant was speaking to the force's media manager at the edge of the cordon. Kidston gathered the growing number of attendees at the outer gates of the property and outlined his expectations:

'Ladies and gents. This is a murder crime scene. No access to the locus unless absolutely required. That will be a small group of investigators and crime-scene specialists. Absolutely no unauthorised access to the house. Sergeant, can you post constables front and rear of the property? Front posting to note names and designation of anyone who enters. No entry without protective clothing and note their time in and time out.'

'Will do, sir,' the young, uniformed sergeant replied.

'DS Stark will remain at the scene to manage the initial stages,' Kidston continued. 'I'll be back later with the detective superintendent and the PF. So let's establish an outer cordon, two houses further back in both directions. These are large properties and I'll be getting search teams to look through the gardens, hedges, and the paths for anything that might be tied to the crime. We'll get the council cleansing van out to work with the search teams, get these drain covers lifted. Wouldn't be the first time a murder weapon was dropped down a stank.'

'What about the cleaner, Inspector?' Chrissie McCartney asked. 'I've taken her set of house keys.'

'Good shout, Chrissie,' Kidston replied. 'What did you get from her?'

'Her name's Audrey Boyce. Confirmed that the front door was locked when she arrived. Been cleaning for Mr Ferrier for over three years. No issues with him as an employer.' McCartney flicked the pages of her police notebook. 'No hints of anyone else staying there for around a year.'

Kidston and Stark took a seat in the panda car beside Audrey Boyce. A mug of hot, sweet tea, provided by a kindly neighbour, seemed to have restored some of the cleaner's equilibrium.

'I'm sorry you had to see that this morning, Mrs Boyce,' Kidston said. 'And I'm sorry you had to wait around a wee bit longer.'

'That's okay, son. Terrible business, I was fair banjaxed. Poor Mr Ferrier. Thon wee polis woman was very kind.' The cleaner sipped the tea. 'I'm feeling a bit more like myself now.'

'You clean every Thursday for Mr Ferrier, is that right?' Kidston asked.

'That's correct, officer.'

'Has he had anyone staying with him over the period?'

'Not since last summer. I would know, you see. From the way the bed was made up and the number of plates and dishes and that.'

'Staying alone for around a year then?'

'Aye, since last July.'

27

'Would you be familiar with Mr Ferrier's kitchen, his glassware, wine glasses and such and maybe his cutlery, knives and forks and stuff?'

'Aye, I would, officer. He had such lovely stuff.'

'And what about payment, Mrs Boyce?' Kidston asked.

'Mr Ferrier would always leave a five-pound note in a brown envelope with my name on it on the kitchen table. He was always very generous at Christmas and the Glasgow Fair for my holidays.'

'What did he usually write on the envelope; "Audrey" or "Mrs Boyce"?'

'Just "Audrey", officer.'

'Thank you, Mrs Boyce, that's all been extremely helpful. We'll be in touch later, one of my detectives will need to take elimination fingerprints, what we call elims, from you, but it's nothing to be worried about, it's purely routine.' Kidston gave the cleaner a reassuring smile. 'I need one more wee bit of assistance from you before I get PC McCartney to drive you home. It will help me with the investigation.'

They kept the lounge door closed, so Audrey Boyce didn't have to witness the horrifying bloodied sight of her employer for a second time. Closely escorted by Kidston and Stark, Mrs Boyce strode purposefully into the kitchen – a woman on a mission – where she ably confirmed that the inventory was missing a Waterford crystal wine glass and an ebony-handled steak knife, one of a matched set. There was no trace of her wages.

'I'm no bothered wi' a' that, son.' The cleaner looked close to tears. 'Poor Mr Ferrier, and besides, I never got to do any cleaning this morning.'

———

Inside the cordon, the police ground was getting busier. The next wave of responders included a search team, dressed in police overalls, and equipped with rakes, sieves, and poles. Kidston addressed the sergeant in charge of the team and requested a full fingertip search of the entire area. Attention was to be paid to gardens, hedgerows, bins and pathways. The drains were to be checked. It would be dirty, demanding work but the force's Support Unit had earned a reputation for their thorough and systematic search techniques of evidence gathering.

'Items of interest include a black wood-handled steak knife, a crystal wine glass and a brown envelope with the name "Audrey", which may or may not contain a five-pound note. Obviously, that's not to exclude any other items that look interesting.'

'All noted, sir.' The sergeant looked keen to get going.

'Anything found to remain in situ until photographed and then flagged to Detective Sergeant Stark, who will be in overall charge of the crime scene until we stand it down.'

Stark raised his hand to show the searchers who their point of contact was.

While detectives conducted door-to-door enquiries in the immediate neighbourhood, SOCOs photographed the locus and boiler-suited officers set about searching the gardens, paths, hedges and drains. A constable on the outer cordon lowered the barrier tape to allow a CID car to enter the police-controlled area. It was Joe Sawyers, accompanied by a grim-faced Sam Brady and Dr Finola Donnelly, the duty pathologist. Kidston greeted the high-powered delegation as they suited up at the foot of the driveway.

'It's a bad one, Sam. Have you been told what to expect?'

'Joe described the scene, but I felt I had to attend this one personally.' Brady's crestfallen face betrayed his emotions. The normally jovial fiscal looked downcast, his handsome features crumpled into a sad frown. At forty-seven, he'd climbed to the top tier of the prosecution service and was tipped to be a future sheriff. 'I asked Finola to accompany us.'

'Any initial thoughts, Luc?' Sawyers asked.

'The body's been violated, mutilated and it's a bloody mess,' Kidston replied. 'Seems like a frenzied attack, but I'd be keen to get all of your thoughts on the scene.' Kidston enjoyed working with Donnelly. They'd had a brief romance five years earlier, when Kidston was separated and awaiting a divorce from his first wife and before he married Grace just over three years ago. He and Donnelly remained on very good terms. The pathologist had a second degree in criminology and in previous cases had proved unerringly adept with her psychological profiles of killers and their motives.

The group comprising two senior detectives, a fiscal and a pathologist stood in silent observation of the grisly scene. Sam Brady was struggling. The ferocity of the violence; violence carried out on a colleague and friend, was hard for him to see. It was the lawyer who eventually broke the silence.

'Monstrous. Poor Ryan. What a ghastly way to die. It looks sexually motivated. What do you think, Finola?'

'It looks like overkill,' the pathologist replied. Donnelly was mid-thirties, a cool, elegant blonde who always tied her shoulder-length hair back at crime scenes. Her clear hazel eyes shone as she probed the deceased's remains. 'Humiliation and degradation of the victim more than lust or sexual desire. Perhaps a level of anger... maybe fury... possibly shame. The genitalia mutilated, penis hacked off and stuffed into the mouth troubles me. That level of sexual aggression is extremely rare.' She spoke in her soft Irish brogue. 'To dominate your victim to that extent... but please remember, I'm here as a forensic pathologist not as a criminal psychologist.' Kidston knew her well enough to know that, behind her surgical mask, she was smiling. She leaned over the body and inspected the wounds on the throat and chest. 'I'm speculating here, and I'll know more tomorrow when I get him on the table, but it looks like the throat was cut first. The blade, or whatever implement was used, has slashed right through the carotid artery. Rapid blood loss of that nature leads to heart failure – his heart would go into arrest in under ten seconds.' *On the table.* Kidston flinched at Donnelly's innocent euphemism for the post-mortem examination that would take place. Kidston grimaced at the prospect. Donnelly straightened up and adjusted her face mask. 'There would be no struggle, no resistance. Ryan Ferrier was already dead when he was stabbed, possibly two or three times, through the heart and before the gruesome butchery was carried out. Everything else is overkill.'

'Good grief.' Joe Sawyers shook his head. 'Such a frenzied attack.'

'Do you gents mind?' Donnelly fished inside her pockets for her personal Dictaphone. 'I'd like to get my initial thoughts on tape.'

'Please do.' Sam Brady had seen enough. He walked to the door with the two detectives. 'Joe, Luc, you must get whoever did this. Ryan's one of our own. I want justice for his killer.'

'Rest assured, Sam,' Kidston replied, 'we'll get the sick bastard responsible for this.'

CHAPTER SEVEN

FRIDAY, 17 AUGUST 1990

Kidston took in the charged atmosphere. The incident room was buzzing. He always enjoyed the thrill of a new investigation, especially on major enquiries. It couldn't get much more 'major' than the Ryan Ferrier case – the grisly murder of a law enforcement colleague. Given the victim's profile, Joe Sawyers had been appointed senior investigating officer and would oversee and co-ordinate the enquiry. As SIO, he would be responsible for the investigative strategy. Kidston would be deputy SIO but, in reality, he would run most of the day-to-day aspects of the case and had allocated the key roles in the investigation team. Kidston had selected DS Gregor Stark as his *collator*, responsible for assessing and collating the various strands of evidence from witness statements and analysing criminal intelligence that might be applied to the case. DS Alison Metcalfe landed the role of *productions officer*, in charge of all physical exhibits. It was a role that few detectives relished – too many opportunities to fuck up, but Metcalfe had performed the job well for Kidston in the past. DC Anthony 'Zorba' Quinn would co-ordinate door-to-door enquiries and had enlisted the assistance of the community policing team, including Peter Costello and Chrissie McCartney. DCs Paul Kennedy and Robin 'Mork' Williams were given the role of *statement readers*. All of Kidston's tried and tested team were in place for what he was sure would be a difficult and challenging investigation.

Joe Sawyers called the meeting of the investigation team to order. A slim and fit forty-seven, the detective superintendent typified the new and emerging breed of senior CID manager. A picture of sartorial style, he was wearing a navy-blue suit, a pristine white shirt, and a wine-coloured tie. Always an elegant speaker, the polite, measured tones of Sawyers' voice were at odds with the information he was imparting. His opening remarks highlighted the known facts of the case, giving an overview of the murder, describing the horrific details of the crime scene, the frenzied nature of the attack on the victim but he started with the deceased.

'Ryan Ferrier was thirty-seven, a career prosecutor and had worked for the procurator fiscal service since graduating law at Glasgow University.' Sawyers pointed to the eight-by-ten-inch glossy photograph of Ferrier affixed to the large whiteboard that dominated the room. It was a professional shot – the type used in annual reports or official publications. The handsome prosecutor smiled out at the group of detectives tasked with catching his killer. 'He was a homosexual, without a current partner at the time of his death. He'd come out as gay at university and wasn't considered promiscuous in his social or sexual habits. Both parents are deceased and there is a brother in Southampton. Steven Ferrier is travelling to Glasgow this morning. He's requested to view his brother's body at the city mortuary and DI Kidston and DS Stark will pick him up at Glasgow Airport. He's scheduled to participate in a 2pm media briefing at force headquarters alongside Sam Brady and me.

'This is a high-profile murder investigation, everyone,'

Sawyers continued, 'the murder of a law enforcement colleague, who many here have worked cases with in the past. The crime-scene pictures have been circulated to this group, but are not to leave this room, so you can all see the horrific extent of the injuries inflicted on Ryan Ferrier. Doc Donnelly described it as "overkill", and I won't disagree with her assessment. It's clearly vital that the nature and extent of the injuries are not made known to the media. So let's keep those aspects locked down, ladies and gentlemen. DI Kidston will update us on what yesterday's initial enquiries gleaned.'

'Thanks, boss.' Kidston stood up. He was dressed in a charcoal two-piece, a crisp white shirt, matched with a silver-grey tie. He fidgeted with his cufflinks. 'Yesterday afternoon's post-mortem confirmed that the cause of death was the victim's throat being cut. There were three puncture wounds to Ryan Ferrier's heart; the probability being that these were inflicted by a steak knife that he'd been eating his dinner with. Only one knife is missing from a boxed set in Ryan's kitchen. The matching fork was on his dinner plate. DS Metcalfe can tell us a bit more, Alison...'

'Yes, thanks, boss.' Metcalfe consulted her folder before speaking. A striking-looking woman, with her androgynous build, clear blue eyes, and prominent cheekbones, she'd worn her blonde hair cropped short since Kidston first met her when they were young detective constables together. She was dressed in a smart navy trouser suit, white blouse, and her trademark sensible low heels.

'High-end set made by a French company, *Forge de Laguiole*. Not your average kitchen knife.' Metcalfe pointed to a table where a black presentation box was laid out. One of the six compartments was empty. 'Knives are polished stainless steel; the handles are black ebony wood and please notice the engraved centrepiece on the handles that make them stand out.

There are photos of the knives for your packs but please have a closer look at them before you leave, check the weight and quality. The search of the locus was negative, all the bins and the drains have been checked with no trace. I've sent notification to all divisions for officers to be aware when searching prisoners. Any knives matching this, we will be notified.'

'And the missing crystal glass, Alison?' Kidston asked.

'Yes. I can understand the killer taking the knife; it's a very nice knife and if he's not disposing of it, he might think of it as a weapon to hold on to, maybe to use again. The wine glass is more puzzling, unless the murderer wants souvenirs. Maybe he took it to dispose of it later because his prints were on it, but it wasn't found in any of the searches. Again, this is a high-end item, Waterford crystal. Mr Ferrier had very good taste in these matters. And again, there are photos of the wine glass in your packs. I've taken elims from Mr Ferrier's cleaner, Mrs Audrey Boyce, and gone over her statement. She is adamant that both sets – the steak knives and the crystal wine glasses – were complete. She saw these items every Thursday when she cleaned the house.'

Kidston watched his DS conclude her part of the briefing with a sense of satisfaction. She was a seasoned investigator with a reputation for being tough, dogged and pragmatic; one of a small group of women that had smashed through the glass ceiling for CID appointments. Kidston had given her an opportunity when an acting detective sergeant's post had opened up on his team – she'd seized her chance and was now coming up to three years in the substantive rank.

'Thank you, Alison.' Kidston continued the briefing. 'We've had a lot of support from Sam Brady, the PF. He's identified a close colleague of Ryan's. A depute fiscal by the name of Sheila Morton. Sheila and her colleagues are working through all the case files that we took from Ryan's home office. She's been able to assist with some additional background on Ryan's personal and social life. Gregor and I are meeting her this afternoon, after we pick up Steven Ferrier. His previous relationship, that we know of, ended around last July and we'll be following up on some details around that later today with Ms Morton.

'The door-to-door, up to this point, hasn't offered anything. No comings or goings that attracted the attention of neighbours. All the vehicles parked in the neighbourhood have been checked out with a negative result. From what we know right now Ryan Ferrier was a single gay man, a dedicated prosecutor who worked long hours. He was popular with colleagues. Gregor, you, and DC Williams have been looking at his prosecution case files. Anything jumping out?'

'Last two years, he's put away three major criminals in separate cases: Chick Torrance for murder, Ralph Bonnar for dealing heroin and Owen Madeley for ringing stolen cars. All three remain currently in Barlinnie but we'll have a look at their main associates.' DS Gregor Stark flicked through the papers in his folder. 'However, if we go back three years, it brings in your case against Phil Canavan and Johnny Boy McManus.'

Kidston nodded to Stark in confirmation and then spoke to the group. 'That was the Gorbals Samurai case. McManus has served a one-year sentence for drugs and firearms. Canavan, although charged with attempted murder was found guilty on a reduced charge of *reckless discharge of a firearm*. The fact that he'd sustained life-altering injuries – an amputated hand – that required a series of surgeries meant that his lawyer was able to plea bargain a two-year suspended sentence.' Kidston paused for a beat, wondering if his old nemesis Canavan could be behind the attack.

Stark went back to his folder and picked up his thread. 'We know that Ryan Ferrier's last meal was fillet steak and chips, washed down with a glass or two of Valpolicella. That's confirmed by the PM and by the packaging found in the kitchen bin. The wine bottle was three-quarters finished. A possible missing wine glass might suggest someone joined him after dinner and drank a glass with him. Not a planned dinner guest. Who visited and why?'

'Theories, anyone?' Kidston always encouraged his team to offer up their ideas on potential scenarios, plausible hypotheses, or even wild outlier theories. Nothing was off the table in these briefings; there were no stupid questions and no wrong answers. 'What is it we don't know that we don't know?' Kidston saw Sawyers' broad smile. He'd nicked that line from his boss.

'We don't know if the killer was someone known to his victim,' Gregor Stark offered. 'We don't know why the nature of the attack was so frenzied.' He looked at his folder. 'We don't know if this was a romantic or sexual liaison gone wrong? Did he use rent boys? DI Kidston and I will explore that aspect with Sheila Morton when we meet her later.' Stark worked his way down a list on his folder. 'Does the ferocity of the attack imply intimacy or were these two people strangers when this encounter started?'

The forthright Metcalfe offered her view. 'That level of violence – the overkill that Doc Donnelly highlighted – does that not suggest a degree of fury triggered by something sexual? Perhaps a homosexual encounter that went too far. Maybe shame.'

'Go on, Alison.' Kidston was encouraged by what he was hearing.

'Cutting off the victim's penis, in all likelihood when he was already dead, suggests to me a need to humiliate... a need to dominate. It's ritualistic but what's the motivation?'

'I agree with Alison,' Stark replied. 'As an MO, ritual violence after the fact is so unusual. It implies a sense of anger...

furious levels of anger... but what we want to know is what triggered that fury.'

'Not a random act. Maybe a homosexual pass gone wrong.'

Kidston attempted to crystallise the key discussion themes. 'It doesn't look like our killer brought a knife with him. That suggests to me that it's not some kind of contract killing. A hitman wouldn't leave the bloody mess we saw yesterday. Possibly not a premeditated act but more a spur-of-the-moment, spontaneous act triggered or provoked by something we don't yet know.'

'Okay everyone, some very good stuff there.' Joe Sawyers brought the briefing to a close. 'Thank you all.'

The detectives, pending enquiries permitting, would return at 7pm for a wash-up debrief. Kidston spoke to the group as they were about to break up. 'I want you all to imagine our colleague Ryan Ferrier being carried from his home yesterday in a body bag... his remains placed in an undertaker's shell and removed to the city mortuary.' Kidston had the room's rapt attention now. 'I promised Sam Brady a result in this one... let's go and get it.'

CHAPTER EIGHT

'Sorry to meet under such dreadful circumstances.' It was a stock phrase, but Kidston conveyed a genuine sadness when he shook the hand of Steven Ferrier. He'd worked closely with the man's deceased brother. The airport cops had brought Ferrier airside and Kidston walked him through the terminal to where Gregor Stark was waiting with an unmarked CID car. Steven Ferrier was four years older than Ryan and Kidston saw the family resemblance between the two men.

Despite the circumstances of his brother's murder, Steven Ferrier was adamant that he wanted to view his remains. The formal identification of Ryan Ferrier had been done by Sam Brady fulfilling the legal requirement prior to the post-mortem. This visit was a courtesy for the surviving family member of the victim. The old single-storey, red-brick and sandstone city mortuary – situated adjacent to the High Court building and across the road from the open parklands of Glasgow Green was a ghastly place for visitors to navigate. Thankfully, the deceased was laid out in a family viewing room – away from the malodorous guts of the mortuary, with its fetid, cloying stench of death; the examination tables, rib spreaders, bone saws and scalpels – and covered with a white cotton sheet. Kidston and Stark allowed Steven Ferrier some private time with his brother. The two detectives chatted with the attendants who could relate the story behind every cadaver. Stark shot a long suspicious glance at the mortuary cat, a well-fed tabby that seemed to have the run of the place. The cat stared back at him, untroubled and oblivious to his machinations.

Steven Ferrier was understandably quiet on the drive to the fiscal's office at Custom House Quay. 'That must have been very difficult for you,' Stark said.

'It was tough,' Ferrier replied. 'I should probably have taken your advice and remembered him from when he was alive.' He started to sob lightly. 'But I wanted to see my wee brother one final time. I'm sorry...' He wiped the tears from his eyes.

'It's okay.' Kidston patted his shoulder. 'When did you last see Ryan?'

'He spent Christmas with my family three years ago. My wife and two daughters absolutely adored him. He hasn't been down since. Work was so full on... but I guess you guys are aware of that being in the same business. Do you think he was murdered by someone from the criminal fraternity?'

'It's one of the angles we're considering,' Kidston said. 'Did he ever talk to you about any threats?'

'Never. We'd speak every month or so. He loved his work, but it didn't leave much time for a personal life.'

'Did you know his last partner?' Kidston asked.

'Douglas Tennant. Just met him once. He was a nice guy, maybe a bit too young for Ryan and I had the feeling that he would break his heart.'

'Did Douglas move on with someone else?' Kidston asked.

'I believe so. He works in London, a job in media advertising. No further contact with Ryan, so far as I know... too raw for my wee brother when it all ended. They'd been together three years by that time.'

'No new partner for Ryan after Douglas departed the scene?' Kidston asked.

'I think he found it hard to find someone new,' Ferrier replied. 'He got back into socialising, but I don't think he got into anything serious on the dating front.'

———

During coffee and cakes with a group of Ryan's former colleagues, Sam Brady offered Steven Ferrier the full resources of the procurator fiscal's office to assist with any aspect of the arrangements. Ferrier was booked into a city centre hotel and the detectives would pick him up ahead of the planned press conference. Kidston wouldn't hand over the keys to his brother's property for another few days. He was always reluctant to hand back a murder house too early. Once returned, the police no longer had control and evidence found would be contested with defence allegations of cross-contamination. Kidston wanted to go back and have one final look at the murder locus – then it would be time.

When Steven Ferrier headed to his hotel the two detectives spent some time with Sheila Morton in a comfortable witness interview room. There were some cakes left and Morton arranged for more coffee. The two detectives had worked through lunch.

Sheila Morton was mid-thirties with shoulder-length auburn hair, a freckled complexion, big brown eyes, and a nervous smile. She was dressed in a grey trouser suit, white blouse and was wearing low heels. 'Steven's very like Ryan, isn't he,' Morton said. 'Very brave of him to visit the mortuary.'

'We did try to talk him out of it.' Kidston nibbled on a Jaffa Cake and sipped his coffee.

'That place gives me the creeps,' Morton said.

'Not a good place for civilians to visit,' Stark said, flipping open his folder. 'Not the ideal way to remember a loved one and that cat gives me the heebie-jeebies.'

The professional aspects were dealt with first. Morton was able to confirm that the files recovered from Ryan's home office were all cases assigned to him and his team. There were no other 'signed out' files unaccounted for. 'We all do it,' Morton said. 'There's such a massive caseload that we all end up taking files home. Sometimes it's the only way we can catch up.'

'Thanks for attending to that so quickly,' Kidston said.

'Absolutely anything this office can do to assist, please don't hesitate to ask.'

'Thank you,' Kidston said. 'Sam Brady says you and Ryan were close friends, would you agree?'

'Yes, we were very close,' Morton replied. 'He mentored me in the fiscal service, and we became good friends.'

'Can you offer us any insight into his personal and social life?' Kidston asked.

'I think you know that he split with his last partner, Douglas Tennant a year ago.'

'We got that from Steven, thanks,' Kidston said. 'He suggests it was Douglas that ended things. Is that your understanding?'

'Very much so. Ryan was devastated. They'd been a couple for three years.'

'How did they meet?' Kidston asked. 'Do you know their story?'

'They met at Bennets nightclub,' Morton replied. 'We used to have some wild nights there.' Kidston had never visited Glasgow's top gay club but knew it was a star attraction in the city's so-called *Pink Quarter*.

Stark wrote furiously in his notepad.

'Did their split come out of the blue?' Kidston asked.

'Ryan never saw it coming. Douglas met someone else and took off for London. It was sudden but it was Ryan's house, so Douglas just packed up his things and moved out.'

'Are you aware of any contact between them since the split?' Kidston asked.

'Douglas was in Glasgow last week,' Morton replied. 'Up for a cousin's wedding and staying with his parents in Mount Vernon.'

The two detectives exchanged a glance.

'Do you know if he contacted Ryan?' Kidston asked. 'Did he get in touch with you?'

'I think he contacted Ryan at the office here, but so far as I know there were no plans to meet up.'

'Do you know if Douglas Tennant brought his new partner up for the wedding?' Stark asked.

'I'm sorry, I don't know,' Morton said, her voice catching a little. 'I'm sorry I can't be more helpful...' She started to sob.

'Easy now,' Kidston said. 'You've been very helpful. I'm sorry we have to ask you so many questions but you're the friend who knew him best.' Kidston pushed a box of tissues towards Sheila who stifled the tiniest laugh as she reached for them.

'Look at the state of me,' said Morton, recovering her composure. 'These are meant for the witnesses we interview.'

'Steven mentioned that Ryan had started socialising again,' Kidston said. 'Was he seeing anyone new? Was he back around the social scene?'

'You know Ryan.' Morton dabbed the corners of her eyes with a tissue. 'He's a very gregarious person. After moping around for three months, he wanted to get back to some kind of social life. We were back clubbing again, Bennets and that new club in Carlton Place, Goodnights. They run a gay night on a Thursday, and we've gone a few times.'

'But no one special or long term?' Kidston asked.

'No one special, no,' she replied.

'Is there anyone else in Ryan's circle of friends or colleagues that we should be speaking to?' Kidston asked.

'He was close with Adrian Harrison. They did their law degrees at the same time at Glasgow University, a few years ahead of my time there. But he practised property law. They played tennis together at Titwood. Adrian was married with two kids, but he was in the closet. Ryan and I knew he was gay for years.'

'*Was* married? *Was* in the closet?' Kidston asked, intrigued by the lawyer's turn of phrase. 'Is he out now?'

'He's dead now,' Morton announced with a sad expression. 'Ryan and I were at his funeral a week ago. Hanged himself.'

CHAPTER NINE

'Adrian Harrison,' Stark said with some urgency. 'A hanging... Maxwell Park address, G-Division, in the last few weeks.'

With Sam Brady nodding his approval, the young paralegal at the procurator fiscal's Deaths Unit fished the buff-coloured folder from an enormous wall cabinet with rotating shelves and handed it to his boss. Brady looked over the contents. 'Gents, as I'm sure you're aware, all deaths without certification by a GP or hospital medic, fall under our remit for investigation. Suicides need to be signed off by CID to exclude any foul play and the standard procedure is to instruct a *two-doctor post-mortem*. This death has been signed off as a suicide by two doctors and by your CID colleagues. Might this merely be a tragic coincidence?'

'It's possible,' Kidston replied, 'but it merits closer scrutiny.' The death of Adrian Harrison may just have been a tragic coincidence, but Kidston didn't believe in coincidences; two friends dying within weeks of each other meant that some serious questions needed to be asked.

The two detectives examined the contents of the folder in

Sam Brady's office. Kidston handed Stark a two-page *Preliminary Death Report* as he read through the main file. Sam Brady read through the post-mortem paperwork submitted by the pathologists.

'Two-doctor PM as per procedure,' Brady said. 'Signed off by Professor Cochrane himself and Dr Harry Marshall. It says, "classic suspension hanging, petechial haemorrhaging to the eyes indicating cerebral hypoxia".'

'The kitchen pulley was ripped from its ceiling mounting,' Kidston said, reading from the report. 'It says, "The rope was looped into a noose which acted as a ligature and tightened around the deceased's neck. A low footstool was situated beside the body indicating a suspension rather than a drop hanging".'

'Did you see who attended from divisional CID?' Stark asked his boss.

Kidston grimaced as his eyes scanned to the foot of the report. 'DI Ronnie Miller and DS Rob Templeton. Why am I not surprised?'

'Oh, come on, Luc. It could all be above board and just a sad coincidence with no actual links between the two deaths.' Sam Brady remembered a spectacular fallout between Kidston and Miller over a high-profile case three years earlier.

'Sam, Sheila Morton has just told us that Ryan Ferrier and Adrian Harrison were good friends, and that Harrison was a closet homosexual. The man was married with children. It's possible he was being blackmailed.'

'Maybe by the same person that murdered Ryan Ferrier,' Stark added.

'I've never met Adrian Harrison,' Brady said. 'He's never worked in the criminal justice system. How do you want to handle it?'

'We'll brief Joe Sawyers before the press conference,' Kidston said. 'We'll do it away from Steven Ferrier, no need to cause additional alarm or upset until we know more. Can you have this file copied for us while we grab another chat with Sheila Morton, thanks.' Kidston handed the folder to Sam Brady. 'Gregor and I will need to visit Mrs Harrison and look into her husband's suicide.'

CHAPTER TEN

K idston and Stark watched the press conference from the seats at the back of the media room in force headquarters. Steven Ferrier stood up well to the barrage of TV and press cameras. A picture of his dead brother, the same image that was affixed to the whiteboard of the police incident room, was positioned on the media backdrop for all to see the resemblance between the two men. He read from a prepared statement that Kidston had assisted him with. His voice faltered just the one time – when he talked about the violent end his younger brother had faced. He'd been briefed not to go into details.

Sam Brady and Joe Sawyers put in their usual performances, consummate professionals. Brady spoke louder and faster than his police counterpart, but he got his message over, the loss of a talented and dedicated career prosecutor would be deeply felt by the entire law enforcement community. Sawyers was quieter, more measured as he spoke about the scale of the investigation and appealed for witnesses, providing a dedicated telephone number for information. He was renowned for his polite articulate manner and refined speaking voice which were as far removed from glottal Glaswegian as you could imagine.

Kidston looked up at the large screen beside the media stage and saw the televisual image of his detective superintendent. Sawyers looked immaculate. His greying hair in a neat side parting, his choice of a dark suit and white shirt portraying the sober, professional image that the occasion required. Questions were fielded with an assured self-confidence. Only one query appeared to ruffle the veteran murder squad detective. It came from a Glasgow tabloid reporter.

'Can you comment on whether Ryan Ferrier's gay lifestyle contributed to his murder?'

Sawyers gave the reporter a withering look and he took a long pause before responding. 'Ryan Ferrier was the victim of a violent murder. It is of no consequence whether he was heterosexual or homosexual. He was murdered. His sexuality is not a factor in this crime.'

The police media manager stepped in and called the press conference to a close.

———

'Given what you told me before the press conference, I may have gone out on a limb a wee bit with my answer about the victim's sexuality?' Sawyers said. 'That reporter annoyed me with that low-ball question.' He was seated in a borrowed CID office in force headquarters with Kidston and Brady. Stark was dropping Steven Ferrier back at his hotel.

'We're speculating about a potential second victim,' Kidston said. 'I think your response was spot on. Gay or straight, it's murder, what difference does it make when a human life is taken?'

Brady agreed. 'I thought you handled it well.'

49

'I thought all three of you handled it great,' Kidston said. 'From where I was sitting Steven Ferrier came over really well. I hope we get some calls to the information line.'

'You'll need to go and see Mrs Harrison.' Sawyers was in full agreement with Kidston's plan. 'I'll deal with the chief officers and the command team at G-Division, but we'll keep it very low profile until we're sure what we're dealing with. Tread carefully... very carefully.'

Joe Sawyers recalled a previous occasion, three years earlier, when he'd offered Luc similar advice. Kidston and Miller had clashed over a high-profile case and the fallout had reached all the way to headquarters. Sawyers was well aware of the hostility between the two detective inspectors. More than once, he'd refereed bouts or calmed eruptions between them. It was unlike Ronnie Miller to miss something as big as this, and maybe it was just a coincidence. But Kidston was right; they had a duty to check it out. And it wasn't just Miller, two doctors had signed off on a suicide, one of them the top pathologist in the country. This entire investigation would need to be handled delicately... very delicately.

Sawyers contemplated the coming storm.

CHAPTER ELEVEN

'Do you think Miller's made an arse of this?' Stark asked. He was driving his boss to the Harrison house in the leafy suburbs of Maxwell Park in Glasgow's Pollokshields district.

'I hope we're wrong, but my detective's instinct is telling me different.'

'Me too,' Stark agreed. 'My *Spidey-Sense* was tingling as soon as Sheila Morton mentioned how Adrian Harrison died.'

'Spidey-Sense! You and your comics, Gregor.'

'Graphic novels, boss, not comics. You're a reader, I bet you'd enjoy Neil Gaiman's *Sandman*. Comics are a higher art form than people would credit.'

'Graphic novels, Gregor.' Kidston laughed. 'What's the story?'

'It's a mix of fantasy, horror, and ironic humour about the lord of dreams, a Morpheus-type character.'

'I think I'll stick to Joseph Wambaugh and John Irving, no offence.'

Both men laughed. It was a much-needed release of tension ahead of a difficult interview with a newly widowed woman. A woman who was about to be questioned about her late husband's personal life.

————

Martha Harrison was surprised to invite two solemn-faced detectives into the comfortable, well-appointed lounge of her detached sandstone villa. She was a petite brunette with a quiet, mousy appearance. Her large blue eyes fixed on Kidston as he explained the purpose of their visit. She was dressed in dark-brown leggings and a sweatshirt of milkshake pink.

'It's a rather delicate matter, Mrs Harrison.' Kidston spoke softly, slowly. 'Adrian's name has come up in connection with a current investigation and we need to ask you some questions.'

A boy and a girl aged around eleven or twelve padded into the lounge, two inquisitive faces peering at the visitors. 'Who is it, Mum?' the girl asked.

'It's not for you, Sophie. It's someone to see me. You and Callum get back to your homework.' Her voice was strident and authoritative. Not so mousy after all. Sophie and Callum did a disappointed about-turn, leaving their mum to offer her two visitors a seat. The detectives declined her offer of tea and coffee.

'We're sorry to intrude on what must still be a difficult period for you and your family,' Kidston said. 'How are you holding up? Do you have the support of family and friends?'

'I'm well supported, thanks. Adrian left us well provided for and I have my job as a primary school teacher. We won't be destitute; we have the house. You should see some of the poor things in my school.' She hesitated and then said, 'My main concern is the children losing their father. I managed to get them to my mother's the day I found him, so they never had to go through the horror of discovering him.'

'We're very sorry for your loss, Mrs Harrison. Did you know Adrian's friend Ryan Ferrier?' Kidston asked.

'I knew Ryan well, almost as long as I knew Adrian.' Martha Harrison folded her hands over her lap. 'I thought someone might be in touch. Are you investigating Ryan's murder? I saw the press conference on the news.'

'Yes. Adrian's name came up today in the investigation. It's at a very early stage.'

'Do you mind if I take some notes, Mrs Harrison?' Stark flipped his folder open.

'Of course, please call me Martha.'

'I'm sure you were asked a lot of questions at the time of Adrian's death, Mrs Harrison,' Kidston said. 'I'm sorry but I do have to go over some of the same ground.'

'That's okay, Inspector.' Her big eyes widened, and she looked directly at Kidston. 'Suicide... nobody wants to use the term, but Adrian's death was a suicide.'

'Have you managed to come to terms with that, Martha?'

'Slowly, but surely... it was such a tragic waste.'

'I'm genuinely sorry to have to ask you this, Martha,' Kidston softened his tone a bit more. 'Why do you think Adrian would take his own life? I understand there was no note. Was there any indication beforehand?'

'There was nothing, Inspector. He was repaving the back garden for goodness' sake.' Her voice began to break. 'I mean... who would do that? Who would finish a paving job, jump into the shower, and then hang themselves from the kitchen pulley?'

'How do you know he had a shower?'

'The shower room was wet; his robe was slung over the door...' After a long hesitation, a puzzled expression came over her face. 'But the funny thing is... why would he change back into the same tennis shirt he was wearing? It would be all sweaty. It was a very hot day, and he was working in the garden.'

'Did you mention this to the detectives that attended at the time?' Kidston asked.

'It's only just occurred to me. Do you find that a bit strange?'

'Taking a shower might seem a bit odd with what he was planning. Did Adrian look as if he'd showered, was his hair wet?'

Martha Harrison's face was a puzzled frown. 'His hair didn't look as if it had been washed, it was matted in sweat. And while I remember it...' Her frown deepened. 'There was a brown envelope with sixty pounds sitting on the lounge sideboard. I never saw that money again.'

'Did you tell the police?' Kidston asked.

'I never realised it was gone until days later. My mind was a total fog. It wasn't in Adrian's possessions, I thought it would turn up in the house somewhere.'

'What was the money for?' Kidston asked. 'Was anything written on the envelope?'

'Not that I noticed. I thought it might be for more slabs or garden stuff. Do you find all this a bit strange?'

'It might be nothing,' Kidston said, 'but it might be something.'

Martha Harrison's large blue eyes widened with curiosity. 'What? What might it be?'

'We'll maybe get to that if you could walk us through what you found when you came home that day but first, and very importantly, what reasons do you think Adrian had for taking his own life? Did he have any financial issues? Any health problems?'

'None.'

'And I'm really sorry to ask, any marital issues between you?'

'Are you hinting at the fact that Adrian was gay?'

'That's what been disclosed to us as part of our investigation. Is that true?'

'I'm afraid it is, Inspector.' Her eyes were suddenly filled with sadness. 'A more accurate term would be bisexual.'

'Was that aspect discussed with the other detectives?' Kidston asked.

Martha Harrison shook her head. 'It never came up.'

'How long did you know?' Kidston asked.

'He told me when Sophie was five. Callum was four. Adrian wasn't a cruel man or a stupid man, Inspector. He wasn't going to abandon his wife and children. At least not until the kids were old enough to understand.'

'You made it work?'

'Of course, Inspector. I loved him. He loved me too. I think he was in love with another boy he went to university with but by the time he met me he'd grown out of it. "A phase", he called it. Turns out it wasn't a phase.'

'It sounds like his homosexuality, or his bisexuality wasn't a matter he would kill himself over. There's no apparent burden of shame or imminent exposure. Was he being blackmailed?'

'There was nothing that I was aware of. He'd seemed very happy recently.'

'Were you aware of any relationships with other men?'

'No, but he had some leeway I suppose. I wasn't constantly checking up on him.'

'Could he have invited a man into the house?'

'That's crazy, Inspector.'

'Could someone have been here helping him to pave the back garden? Maybe that's what the money was for.'

'That doesn't sound so crazy. Are you saying that Adrian may not have killed himself? Is that what you meant when you said, "it might be something"?'

'We'd like to look into it more, Martha, if you're comfortable with that.'

'Of course. I want to know what happened. I don't want people to believe Adrian killed himself out of shame.' Kidston heard the pride in Martha Harrison's voice. A note of anger there too. 'He had nothing to be ashamed of. He was a loving husband and a loving father. I want the truth of it.'

Martha Harrison walked the two detectives through the scene she'd discovered that fateful afternoon on her return from work. The pulley mounting had been repaired but she laid out the footstool where she'd found it and indicated the position of her husband's body. She confirmed that the pulley rope had been tightly fastened around her husband's neck and calmly described the horrific sight of his eyes and tongue. Her eyes glowed with possibilities. A sense of wonder, as slowly, surely, she began to imagine a different scenario to the one she'd originally accepted. Her late husband's bathrobe was still hanging in the shower room – she hadn't got around to removing Adrian's stuff yet.

Kidston and Stark examined the thick blue cotton robe. The unmistakable silvery staining of dried semen glinted at them from inside the garment. Kidston removed the rope belt from the loops and walked back through to the kitchen. Stark loosened the pulley rope producing sufficient length for a comparison. The braided belt was almost identical in thickness to the pulley rope.

'We'll need to take possession of Adrian's robe and a length of the pulley rope. We'll try and rig it up again for you.'

'That's okay,' she said. 'You can take the entire thing down if you want. I was intending to get rid of it anyway.'

Stark went out to the car and returned with three evidence bags. He cut a substantial length of rope from the pulley line but was able to secure the apparatus in the 'up' position.

'We'll need to send a full scenes-of-crime team tomorrow to take some photographs and fingerprints,' Kidston said. 'Was the house busy after the funeral?'

'Not overly busy, just my mum and my sister and brother-in-law. We didn't bring people to the house for the funeral because it happened here... too morbid. We held the funeral reception at the Sherbrooke Castle Hotel.'

'That might help us, Mrs Harrison,' Kidston said.

'Martha, please.'

'I'm sorry you had to revisit all of this, Martha.' Kidston handed her his card. 'You've been a great help and we'll reinvestigate Adrian's death based on what you've told us. Please contact me if you call anything else to mind.'

'Are you saying Adrian was murdered?'

'I can't say that at this point but I'm not ruling out that Adrian's hanging was staged.'

CHAPTER TWELVE

'We've missed Joe's debriefing at the office, but we should catch him before he leaves for the night.' Kidston checked his watch as Stark drove them back to the office. 'First up, I'm famished. Let's get some dinner. How about a fish supper from The Unique? My treat.'

'Brilliant idea, best fish and chips in the city.'

Their route back from Pollokshields took them via the south side institution in Allison Street. As usual, there was a long line of black hackneys outside. It was where many of the city's taxi drivers ate their dinner. Thankfully the taxi men were all seated in the café-cum-restaurant through the back and there was no queue at the counter.

Gregor Stark burst into the brown paper wrapping that held both meals and scooped a few chips from his supper before restarting the ignition. The wonderful aroma of hot freshly battered cod filled the car like a sweet bouquet. 'How is a growing boy like me supposed to survive on three Jaffa Cakes and cups of coffee?'

'It's been a long one, Gregor, but an eventful one.' Kidston laughed. 'But we've got something to go on with Adrian

Harrison and I think it will link us to Ryan Ferrier. I don't believe in coincidences.'

'You realise you're about to blow Ronnie Miller's original enquiry out of the water?'

'If you could even call it an enquiry.' He snuck a chip from where Stark's wrapper was open at the corner. 'Look what we managed to achieve with just some gentle probing. The bosses can deal with Ronnie, but we'll also need to deal with the pathologists.'

———

Stark brewed two mugs of tea and they spread their suppers over the refreshment-room table. They ate quickly from the greasy paper, devouring the thick battered cod and well-fried chips. Stark licked the salty and vinegary remnants of his supper from his fingers. Newspapers were discarded across the table. Stark flicked through the nearest tabloid and sneaked a look at the page three glamour shot.

'Anything interesting?' Kidston asked with a mischievous smile.

'Full of the Iraqi invasion of Kuwait,' Stark began. 'Middle East, UN Security Council... riveting stuff.'

'That's what drew your attention?' Kidston teased.

'That and the cartoons.' Stark laughed.

Joe Sawyers came in with a mug of tea, just in time to rescue a portion of Kidston's dinner.

The superintendent caught them up with his 7pm debriefing; there was nothing of note to report. The lab would have some analysis for them by tomorrow. The hotline had taken nine calls, most of them expressing sympathy for the victim. Six detectives had gone back out to follow up on them and conduct some additional door-to-door enquiries.

Kidston updated Sawyers on their interview with Martha Harrison and showed him the dressing gown and the pulley rope. The veteran detective's eyes lit up when he heard about the shower and the missing money.

'None of that made it into the death report from what I've read,' Sawyers said as he dried off his hands with a tea towel.

'No. We had to walk Mrs Harrison through it again, but I can't help thinking if the initial investigation had been more thorough... if some additional enquiries had been carried out.'

'I'll need to brief Colquhoun and the command team,' said a perturbed Sawyers. Assistant Chief Constable Farquhar Colquhoun would need to be told about something this important, with the potential to embarrass the force. As ACC Crime, the man known as 'Q' was the force's de facto senior detective and ran his executive portfolio with a very firm hand. He hated being out of the loop. 'We'll need to be extremely tactful in how we broach this with Prof Cochrane and the pathologists.' Professor Allan Cochrane was the country's most eminent pathologist. His forensic pathology department at Glasgow University shared its time between teaching student doctors and assisting the procurator fiscal with enquiries into sudden or suspicious deaths. Cochrane and his team were not known for their mistakes.

'Think about it,' Kidston said. 'The Prof was presented with a report, signed off by a detective inspector and a fiscal as non-suspicious. I imagine that Adrian Harrison's injuries were consistent with hanging. Maybe our suspect did hang him after choking him.'

'Well, if we have a suspect, we'll need to rely on him telling us how he did it,' Sawyers said with a wry smile. 'There's no second post-mortem for Adrian Harrison. He was cremated.'

Gregor Stark smiled. 'No chance of any comeback on Professor Cochrane then.'

'Are you guys heading home?' Sawyers asked. 'It's been a long day for you.'

'Not quite yet,' Kidston said. 'I'm going to take Gregor to the murder house for one last look around. Forensics are finished with it. I want to give Steven Ferrier the house back soon. Do you want to join us?'

'I had a final walk through earlier with Martin Reynolds before the IB people finished. They've done their usual thorough job.' Reynolds was the head of the force's Identification Bureau, known to cops and detectives as IB. With their detection rates on fingerprint lifts and successes with blood, hair, and other forensic samples, Reynolds and his team had solved as many crimes as the force's best detectives.

'I just want to phone Grace before we head over there,' Kidston said. 'Let her know I'm going to be a bit later tonight.'

'Good man,' Sawyers said. He'd seen a massive change in Kidston since he'd remarried and started a family. His best DI still put the hours in and still solved big cases but his days of hanging around the CID office at night were over. Kidston had something to go home to now.

———

Kidston stood in the middle of the big lounge and stared at the bloodstained chair. He recalled Ryan Ferrier's gruesome bloody corpse and the ferocity of his murder. He'd known Ryan, worked cases with him, consulted on prosecution strategies, evidential tactics. He was a conscientious, professional prosecutor... a friend. That bloody corpse had been a shadow of Ryan Ferrier and now his house, this murder house, was a poor imitation of a home; cold, inhospitable, vacant, and derelict of spirit. The lounge walls, especially around the doors and light switches, were blackened in large patches with fingerprint dust.

The ferric oxide used to lift latent impressions left an ugly sooty residue. Dusting for prints. *Remember, Man, that thou art dust and unto dust thou shalt return,* Kidston thought, echoes of his Catholic childhood. Everything goes to nothing in the end.

'What do we know now that we didn't know yesterday morning?' Kidston asked Gregor Stark as they walked through the house one final time.

'We know much more about the victim, more about his personal life, his family and colleagues. We know where he played tennis and the clubs he socialised in,' Stark said. 'We know that he was close friends with Adrian Harrison, another gay lawyer, who may have been the victim of an earlier murder and too much of a coincidence–'

'We don't believe in coincidences, Gregor.'

'And we're not wild about any possible hitman theory. A professional killer wouldn't take the chance that he'd find a suitable weapon in his victim's home. They may have shared a bottle of wine suggesting familiarity plus the fury and frenzy of the murder act points to intimacy. We think our killer was known to Ryan Ferrier... a friend or acquaintance... possibly of both men.'

'What's our next steps in hunting down that friend or acquaintance?'

Stark took a moment to order his thoughts. 'A trace, interview and eliminate on the ex-boyfriend. We don't know how long Douglas Tennant is going to be home and we want to sit him down face to face. We need to check if he has any links to Adrian Harrison.'

'Good thinking, Gregor. And after that?'

'Titwood Tennis Club and Bennets or Goodnights nightclubs?'

'Correct. We'll head to Mount Vernon tonight. Tennant's sister is getting married tomorrow. We'll do the various clubs tomorrow night. After we've explained ourselves to the pathologists. What's your *Spidey-Sense* telling you now, Gregor?'

'We're dealing with a double murder.'

'I think your *Spidey-Sense* is on the money.'

CHAPTER THIRTEEN

Douglas Tennant didn't seem too surprised to find two detectives knocking on the door of his parents' neat semi-bungalow. Following introductions, the detectives were seated on a large black leather sofa in the front lounge. The offer of tea or coffee from Mrs Tennant was declined and she went to join her husband in the small TV lounge at the rear of the house. Stark flipped his folder open, ready with pen in hand.

'I wondered if someone would be in touch,' Tennant said as he sat in the armchair facing his interviewers. He was tall and slim, in his mid-thirties with dark cropped hair and a handsome smile.

Stark eyed Tennant up and down as if measuring him for a police cell. 'Why do you say that?'

'I heard the news about Ryan, I saw the press conference and imagined my name would come up as an ex-partner.' He had a soft, polite speaking voice.

'You live and work in London now,' Kidston said. 'In media and advertising, is that correct?'

'Yes.'

'And you're with someone else now?' Kidston asked. 'Is it the same person you left Ryan for?'

Tennant's handsome face crumpled as he sighed heavily and bit his lip. 'I'm with Dennis now, and yes, he's who I left Ryan for. We live together in Elstree. He couldn't make this wedding trip due to work commitments.'

'But you called Ryan earlier this week?' Kidston said. 'What was that about?'

'I thought we could fit in lunch or dinner while I was home. It was sentimental of me.' Tennant was crying now; a solitary tear ran down his left cheek. He wiped it away. 'I was very fond of Ryan.'

'Did you meet up?' Kidston asked.

'Ryan didn't want to. Told me our split was still too raw and he was struggling to move on.' Tennant's tears flowed freely now. He held his head in his hands and wiped his face before looking imploringly at his interrogators. 'Do we have to do this?'

'I'm afraid we do, Mr Tennant,' Kidston said. 'Can I ask you where you were on Wednesday?'

'I was with my sister and my parents all day. We went into town for a meal, came back here for a few drinks. I spent the night in my old bedroom.'

'When you spoke to Ryan, did he mention whether he was seeing anyone else?' Kidston asked. 'Did he disclose anything about his personal life that could assist our enquiries?'

'I asked about how he was doing and whether there was anyone new.'

'And?' Kidston asked.

'Mentioned that he'd played the field a bit but was getting too old for one-night stands. He was getting back into the club scene, Bennets, and Goodnights. But there was no one permanent, no new romance. He certainly never mentioned anything that suggested he was in any danger or that someone was out to kill him.' Tennant regained his composure. 'I wondered if one of the criminals he'd put in jail had exacted some dreadful revenge. I assume the police would check that.'

'It's part of our investigation, Mr Tennant,' Kidston said. 'DS Stark will take a note of your London particulars while I just have a quick chat with your parents to verify your alibi.'

———

Back in the car, the two detectives exchanged their thoughts on Douglas Tennant. His alibi had checked out and, under a fair degree of scrutiny, his emotional interview had convinced both detectives that he was a grieving former partner.

Stark only had one doubt. 'Sentimental, my arse. I think he was hoping for a wee romantic reunion with his ex-boyfriend. He was up for his *Nat King Cole*.'

Kidston didn't offer any disagreement and smiled at his sergeant's language. Stark was using one of their former detective sergeant colleague John Wylie's stock phrases from his expansive book of Glasgow rhyming slang. Wylie was a master of the art.

'Not a suspect though,' Kidston said. 'Genuinely grief-stricken and a stonewall alibi. We need to be looking elsewhere.'

CHAPTER FOURTEEN

SATURDAY, 18 AUGUST 1990

Joe Sawyers had arranged the 10am meeting with the pathology team at their offices in University Gardens. As the CID car climbed Gilmorehill, Kidston took in the picturesque sight of the university's iconic tower and spire that dominated the city's west end skyline. The Gothic revival splendour of Glasgow's ancient seat of learning shimmered in the morning sunshine, the reflected light dancing on its pale-brown sandstone edifice. The magnificent structure brought back happy memories for Kidston; he and Grace had their wedding there in the spring of 1987. Before teacher training college, she'd completed her English literature degree at Glasgow, and used her graduate's privilege to be married in the university chapel. Kidston occasionally marvelled at the names of Grace's more notable former alumni: Adam Smith, James Watt, Lord Kelvin, John Logie Baird, and Joseph Lister were the names he was familiar with, but Grace also talked about three UK prime ministers, a signatory to the US Declaration of Independence, and numerous Nobel laureates whose names he struggled to remember. With his three O-Grades, Kidston was never likely to trouble the place. *But you went to the University of Life*, he could hear Grace teasing.

Gregor Stark joined Kidston and Sawyers in making up the CID delegation. The pathologists had given up their Saturday off, but this was an important get-together. Professor Cochrane had been adamant; the meeting couldn't wait. On Monday morning the department would be inundated with all the so-called *fiscal deaths* from across Glasgow's seven police divisions. The mood was apprehensive.

Cochrane sat in the centre of the paper-strewn office, files and folders covered every desk, and was reading through the report concerning the death of Adrian Harrison. Dr Harry Marshall and Dr Finola Donnelly were also flicking through various associated paperwork. Kidston was pleased to see Donnelly there; she'd been a strong ally in previous cases. He noticed that she was wearing her hair down, and that her skin had its familiar natural healthy glow. She'd probably managed to fit in one of her regular runs around the nearby Kelvingrove Park. Everyone had tea or coffee and a plate of digestive biscuits lay on the only table not covered with files.

Allan Cochrane was in his early sixties, a big man with long straggly grey hair swept back off his forehead. He had long frizzy sideburns and if it wasn't for the silver-rimmed bifocals perched on the tip of his nose and the man's penchant for colourful bow ties, he could easily have been mistaken for an ageing rock star. His normally booming voice was quiet when he spoke.

'This is not an ideal scenario by any stretch. Harry did the initial exam and called me in as corroboration. The police report, bottom line, states: "No suspicious circumstances", and that's been signed off by a detective inspector.

'The injuries we found in the exam were consistent with a hanging,' Cochrane continued. 'Obviously we can't state whether the deceased hanged himself or was somehow coerced or forced to do it like an execution. Dr Marshall, would you like to elaborate?'

'Yes, thank you, Professor.' Marshall was much younger than his boss. A kind face and an eager expression. He was casually dressed in a maroon sweatshirt, blue jeans, and Nike trainers. 'Normally in such cases, we need to differentiate between two different methods of hanging: suspension hanging, where the body is suspended at the neck or a drop hanging. Think about the so-called "long drop", the method used in executions. This is where a calculated drop is designed to break the neck. There was no such injury in this case; the U-shaped hyoid bone survived intact, which is not that unusual. Adrian Harrison's post-mortem injuries were fully consistent with a suspension hanging.'

'But you have an alternative theory now, some new suspicions?' Cochrane directed his question at Sawyers before dooking a digestive biscuit into his mug of tea.

'Luc and Gregor picked up on the Adrian Harrison case in the initial stages of their investigation of Ryan Ferrier's murder,' Sawyers said. 'And there are zero doubts about that one being a murder.'

Three pathologists nodded in agreement. They'd all viewed Ferrier's remains in the mortuary.

'The police lab has confirmed that semen stains inside Adrian Harrison's bathrobe do not contain his DNA based on the post-mortem samples we got from the mortuary.' Sawyers continued. 'We are considering that the subject of this DNA profile could be a suspect in the Ryan Ferrier murder investigation and that he's responsible for two murders.'

'We believe that the hanging scene was staged by the suspect,' Kidston said. 'I'm hopeful that by Monday the lab will identify and confirm Adrian Harrison's DNA from skin-cell deposition on the cord from his dressing gown. The cord is almost identical in thickness to the rope from the kitchen pulley.'

'It looks like you do, indeed, have two murders to investigate, Detective Inspector Kidston.' Cochrane adjusted his bifocals and got to his feet. 'Can I borrow you, DS Stark? Come over here, please.' Stark, a curious expression on his face, crossed the room to where Cochrane now stood. 'Take off your tie please, Sergeant.'

Stark slipped the knot and handed his blue silk tie to Cochrane.

The big pathologist held the tie at both ends. 'This works better if you're kneeling, Gregor.' Stark knelt on the floor facing Cochrane. 'If I wrap this tie around your neck and step around behind you...' The pathologist made his move and now towered over the young DS from behind, his feet planted either side of Stark's kneeling legs. 'And if I cross this tie behind your neck...' He demonstrated the action. 'And now... if I pull you up, lift you by the neck...' Thankfully for Stark this element was simulated, and Cochrane did little actual pulling. 'If I pull up, hard and tight, it wouldn't take too long, or too much pressure to compress your carotid artery, your jugular veins, or your airway. You would lose consciousness in under a minute and, ultimately, a few minutes later you'd be dead. And you can see from the line of the tie where the post-mortem ligature marks would be.

'Okay, Gregor, thank you.' He tapped Stark's shoulder. 'Hopefully not too tight... I was thinking about that traffic cop who gave me a speeding ticket last month.'

Stark jumped to his feet and rubbed his neck. 'That wisnae me... thankfully.' Stark laughed as he looked over his heavily creased silk tie. The 'hanging' demonstration had eased much of the earlier tension.

'Gentlemen, it looks very likely that Adrian Harrison was

hanged by your suspect.' Cochrane picked up the post-mortem report. 'Death was due to cerebral hypoxia from application of a ligature around the neck compressing the carotid arteries and jugular veins. This was evidenced by petechial haemorrhaging in the victim's eyes, a dry and protruding tongue and furrowed ligature markings on the neck and jaw.'

'All consistent with our murder hypothesis,' Kidston said. 'Martha Harrison mentioned the tongue. It must have been horrific for her.'

Dr Donnelly looked up from the file she was reading, her clear hazel eyes scanning the entire group. She ran a hand through her hair. 'From reading the police reports the demonstration might have been right on the money. Before the Prof moved behind Gregor, their position was consistent with the kneeling man fellating the standing man. You've got a semen stain inside the robe. Something during or after the sex act has angered the suspect and provoked this attack.

'If I can extrapolate and include the Ryan Ferrier crime scene that I attended, the overkill that I witnessed, also sexually motivated, but with a heightened level of anger... to a violent fury, we may have a suspect who's repulsed by the homosexual sex act. Maybe the victim's pushed things too far or the suspect is heavily conflicted about his homosexuality.'

'Yes,' Kidston agreed. 'Shame is one of the motivating factors we'd been considering for the Ferrier case. You agree this is a credible theory, Finola?'

'I do but remember I'm a pathologist. I'm crossing my lane here and encroaching into the world of forensic psychology. I'd be unable to offer this as a professional opinion.'

'Come on, Finola,' Cochrane boomed. 'You're as qualified as the next person, you've done extensive research and study in this area.'

'Would you be minded to offer a profile of our killer?' Sawyers asked.

'It would be conjecture, no more than my subjective, unqualified opinion.'

'But, Finola,' Kidston said, 'unless his prints or DNA are on our files, it's all we've got to go on right now.'

'I'd guess he's aged between eighteen and twenty-five, probably younger than his victims, tall, powerfully built. I think Allan's demonstration confirmed that for me. He's heavily conflicted about his homosexuality, possibly bisexual and early into experimenting with men. Men who are a bit older than him but not old men. Maybe...' Donnelly tailed off.

'Maybe what?' Kidston asked.

'I'm no profiler, remember,' Donnelly replied, a grave look on her face. 'If he enjoyed the first killing and the second murder saw that escalation of violence, the next murder could jump to another level.'

'Christ, Finola,' Sawyers said. 'You saw Ryan Ferrier. Is there another level? A third murder takes him to entry-level serial killer.'

CHAPTER FIFTEEN

'It was a Friday afternoon in mid-June,' Amanda Devlin said. 'I checked my diary to confirm after you called. It would be the fifteenth, just over two months ago.'

Devlin and fellow member, Tricia Mathieson were hosting Kidston and Stark in the impressive clubhouse of Titwood Lawn Tennis Club. The detectives had opened the meeting by offering commiserations to both women who'd been friendly with the two deceased members. Titwood was one of the oldest and most prestigious clubs in the city and was located around a three-minute walk from the Harrison family home. They'd provided coffee and sandwiches, which both detectives were grateful for. Stark had made enquiries earlier through the fixtures secretary to establish who had played with either Ryan Ferrier or Adrian Harrison in recent weeks. It was Devlin who'd called Stark back with an account of two non-members, who'd hit some doubles with the men. Tricia Mathieson had been her playing partner.

'On the phone you said they were outsiders,' Stark said, sitting with his folder open, pen at the ready. '"Gatecrashers", you called them. What made them so out of place?'

Devlin looked at Mathieson before answering. 'Everything was a bit off. One was playing in red football shorts, the other had on baggy blue beach shorts. We've got a dress code and I'm afraid that's not it.' Devlin spoke with a refined accent. Her clothing, hair and nails screamed money. Mathieson wore a sleeveless dress that showed her tanned, muscular arms to good effect. They were both around forty and looked fit and athletic. Kidston knew several similar women in his own club. He was thinking they'd probably give him a decent game.

'When we came out of the clubhouse around 2.30pm all the courts were in play.' Mathieson sipped her coffee before continuing. 'The club rule is no singles play when the courts are full. Players are expected to partner up and play doubles.'

'Same rule at Newlands,' Kidston agreed. 'For every club I imagine.'

'That's right, you play, Inspector, Sergeant Stark did say.' Mathieson placed her coffee down and crossed her legs, displaying her well-toned calf muscles. 'You must have played here.'

'A few times, back in the day, an interclub league match. My game's not up to it anymore, I'm afraid. What about our two interlopers?' Things were becoming a bit too convivial, and Kidston was keen to return to their enquiry. 'How did it play out?'

'When I reminded them of the rule, which they had no idea about, we hit mixed doubles with them for a few games and then Ryan offered them a game of doubles with him and Adrian.'

'Definitely not members?' Kidston asked.

'No chance,' Devlin said. 'Never seen them before or since.'

'Could they play?' Kidston asked.

'They were pretty good,' Devlin replied. 'The tall one, with the red shorts, was very good. A lefty with a ferocious serve if I remember. The smaller guy was a bit embarrassed, I partnered him for a few games. Red Shorts was smashing body shots at me. I was more than capable of dealing with them, but it was poor etiquette. He was so bloody competitive, but his pal kept apologising to me. We were still playing in the next court when they paired up with Ryan and Adrian.'

'Ryan was coaching Red Shorts, showing him how to do a backhand slice... I remember that,' Mathieson said. 'He was showing him how to improve his ball toss. Ryan was very tactile with him... I mean... it's very tough to say and probably inappropriate...' She tailed off.

'No, please go on,' Kidston said. 'Think about the relatives.'

'Well... you know Ryan was gay–'

'Yes.'

'He was *very* gay, and I mean that in a nice way,' Mathieson continued, the faintest crack in her voice showing the first signs of emotion. 'Outgoing, flamboyant, great fun, brilliant company.' Kidston saw the tears in her eyes. 'I'm so sorry, but I think Ryan was flirting with the tall one, Red Shorts.'

'Did he flirt back?'

'He looked very comfortable with it, high fives, back slaps and such,' Mathieson replied. 'Do you think these two boys had something to do with Ryan's murder?' She was sobbing now.

'I'm sorry,' Kidston said. 'This must be very upsetting for you both. Would you like to take a break?'

Mathieson dabbed her eyes. The two women exchanged a glance and confirmed they were okay to continue.

'Was Adrian involved in any flirting?' Kidston asked.

'It was mostly Ryan but the tall one with the red shorts was lapping it up, encouraging it almost.' Mathieson recovered her poise. 'Can I ask if Adrian Harrison's suicide is being reinvestigated? We saw the forensic people going back into the house.'

'I can't really comment beyond that we're investigating the Ryan Ferrier murder and his close association with Adrian links with our enquiry.'

'Poor Martha,' Mathieson said. Devlin nodded her agreement.

'I always wondered if Adrian Harrison might be gay,' Devlin announced much to the surprise of Mathieson who spluttered into her coffee. 'I know he and Martha had two lovely kids, but it was just a sense of him. I think they call it *gaydar*.'

'Did you have a similar impression, Tricia?' Kidston asked. 'Was there any talk amongst members about Adrian?'

'No,' Mathieson said. Both women shook their heads.

'If we can go back to the tennis,' Kidston said. 'Did you see any of the four of them leave together?'

'No, we finished our game before them.'

'Can you remember their names?' Kidston asked.

The two women exchanged a puzzled look. 'There were nicknames, but I can't remember them, I'm sorry,' Mathieson said.

'I think the tall one was Nicky or Ricky or even Micky,' Devlin said. 'The short one I have no memory, I'm sorry I can't be more helpful.'

'What about ages, descriptions?' Kidston asked.

'I have Red Shorts taller and younger, around eighteen to twenty-one, not much older than that,' Mathieson said. 'Very good-looking, thick, brown, longish hair, worn over the ears and the collar. He's about six feet two, impressive physical specimen. Muscular, very fit. Broad shoulders, narrow waist. Great build for tennis.'

'The other boy?'

'Red hair, pasty complexion, around five six,' Devlin said. 'Much quieter. I had a sense that he knew they were gatecrashing. As if he was expected to be chucked off the court at any minute. Played with an old wooden Slazenger. I had one when I was a girl.'

Mathieson nodded her agreement.

'The other tennis racket?' Kidston asked.

'Wilson, aluminium, early model,' Mathieson answered.

Stark scribbled furiously on his notepad.

'Accents?' Kidston asked.

'Local, both. Glasgow housing scheme, a bit common,' Mathieson said sniffily.

'What about you, Amanda?'

'I'd go with Tricia's description,' Devlin said. 'She played on the same side of the net as him. I'd be struggling to add to that. I would add one thing though that I do remember.'

'What's that?' Kidston asked.

'I have a son not much younger than the Nicky or Micky one and if he'd behaved like that, I would have had serious words with him.'

'What did he do?'

'He was smashing balls, cursing and swearing and throwing his racket about when he lost a point or made a mistake,' Devlin said. 'He had an angry temper, didn't seem able to filter it out.'

———

Kidston's extension rang. It was Miller.

'Martha Harrison's just told me her theory about how her husband was murdered,' Miller said. 'Why are you giving a grieving widow false hope, putting her through an emotional ringer like that?'

'Are you joking, Miller?' Kidston couldn't believe the audacity of the man. This was the cover-up call, damage limitation. *Please, don't make me look too bad.*

'Look, Kidston, we didn't have what you had. We didn't

know anything about the shower or the missing money. You have to admit the scene was staged pretty good.'

'Good enough to fool you.' Kidston simmered. 'If you'd bothered to sit Martha Harrison down, walk her through her husband's last hours, you'd have seen the contradictory evidence staring you in the face.'

'Don't fuck me over, Kidston. I'm warning you.'

'Don't threaten me, you fuckin' cockroach. You know that's what they called you after your last major fuck-up, when you scurried back to headquarters and let everyone else clean up your mess. "The Cockroach"; survives disasters and nuclear fallout. Let's see how you survive this one.'

The phone line hummed with hatred and loathing. The callers fortunate not to be in the same room or they'd surely rip each other apart.

'I'll fuckin' end you, Kidston. I'm warning you.'

'Admit your mistake, Miller, own your failure. Step aside and leave Mrs Harrison alone. I'll find her husband's killer.'

Kidston slammed down the phone.

CHAPTER SIXTEEN

Stark pointed the car towards Bennets. A trip to the Merchant City was a journey into the dark heart of the Second City of the Empire, where the whispered street names recalled plantation slavers and merchants from Virginia and the West Indies. The Merchant City district stood as a memorial in stone and steel and glass to Glasgow's ancient mercantile wealth and its links with the Atlantic trade in sugar, tobacco, and the soul-crushing misery of human slavery.

There was little human misery on display as the two detectives made their way through Glasgow city centre. The town was teeming with Saturday night revellers, moving between the city's pubs and clubs and all dressed for the lovely August weather. Young men in shirtsleeves or T-shirts, young women wearing as little as they could get away with. The heady mix of alcohol and warm weather contributed to a summer party atmosphere.

Stark had to slow the CID car at one junction as a loud and sizeable hen-night party badly navigated the crossing, ignoring the pedestrian lights. A young woman dressed as the Bride of Frankenstein, her costume paired with Bunny Girl's rabbit's ears, tail and bow tie and completed by 'L' plates and garish Halloween make-up, was being dragged before any willing male passers-by, who were commanded to kiss the bride. For those brave enough, a cash donation was required to be dropped into a plastic bucket wielded by a bridesmaid. With both front car windows wound down to enjoy the warm summer night air, Kidston and Stark recoiled at the clanging of pots and pans that provided the discordant soundtrack to this colourful and noisy spectacle.

The tuneless racket of the bridal party competed with a drunken rendition of 'Nessun Dorma', from an old dosser with a surprisingly fine tenor voice. The drunken recital was emblematic of the battle for Glasgow's soul; in a city known for drunkenness, violence, religious bigotry, unemployment, poverty and rain, new cultural touchstones were emerging in the City of Culture. Puccini's aria was everywhere; aided by being used as an anthem for TV coverage of the recent summer World Cup. Pavarotti had played the city back in May, and big Luciano was, it seemed, *Top of the Pops*, for Glasgow's street singers. Glasgow's fine Victorian buildings shimmered in the late evening twilight – many had been blasted free of soot and grime to celebrate the city's reign as European culture capital. The year-long City of Culture celebrations were attracting many star performers to Glasgow, but few could compete with the enthusiasm of native Glaswegians and their weekend theatre of the street.

Kidston quickly realised that removing their ties had made little difference; they both stood out like sore thumbs. Two straight men lost in a loud, vibrant world of gay. The repetitive electronic dance beat pulsated through the entire building. Bennets was all low lighting, high energy and absolute bedlam on the dance floor. Stark's head was set to constant swivel as he took in the atmosphere and checked out the revellers. Naked torsos, leather waistcoats, gold lamé trouser suits and a man dressed as Marie Antoinette. The joint was jumpin'.

The manager, who went by the name of Jason, led the two detectives through the throng of clubbers to a staffroom where he'd gathered a mix of stewards and bar staff.

'Please don't keep them any longer than necessary,' Jason said. 'It's very busy tonight.'

Stark passed around pictures of Ryan Ferrier and Adrian Harrison. Only one of the group could assist them. 'The dark-haired one, Ryan I think, I recognise him as a customer,' Yvonne, the bar worker with magenta-streaked hair said. 'The other guy's familiar but you should ask Dusty.'

'Who's Dusty?' Kidston asked.

'Dusty Springburn,' Jason said. 'One of our resident drag queens. Performing downstairs just now. Tonight's a drag night.'

'I work downstairs when the drag nights are on,' Yvonne said. 'That guy Ryan was always here to watch Dusty. I think they might have been friends.'

Jason led them to the basement. Someone nipped Stark's bum as they pushed through the crowd. When he turned around a man in an indecently low-cut Elvis jumpsuit beamed at him. Stark smiled back but pushed on. The young DS was getting second glances from all quarters for his boyish good looks. Kidston heard the strains of a song he recognised at once. 'I Close My Eyes and Count to Ten'. The singing was incredible. Raw and vulnerable. This Dusty sounded like the real deal.

'Quite a singer,' Kidston said.

'Brilliant,' Jason agreed. 'Dusty's quite the torch singer. No lip synching for her, unlike the other queens who perform here. Wait till you hear the finale. It should be the next song.'

At the bottom of the stairs Kidston caught his first sight of the performer known as Dusty Springburn. The platinum-blonde beehive caught the stage lights which reflected off a long silver-sequinned column dress. It was encore time as the singer slipped behind a backstage curtain. The crowded basement audience chanted her name in unison.

'Dusty! Dusty! Dusty!'

The singer reappeared to a massive cheer.

'Thank you, Bennets,' Dusty said with a breathy sensuality. 'I appreciate everyone coming out to see me.' She blew the audience an extravagant kiss. 'I think you all know this one.'

The audience were rapt, hushed in anticipation as Dusty's act reached its encore; 'You Don't Have to Say You Love Me'. The boobs, hair and nails were fake, but her voice was the real thing, and she sang with the heart of a wounded lioness. Starting the song with a slower introduction, the vocal was almost conversational. *Singing about someone leaving after they said they'd stay forever.* It sounded accusatory – it seemed every audience member knew that conversation as they nodded in collective agreement. Dusty sang like she meant every word. It wasn't hard to believe that she'd encountered serious heartbreak somewhere along the way. The musical accompaniment from a backing track kicked in for the second verse and Dusty's voice soared with the lyrics. The torch song that flames and burns and reduces all others to ash had the audience singing along with gusto.

Kidston and Stark watched in amazement as more of the crowd joined in the song's chorus, singing louder, whooping and shrieking. Many were overcome and in tears as the words tore at their hearts.

Jason led them to a backstage staffroom which was doubling up as a dressing room. A rail of glamorous colourful dresses stood close to the white-painted bare-brick wall. A side table was strewn with extravagant wigs; blonde, ginger and brunette. Dusty sat at a mirrored vanity dresser and was adjusting her hair grips when the detectives entered.

'Some people to see you,' Jason said. 'Brilliant show, fabulous finale.'

'Thank you, sweetie,' Dusty said. 'Who do we have here? Hollywood calling? London West End?'

'Strathclyde Police CID,' Stark said in a very formal voice, showing his warrant card and making the introductions. Jason pulled up a couple of orange plastic chairs and left them to it. Dusty swung around her chair and picked at the final two kirby grips holding her wig in place.

'What a disappointing end to the night,' Dusty said with a mock pout. 'You need to let a girl down a bit more gently, Sergeant.' She laughed heartily at her own joke. 'They should have sent a couple of ugly coppers, you two are far too good-looking.'

'Brilliant performance.' Kidston took over. 'We just caught the last two numbers. That's quite a voice you've got.' Establishing rapport was an old hostage negotiator tactic. Even though he was being genuine, it wouldn't do any harm to get a potential witness onside.

'Oh, thank you for saying that.' Dusty, giddy and on the edge of tears, fanned a handful of long elegant fingers in front of her face. 'It gets a bit emotional, takes a while to come down from an audience like that.'

'I can imagine,' Kidston said. 'I'm sorry I missed the rest of your set. Maybe another time. Love a bit of Dusty and that's a helluva tribute.'

'Homage, darling, homage, but thank you, I really appreciate you saying that,' Dusty said with a flirtatious smile. 'You can be on my guest list anytime.'

Stark gave his boss a puzzled look. Kidston laughed and said, 'Better get down to business.'

'What can I help you gentlemen with?' Dusty asked.

'We're making enquiries into a murder south of the river,' Kidston said. 'Ryan Ferrier, who we believe frequented Bennets and watched your shows. We think he might have brought another man with him, a lawyer named Adrian Harrison.'

Stark handed over pictures of both men. He noticed the singer's elegant hands, and long, glittery varnished nails.

Dusty handed the pictures back. 'I knew them both, Ryan better. He started bringing Adrian along to my shows more recently. Poor Ryan, I heard on the news he was murdered. Was Adrian murdered too?'

'That's all part of our investigation,' Kidston replied. 'Anything you could help us with would be appreciated... anything at all.'

'Of course.' With the platinum beehive wig removed, Dusty pulled off his hairnet to reveal a thick mane of blond hair which he expertly fashioned into his everyday style. Kidston was struck by his incredibly handsome face, perfectly symmetrical features, and wide toothpaste advert smile. Behind the heavily mascaraed panda make-up, Kidston saw the big blue eyes, clear, bright, and engaging.

'I don't really know too much about Adrian. I remember Ryan teasing him about being in the closet and that he was married with kids. I think he only came to one or two of my shows. I've known Ryan much longer from around the gay scene.'

The room door was pushed half open. The face that peered in was heavily made up and accompanied by a vivid scarlet wig. 'Great show, baby girl. That's why you're top of the bill.'

'Thanks girlfriend,' Dusty called back. 'Give me fifteen

minutes, I'm with CID. Sorry, that was Scarlett Mascara, one of the other queens. She's very good.'

'Back to Ryan and Adrian,' Kidston said. 'Did you notice anyone else in their company on the most recent visits?'

'Around two months ago there was a guy with them for part of the night. I don't think they came in together, but they spent a lot of time on the dance floor.'

'Do you know the guy?'

'I know of him. He's a bit of a hustler. Everyone knows him as "Big Nicky". I'm not sure if it's his first name, Nicholas, or from a surname like Nicol, or Nicolson. I'm sorry.'

'What kind of hustler?' Kidston asked while Stark scribbled in his police notebook.

'He's always preying on older, richer men for money. I'm not even sure if he's gay. He's a handyman type, a bit of landscape gardening, painting, and decorating. Always pleading for money to pay for trips abroad. I think he lives in Toryglen or Rutherglen.'

'Can you describe him? Em...' Kidston hesitated, 'I'm sorry, what do I call you?'

'I'm good with Ms Springburn, Detective Inspector.' Dusty affected a haughty star pose, brushed an imaginary strand of stray hair from her forehead and then laughed. 'I'm only joking. My real name is Marc Monaghan, but everybody calls me Dusty.' Stark wrote his full particulars into his notebook. 'Springburn was an obvious name choice; my love of Dusty and the fact that I was born and raised there; technically I'm a Balgrayhill boy. Not easy to be a young gay man in a Glasgow housing scheme, that's why I tried London and then moved to the west end of Glasgow. Essentially, I'm the Jimmy Somerville character in that Bronski Beat video for 'Smalltown Boy'. Things are much easier in the big city.'

Kidston noticed how easily he shifted between male and

female personas. He could turn the camp accent and the flamboyant body language up or down as required but the hands were always engaged. His normal accent was polite Glaswegian with little trace of his stage character from earlier.

'Describe Nicky for us please,' Kidston said.

'He's about your height and build, Inspector, say six two? Age twenty-one or twenty-two, light-brown hair, medium length just over the collar.' He demonstrated with his hands. 'Very good-looking boy, impressive physique. I've seen him dancing without a shirt, he's ripped.'

'What about his eyes?'

'Dark... Dark and scary. I swear he's got the most unsettling blank eyes. It's like there's nothing behind them. Like looking at a dead fish.'

'Any of his hustles, here at Bennets, that you can tell us about? Has he been in trouble with the police or been barred or thrown out of here?'

'Not that I'm aware of,' Dusty said. 'I think his thing is blow jobs or hand jobs with older guys. For money. I think he may be hung up about his sexuality.'

'How so?' Kidston asked.

'He's been coming here around eighteen months, so far as I know he's not been in a relationship with any man, he might be bisexual. He might be straight, and experimenting or just dicking around with gay men. But you hear things.'

'What things?'

'He's not called "Big Nicky" for just his height. The rumour is that a guy paid thirty pounds to blow him off.'

'What guy?'

'I really don't know. It's just the talk you hear working in a place like this.'

'Where would he be on a Saturday night if he's not here?' Kidston asked.

'Hard to say. Plenty of clubs and pubs to pick from. There's a gay night on Thursdays at Goodnights across the river in Carlton Place. I've seen him there. It's got a decent vibe over the weekend too. If he knows the police are looking for him maybe he's lying low.'

'He doesn't know... yet,' Kidston said. 'And we'd like to keep it that way, so not a word about what we discussed.'

'I understand,' Dusty said.

'Thanks for all your help. What is it you do when you're not singing in clubs?' Kidston asked.

'I'm a teller with the Clydesdale Bank.' Dusty sighed. 'Where all good queens go to see their dreams of stardom fade and die.'

'You shouldn't give up too easily,' Kidston said. 'My wife sang in a country and western group until our daughter was born. We went to Nashville three years ago and she sang in a couple of honky-tonks. For tips. But to her, that was like making the big time.' Kidston handed over his card. 'Please get in touch if Nicky shows up or if you can think of anything else.'

'Wow! You're married to a singer.' Dusty accepted the card. 'I'll make some discreet enquiries and be in touch if I hear anything. Now I need to remove my war paint and armour, could one of you two kind gentlemen unzip me at the back, please, I'm dying to get these tits off.'

Stark looked mortified. Kidston saw his discomfort and nodded an instruction that he should attend to the request. The young DS hesitated, seemingly frozen to the spot. His face was a picture when a smiling Kidston stepped behind Dusty and expertly undid the fastener.

'A wee bit uncomfortable for you there, Gregor? You seemed a bit out of sorts.'

'A man in a dress, boss,' Stark said. 'It's a bit of a freak show. Found it hard to get past the fact I was interviewing a man dressed as a woman. Not to mention the wig, the false boobs, and those nails.'

'It's not contagious, Gregor.'

'I was watching my P's and Q's. Didn't want to cause any offence. And what about all that flirty stuff with you? What was that about?'

'That's how gay men, or some gay men behave. Dusty's a drag queen, so it gets ramped up or camped up a good bit. But you saw the change when the wig came off. Then we met Marc Monaghan.'

'So is he a transvestite?'

'He might be, but I seriously doubt it. Don't stress about it. Marc, or Dusty, is a gay man who is also a singer and performance artist. A very good one.'

'Too strange for me. All that flirtatious stuff. How come you're so comfortable in that setting?' Stark looked sheepish when he realised how he'd phrased his question. 'I don't mean anything by that, you just seem to know a lot about it... understand it better.'

'My young brother is gay,' Kidston said. 'He's not strange, just different.'

'I'm sorry, I didn't mean to cause any offence.' Stark grimaced, his embarrassment clear.

'Honestly, Gregor, don't stress it. This will be a difficult investigation. It might require some sensitivity if we're to deal with gay men and their families.'

'What does your brother do?' Stark asked.

'He's an actor, a performer, based in London. Been in a few

West End shows. Left Glasgow when he was nineteen. Living his best life, doing what he always wanted to do.'

'Was it difficult for your folks when he came out as gay?' Stark said. 'If you don't mind me asking.'

'My dad had a little wobble, but Sean was fourteen when he came out. Prior to that it had been girlfriends all the way.'

'What about all that AIDS stuff? Did that not have people worried?'

'It was concerning for my parents, but Sean's sensible. He took precautions, looked after himself properly.'

The young DS changed the subject. 'What about this Nicky guy?'

'We have a name and a description similar to what Amanda Devlin and Tricia Mathieson gave us. We may have a general area for his address, an idea of what he works at. The landscaper theory ties in with Adrian Harrison,' Kidston continued. 'I'm praying the lab tells us by Monday that the semen stain is from this Nicky guy, but we still need to piece it all together. We might need to get Amanda and Tricia to help with a photofit, show it to Dusty and see if we're close. We need to check out Goodnights.'

'Phil Canavan's place,' Stark said.

'Sarah Canavan's, more accurately,' Kidston began. 'Phil's just managing it for his sister. Any reports on how that place is being run? Hard to believe Phil Canavan is out of the drugs game completely. A leopard never changes its spots.'

'Blames you for that tin hand.' Gregor Stark absentmindedly ran a forefinger over the small dent in his forehead. An automatic response. A reminder of the fateful night he and Kidston had faced down an armed Phil Canavan.

'Phil has only himself to blame for his misadventures. I suppose the emergence of Nicky as a suspect pushes Canavan well down the list. I can understand him having motive for Ryan Ferrier but what's his connection with Adrian Harrison?'

'I agree, seems very slim,' Stark said. 'Word is Sarah Canavan is very strict on her no drugs policy but I'm not sure all her clients will be on their best behaviour.'

'I imagine Saturday is a better night to check it out than Sunday. What do you say, one more stop before we clock off?'

CHAPTER SEVENTEEN

'I s Sarah or Phil Canavan on tonight?' Kidston flashed his warrant card at the dinner-suited steward on the front door of Goodnights.

'Mr Canavan is in the lounge. Who shall I say is calling?'

'Gorbals CID.' Kidston pushed past the steward. 'It's okay, we all know each other.'

The two detectives walked through a brightly lit foyer decorated in a heavily embossed gold wall covering. The lighting changed dramatically when the double doors opened to the semi-darkness of a busy club. The noise levels changed too; Kidston's ears were greeted by a heavy disco beat and the recognisable sound of Donna Summer's 'I Feel Love'. It was a big improvement on what they'd been playing in Bennets. Canavan was standing at the edge of a throng of drinkers, on an elevated lounge bar area, and looking down on the busy dance floor.

'Can we speak in your office?' Kidston asked, realising he wouldn't be able to compete with the heavy disco music. He noticed that Canavan's prosthetic was conspicuously absent from view, tucked into the right-hand trouser pocket of an expensive-looking suit.

Canavan led them downstairs towards his office. Kidston noticed the signing on the adjacent door.

'VIP rooms. Phil, you and Sarah seem to have a decent little club going here. What happens through there?'

'Champagne bar for our VIP customers, Mr Kidston.' Canavan could barely contain his sneer. 'Might be a bit rich for your blood, even on a DI's salary.'

The door to the VIP room opened and two stunning young women stepped out into the hallway. Both were dressed in glamorous evening gowns and smiled as if to greet visiting clients.

'Ladies.' Kidston nodded politely. Stark's eyes were out on stalks as he eyed the two gorgeous women.

Canavan took that as his cue. 'Gents, can I introduce Cassandra and Heidi, two of our VIP hostesses?'

'Good evening, gentlemen,' Cassandra greeted them. She was tall and leggy, with beautiful dark skin and spoke with a soft Caribbean lilt. 'Can I offer you gentlemen a glass of champagne?'

'We're here on official police business, but thank you,' Kidston said.

'Oh, that's a shame.' It was Heidi, a petite, long-haired blonde, speaking in strongly accented English. 'Maybe some other time.'

Canavan ushered the detectives into his office. It was plush, well equipped, with a mahogany desk and wall cabinets. Kidston noted that one wall was fully mirrored, possibly a throwback to when the room had been a small dance studio. The two detectives sat in a big brown leather sofa. Canavan sat on a matching armchair on the visitors' side of his desk. 'Would you like a glass of champagne, or I have a bottle of Laphroaig open or maybe something else?'

'No thanks, Phil,' Kidston said. 'Charming hostesses, I'm sure they'll keep the champagne flowing. I know how it works.'

'Some lovely girls that Sarah kept on when she sold her salons.' Canavan seemed a bit jumpy. 'Are you sure I can't get you a coffee or something?'

'No thanks. We're here on a murder inquiry.' Kidston scrutinised Canavan's reaction to his announcement but the career criminal never flinched.

'What murder would that be, Detective Inspector?'

Stark got the nod and produced photographs of the two murder victims.

'Either of these faces familiar, Phil?' Kidston asked. 'More likely to see them on a Thursday when you run your gay night.'

Canavan bristled, a look of disgust. 'It's not my fucking gay night, nothing to do with me. That's all down to Sarah and her love of the pink pound. I can't abide all that camp hysteria; you won't find me here on a Thursday.'

'Well, it is Sarah's club, or so I understand.' Kidston pushed the knife a little deeper.

'That's correct, Inspector.' A wounded Canavan sneered at Kidston. 'Let me get my door staff to look at the pictures. My chief steward, Billy Bannerman's on the door.' He picked up the phone. 'Billy, you and Johnny Boy get down here now, I've got the CID in.'

Two minutes later, the steward who'd greeted them at the front door appeared with Johnny Boy McManus. He was Canavan's frizzy-haired chief enforcer, sometime bodyguard and principal driver and looked ridiculous. His bulky, bantam frame was bursting out of a dinner suit, two sizes too small for him. The ruffles on his shirt made him look like a sub-standard Prince tribute act. Kidston exchanged a sly look with Stark.

'Nice ruffles, Johnny Boy,' Kidston said. 'Long time, no see. I hope you've been behaving yourself since your last stretch in Barlinnie.'

'Aye, Mr Kidston, keeping my nose clean these days.' The little enforcer lowered his head, tucking his chin behind an oversized velvet bow tie. Avoiding eye contact. A habit formed from a lifelong mistrust of the polis and hatred for the CID. He wanted this interview to be over quickly.

Canavan passed the two photographs to Billy Bannerman. In contrast to his fellow steward, Bannerman wore his dinner suit with a sense of suave style. The two stewards looked at both pictures.

'Don't know either of them,' Bannerman said.

'Thursday nights,' Canavan said. 'Homos.'

'I never said they were gay,' Kidston corrected him. 'Both these men are murder victims.'

'Ah'm no' here on Thursdays,' said a relieved Johnny Boy.

'Not ringing any bells.' Bannerman was holding a picture in each hand. 'Even on a Thursday, I normally work with Sarah.' Something in his mannerisms, the way he looked at Canavan, told Kidston he was lying.

'What about a young guy called Nicky, maybe known as Big Nicky?' Kidston asked. 'Six two, aged around twenty, twenty-one or twenty-two, brown hair, dark eyes, athletic build. Probably works as a landscaper or decorator, enjoys a game of tennis. Might live in the Toryglen, Rutherglen area.' Kidston kept his gaze on Bannerman whose eyes revealed a flicker of recognition. 'Possibly comes here at the weekend as well as a Thursday.'

Bannerman shook his head. 'No, I'm sorry, Inspector.'

'Sorry, we don't know each other.' Kidston's pale-green eyes considered the suave bouncer. 'I know these two well, but I don't think we've met.'

'I'm Billy Bannerman, the chief steward.'

'Have you worked anywhere else, Billy?'

'Here and there.'

'Here and where?'

'Um, Maestros, Shuffles, The Cotton Club. I used to do the Northern Soul circuit.'

'I'm told Sarah Canavan runs a very strict policy for underage drinking and drugs. I hope there's nothing going on here that would put that at risk.'

Canavan looked sick.

'If any of you encounter Nicky over the next few nights, I want to be informed. Is that understood, Phil?' Kidston glared at Canavan. 'If I find out he's been frequenting Goodnights and you've not told me, I'll bring a world of pain on this place. I'm sure if I bring the drugs dogs in to check your toilet seats, we'll find traces of white powder. Sarah won't be pleased if I close this place down. Neither will the courts. Canavan, you're on a suspended jail sentence. This could mean a long stretch in Barlinnie for you.'

Canavan's look was turning to anger.

Spiralling to fury.

———

When a tired Kidston arrived home just after midnight, he saw that their bedroom light was on. Grace often slept with a light on – a throwback to a childhood fear of darkness that had plagued her into adulthood. As he entered, he found Grace was waiting for him. She was lying in bed reading the latest Danielle Steel paperback while listening to Joni Mitchell's *Hejira* at low volume on a bedside CD player. The song playing was 'Amelia', a favourite of Grace's and one she often played on her guitar. Tallulah was lying half asleep in her basket. She raised her head long enough for Kidston to nuzzle her neck before lying back down to resume her doggie dreams.

'I'm sorry it was such a late one, Gracie.' Kidston spoke as he hung up his suit. 'The Ferrier case is starting to move into some possible lines of enquiry. How did my girls get on today?'

'Everything's good, thanks, but you've had such a long day.' Grace spoke softly and ran her hand through her thick mane of long red hair. Her smoky-grey eyes sparkled in the light of the bedside lamp. 'Did you get anything to eat?'

'Managed a sandwich earlier.'

'Florrie missed you reading her favourite bedtime story.'

'Did you do the Bear Hunt with her?'

'We did, but I think she prefers all your funny voices.'

'I promise I'll read it tomorrow night.' He slipped in beside Grace as she closed her paperback and switched off the lamp. He wrapped his arm around her shoulder, and she rested her head on his chest. He talked her through the main points of his day and where he thought the enquiry might be going. They laughed at Gregor's nervy encounter with a drag queen. Grace was a very good listener and Kidston always felt the benefits of these conversations. Decompression, they called it.

Grace slid up his torso and reached out in the darkness to caress his cheek. He kissed her gently on the forehead. 'Poor Luca,' she whispered. 'I missed you and I worry when you don't come home.' She kissed him full on the mouth; it was a slow, soft kiss, full of late-night intent. 'Are you tired?'

'Not so much now,' Kidston mumbled as he felt his tiredness wash away, his body responding to Grace's touch. A familiar stirring sensation. Grace swung around and sat astride him, fumbling under the sheets until she found what she was looking for. Kidston let out an involuntary moan as she slid onto him in a deft, rocking movement. In the throes of arousal, they covered each other's mouths with their hands; Tallulah was more likely to wake up than Florrie but with no little effort they managed to keep the noise down.

Their favourite kind of decompression.

Five minutes later, Grace was fast asleep.

Kidston wasn't too far behind his wife but, just before he fell into a deep sleep, his tired mind remembered the look of fury on Phil Canavan's face.

CHAPTER EIGHTEEN

SUNDAY, 19 AUGUST 1990

'We can rule out Torrance, Bonnar and Madeley,' Stark announced. 'No chance any of them are looking for reprisals.' The three main career criminals serving jail time after Ryan Ferrier's prosecutions had all been eliminated. 'All three accept jail as an occupational hazard.'

'Any update from the lab on the dressing gown, Alison?' Kidston asked.

'There was sufficient deposition for a viable sample,' Metcalfe replied. 'We should have a DNA result tomorrow.'

Half the team were in the office. The big table was laid out with tea, coffee, and hot filled rolls. The aroma of cooked bacon wafted through the room. Kidston wanted a recap and a discussion on next steps. He asked Stark to update the group on the suspect known as Nicky or Big Nicky. The young DS walked the group through the guts of the information gathered from Amanda Devlin, Tricia Mathieson, and Marc Monaghan. Stark also updated the meeting on the visits to Bennets and Goodnights.

'I ran Billy Bannerman through the computer,' Stark said. 'He's got form for drug dealing as you suspected, boss.'

'Shifty character,' Kidston said. 'Got a sense he was holding back last night. What about our "Nicky" with a Toryglen or Rutherglen address?'

'Nothing on any of our files or systems,' Metcalfe said. 'Zorba and Mork are working through the various postcodes in Toryglen and Rutherglen from the voters' roll but it's a massive area and Nicky might not be registered to vote.'

'If we don't get a DNA hit for the dressing gown from the lab tomorrow, we'll arrange for Devlin, Mathieson, and Monaghan to work up a photofit,' Kidston said, stifling a yawn with the ball of his hand.

Kidston spent two hours reading through all the statements, personal descriptive forms, bulletins, and briefing notes connected to the investigation. He updated his *Murder Book*, a master file that Kidston liked to maintain for his homicide enquiries; a running chronological log highlighting key policy decisions and developments in the investigation. Stark updated all the other ongoing enquiry files. Work duties allocated for Sunday included further door-to-door enquiries at both the Ferrier and Harrison addresses, and a return visit to Titwood Lawn Tennis Club. Kidston arranged teams of detectives to revisit both Bennets and Goodnights and show pictures of the two deceased to their Sunday evening patrons. It might jog the memory of other clubgoers and bring the mysterious Nicky into sharper focus. Even though a picture of a viable suspect was starting to emerge – he was little more than a shadow.

Kidston ordered Stark home. They'd been surviving on fish suppers, sandwiches and other scraps and little sleep since Thursday. Kidston felt the need for a home-cooked meal, a run with Tallulah and an early night.

———

It was a lovely afternoon for a run with Tallulah in the park. The striking grey-and-white husky with its piercing ice-blue eyes and lupine face had been rescued as a puppy by Luc and Melanie and they'd shared her for years after their marriage split. When 'Auntie' Melanie saw the connection between Florence and Tallulah, she'd offered that Luc should keep the husky. Tallulah was now part of their family.

Glasgow, *the dear green place*, could fool you on a sunny day. Kidston changed into his running gear and loaded a Prince cassette tape into his Walkman. The nearby Rouken Glen Park on the boundary between Glasgow and East Renfrewshire was his favourite running destination. Designed around a natural glen, it featured a spectacular waterfall, surrounded by steep woodland with criss-crossing trails and paths. He'd been going there since his childhood; playing pitch and putt or larking around with his pals on the boating pond until the angry parkie shouted his number to call in his boat.

He parked close to Whitecraigs railway station at the northeast corner of the park. 'Sign 'O' the Times' played through his headphones as Kidston started with a gentle-paced run around the pond. Tallulah was straining on her lead but ran alongside him at his pace. She ignored the other dog walkers circling the pond at a more leisurely stride. Picking up speed, he headed through the glen towards the waterfall. Tallulah seemed to be enjoying it as much as he was. Running with his husky was another form of decompression; it helped to clear his head and focus his mind on his cases. They stopped at the falls, both glad of a break in the warm sunshine. Fascinated by the thunderous roar of the cascading waters, Tallulah joined in, performing a light, low howl to accompany the crashing sounds of the waterfall.

As they resumed their run, Kidston reflected on his current investigation. It wasn't looking likely now that Ryan Ferrier had been killed by one of the many criminals he'd sent to jail – that was always a long shot. The link to the Harrison murder, and he was certain now that it was a murder and that both men were killed by the same hand, would have repercussions. Why did it have to be Ronnie Miller again? The two men seemed destined to clash throughout their careers. Their last big confrontation over the Ellie Hunter case had caused ructions in headquarters and the fallout had been considerable. The bosses would need to rule on Adrian Harrison's death, but Sawyers had already directed that it was now a twin investigation. Miller would need to suck it up. Professor Cochrane had provided an element of mitigation for how a murder could look like a suicide, particularly when the crime scene was well staged. Kidston would have carried out a more thorough investigation. The mysterious Nicky was in the frame, and he was hopeful that Martin Reynolds' lab rats could identify him from his DNA. Tomorrow was going to be a big day.

Nearing the car at the end of their run, Kidston broke into a final sprint. Tallulah loved to finish with a full speed burst and went full pelt alongside him. Now off her lead, she stayed close to Kidston, turning her head regularly to check his progress. There would only be one winner; the husky could go on forever, and as Kidston neared the end of the final track, he shouted the command.

'Tallulah up!' She braked, effected a quick spin turn and with a dramatic twist of her torso, pushed off her hindquarters and leapt into his waiting arms.

'Good girl, you win again.' Kidston nuzzled into her neck fur, patted her pretty head, and carried her back to the car.

———

The old version of Kidston would never have taken a Sunday evening off in the middle of a murder enquiry. This new and improved version appreciated his life away from the job and the fact that he would pick up the reins of the investigation tomorrow, refreshed, and reinvigorated. How many investigations had he laboured through, tired and exhausted, making bad judgements, wrong calls, or poor decisions? He much preferred this version of himself.

He sat on the edge of Florrie's bed. Grace sat on the other side with Tallulah curled up on the bed beneath Florrie's feet. Kidston's toddler daughter was captivated by the various funny voices and comical noises he used to describe the action in her favourite Michael Rosen book. From the exaggerated swishing of the long grass to the splashing sounds of the river and the squelching noise of oozy mud, Florrie giggled at her daddy's highly animated performance.

She went to sleep a very happy little girl.

'That was quite a performance you gave,' Grace said when they had returned to the lounge to finish off the nice bottle of Barolo they'd opened at dinner. 'She's gone out like a wee light.'

'She's not my most critical audience.' Kidston laughed.

'But you do put a lot into your performance. Much like last night's, which, if I'm honest, was a bit more to my taste.' Grace smiled as she pushed an errant strand of flame-red hair behind her ear.

He recognised a familiar twinkle in her smoky-grey eyes. 'Early night?'

She was already draining her wine glass, taking his hand, and leading him to the bedroom.

CHAPTER NINETEEN

MONDAY, 20 AUGUST 1990

Joe Sawyers asked Kidston to step into his office. 'Congratulations, Detective Chief Inspector Kidston.' A beaming Sawyers walked around his desk and extended a warm handshake to his friend and colleague. 'A well-deserved promotion.'

'Where am I going?' Kidston's head spun with the possibilities of a move. His priority was his current case.

'You're staying here at the South, as my deputy,' Sawyers announced. 'I'm absolutely delighted for you.'

'Thanks, Joe. I'm well chuffed with that.' He punched the air, a massive smile on his face.

'There's a slight complication. I'd better explain.' It sounded ominous.

The two men took a seat and Sawyers continued.

'You're aware of the arrest and conviction of Robert Black for the Scottish Borders child abduction?'

Kidston nodded. 'Six-year-old girl bundled into the back of a blue Transit van. Tied and bound inside a sleeping bag. Arrested around the time of the Glasgow Fair holidays. Convicted last week.'

'Black is an evil bastard who travelled the length and breadth of the country in his work's van, including Glasgow and various parts of Strathclyde. He's uncooperative by all accounts but we're looking at him for several murders across the UK. Lothian and Borders are looking at him for Caroline Hogg.' Sawyers hesitated before continuing. 'Colquhoun and the chief want me to co-ordinate the Strathclyde side of it. I'll be spending a lot of time in Edinburgh... at least initially until the enquiry is established.'

Kidston's blood ran cold as he remembered the pretty face of the five-year-old schoolgirl, whose image had been posted in police stations and public buildings all over the country. Caroline was abducted and murdered after being last seen playing on Portobello Promenade. Her body was found ten days later in a ditch in Leicestershire. It was chilling to imagine Florence, only a few years younger, falling into the hands of a vile predator like Black.

'What about the Ferrier and Harrison case?' Kidston asked. 'It was just the other day you were speculating about a serial killer.'

'It's yours, Luc,' Sawyers said with a reassuring smile. 'You'll be SIO now. You have Colquhoun's full confidence. More importantly you have the confidence of Steven Ferrier, Martha Harrison, and Sam Brady. And I'm at the end of a phone, if you need me.'

'And my post at the Gorbals?'

'Colquhoun normally gives me a bit of leeway with senior CID appointments but since you're going to be running the show it seems fair that you have some input.'

'Options?'

'There are four. Two promotions from DS and two sideways transfers, substantive DIs.' Sawyers pulled a sheet of A4 from a manila folder. 'The DIs are Benny Esposito coming back from the College and Kenny Strickland from the Crime Squad.'

'Both solid citizens, safe pairs of hands.' Kidston had a look that said *I won't be making any selections until I know all the picks.*

'No?' Sawyers shook his head mischievously.

'Well, if I can be slightly controversial, Benny's a serial shagger and Kenny's slower than a fortnight in the jail. Who are the promoted DIs?'

'Jimmy Gabriel, from crime policy and Janine Stewart from Paisley,' Sawyers said. 'New blood, both up and coming.'

'I know *The Archangel* Gabriel well. Jimmy would be a good fit.'

'From my discussions with Colquhoun, I think he'd like Gabriel here, where you and I can develop his career.'

'Do you think Strathclyde Police is ready for a gay detective inspector?'

'Mr Colquhoun insists we are, and an openly gay detective inspector would be a great asset for your current investigation.'

'I was thinking the same thing,' Kidston agreed. 'It has to be Jimmy.'

'There you are, Luc. Your first decision as a DCI, and you've made the right one.'

'The one you and Q wanted me to make, you mean.' Kidston laughed. 'Jimmy will be great but if we're shuffling the pack, I need you to approve my next decision.'

'What's that?'

'Gregor Stark moves with me. I'm mentoring him for the inspector rank. He's not quite there yet, but he's coming along brilliantly.'

'That's your shout, no problem,' Sawyers said. 'You're up in front of the chief at 1pm, I don't suppose you've got much time for a haircut.' He sized up his new DCI's appearance and gave him a stern look. 'You can at least put a brush through it.'

Kidston pushed both hands through his unruly mop of raven hair and smiled. He'd always worn his hair longer than regulation length during his time in CID. As a uniformed officer, he'd worn it cropped short. 'I'll try not to embarrass the division. One downside of Jimmy coming; means that you'll no longer be the best dressed detective in the South.'

'I thought that was you?' Sawyers grinned mischievously.

'You've always been the benchmark.' Kidston smiled as he thought about the sartorial standards that Sawyers had brought to divisional CID after a stint in Special Branch. In *the Branch*, he'd explained, the idea was to blend into the background, in among the civil servants, royal household staff and armed close protection officers from the Met. No one wanted to stand out in a pale or flashy-coloured suit, and it was more difficult to conceal the fact that you were carrying a firearm. If black, charcoal and navy were an adequate colour palette for the Branch, then it should suffice for divisional detectives. Kidston recalled one incident when a young cop turned up for his CID secondment wearing a navy-blue blazer and grey flannel slacks. Sawyers had told him, "That might be good enough for the bowling club, constable, but not for the CID". The young wannabe detective was despatched to Ralph Slater's vast suit emporium in Howard Street, where an account was opened, and a small monthly payment arranged.

'Is it true Jimmy blew a month's salary on a Savile Row suit?'

'True,' Kidston confirmed, 'Tommy Nutter, cobalt-blue three-piece. Very impressive bit of bespoke tailoring. I'd love to have one.'

'Christ, you're as bad as he is.'

'Not these days, Joe. I've got Grace and Florence to think about now. There's a baby seat in my BMW.'

'I suppose, changed days for you.'

'Who else is up?' Kidston asked about the promotion parade.

'John Wylie is coming here as a uniform inspector initially,' Sawyers began. 'Probably DI at some time in the future. He's getting the community policing team at the Gorbals.'

'Good for John, I'm pleased for him.'

'No issues between you two after the fallout from the Ellie Hunter case?' Sawyers asked. 'I seem to remember that he sided with Ronnie Miller on that one.'

'I'm sure he did but it wasn't something I had to broach with John. He was supporting a colleague and a good friend. I suppose it was a betrayal of sorts, but it was hardly Gethsemane or Fredo Corleone.'

Sawyers laughed at his new DCI's comparisons.

Three years earlier John Wylie had been the senior DS on Kidston's team but had performed badly on a promotions board and been rotated out of CID and back to a uniform sergeant's role. Just prior to his transfer, Wylie had gone to seed, embittered by his lack of promotion, and was drinking heavily. It looked like he'd managed to turn things around and was getting closer to the detective inspector's post he'd long craved.

They chatted through the various promotions and transfers. It was always a popular topic on promotion parade days. Careers moving on, careers stalling. All the whys, and wherefores. Some tipped for the very top, others in freefall. Observers were always watchful for those using their connections to get on. *Semper Vigilo*. In police circles the term used for a high-ranking personal sponsor supporting a junior officer's promotion was 'a wire'. They'd probably use the term for Jimmy Gabriel, who as part of Colquhoun's crime policy unit would have worked very closely to his wire, the assistant chief.

'Everybody back here for a 3pm briefing,' Sawyers said. 'We're officially launching the enquiry as a double murder investigation. You'll have detectives from both divisions working on the investigation. Colquhoun is livid over the Adrian Harrison case. He'd never say this out loud but it's worse because it ties to the Ferrier murder. If it was A.N. Other, maybe a single missed murder, his wrath would have been less but now he's gearing up for a serial killer investigation, some nutter murdering all the gay lawyers.'

'That's a bit of a jump,' Kidston said. 'You know I'm a man for thinking through worst-case scenarios, but even I haven't gone there... yet. Not a lot of serial killers from Glasgow.'

'You'd be surprised. Plenty from here or hereabouts or at least passed through the city; maybe this child molester, Robert Black, is the latest. We did have Peter Manuel, Ian Brady, and Bible John. Just because they were before your time doesn't mean there's no threat.' Sawyers had worked the Bible John murders as a young detective. Glasgow, and in particular the city's women had been gripped by fear as the murder count reached a horrific total of three. He grimaced at what he was about to say. 'Glasgow's overdue another serial killer.'

'Well, let's make sure it's not this guy,' Kidston said. 'Serial killers only achieve their status and notoriety due to a failure of policing... poorly run investigations... bad intelligence gathering. That's not going to happen with our case. Unless our guy's done more that we're not aware of, he'll be stopping at two.'

'I hope you're right, Luc,' Sawyers nodded gravely, 'I seriously hope you're right.'

CHAPTER TWENTY

Gregor Stark was in the detective inspector's compact office, typing up his case notes, away from the main CID room. Kidston had been summoned for an early morning briefing with Mr Sawyers and the bosses at divisional headquarters. He'd been away all day.

A pewter-framed picture of Kidston's wife and daughter with the family husky was on the desk. Stark reflected on the change in his boss since his daughter Florence was born. Kidston had made him take last night off. It was a good shout; he hadn't seen his girlfriend Marianne, in over a week and she was starting to give him a hard time. As a couple they might be running out of road.

A knock on the door interrupted the furious click-clack of Stark's typewriter.

'Come in!' Stark shouted and was surprised to see the face of his former detective sergeant colleague, John Wylie. 'Inspector Wylie, looking good, John.'

Wylie was dressed in his newly promoted inspectors' uniform. 'Thanks, Gregor. Is Luc not around?'

'He's over at DHQ, back later.' Stark walked around the

desk to proffer a warm handshake. 'Those pips look good on you, John. You're looking brilliant.' Stark estimated that Wylie had lost over two stones in weight. The old Bobby Charlton comb-over was gone, replaced by a shaven head that gave Wylie a much more formidable presence. Patting Wylie's shoulder with the handshake, Stark was aware of how much his colleague had bulked up. He caught a whiff of Wylie's aftershave – '*the great smell of Brut*' – some things would never change. 'You've been working out, John.'

'I have, Gregor. It's all down to Joanne, she's got me running and swimming and we go to our gym together. And I've sworn off the hard stuff.'

Stark had heard that Wylie had taken up with a widowed traffic warden at his last station. Going by his colleague's invigorated appearance, the woman had obviously been a good influence on him.

'I heard you'd been promoted back to the South,' Stark said. 'Where are they posting you?'

'I'm back here to head up the community policing team,' Wylie said. 'I'm hearing on the grapevine that Luc is being promoted to DCI today. I hoped that I might have a shot at Luc's vacancy, but I'm told I'll be considered for future DI posts.'

'That would make sense.' Stark smiled for his colleague but the voice in his head panicked at the thought of losing his mentor. 'Do you know where Luc's heading?'

'Sorry, I don't. I haven't seen any lists. The chief had us all in at different time slots for the handshake. I'm delighted with my posting.'

'The community policing team works closely with CID, as you know. You'll have big Peter Costello and Chrissie McCartney and that crowd. They've been assisting us on the

Ryan Ferrier murder enquiry. Some great cops and big characters.'

'I'm looking forward to getting in about it, Gregor. I was surprised by how much I enjoyed being back in uniform.'

'Well, it looks as if it's been the making of you.'

'That's mostly been down to Joanne.' Wylie turned to leave but hesitated. 'Before I go, Gregor, I need to say thanks to you as well.'

'What for?' Stark asked, surprised.

'That day you took me home when I was the worse for wear. That was my lowest ebb. Getting bounced back into uniform after that could have destroyed me if I'd just gone off and drowned my sorrows in whisky.' Wylie gave his former fellow DS a thoughtful look. 'But I remembered the pep talk you gave me. It was a brave and decent thing you did.'

'I was just worried for a colleague.' Stark well remembered the day his fellow DS had gone on a lunchtime bender on hearing the news that a junior female DS was being promoted to detective inspector ahead of him. 'It's good to have you back, John. New and improved and fighting fit.'

'What about that fabulous World Cup?' Wylie, a football fanatic, said, changing the subject. 'Great tournament. I backed Italy to win but you can never rule out the Germans. I won a few quid on wee Totò Schillaci as top goal scorer but I wanted them to win it.'

'Brilliant tournament,' Stark agreed.

'"Nessun dorma", Gregor. "Nessun fucking dorma".'

Stark laughed at Wylie's reference to Luciano Pavarotti's version of Puccini's aria that the BBC had used for their World Cup coverage and remembered the drunk street singer's version, the night he and Kidston had visited Bennets. 'I'm still having nightmares about Scotland losing to Costa Rica,' Stark said. 'As usual we flatter to deceive.' June and July had witnessed a festival of international football: Italia '90. Scotland had failed to make it out of the initial group stages; like always.

'I thought Mo Johnston and Ally McCoist did well for us.' Stark had allowed Wylie the opening he needed to talk about one of his favourite topics: Glasgow Rangers FC. His club had caused a footballing sensation the previous summer, when they signed Mo Johnston, the former Celtic striker from French club Nantes for 1.5 million pounds. The fact that Johnston was a Roman Catholic and had been on the verge of returning to Celtic made the move highly controversial and fuelled the sectarian divide between the two tribes of supporters in one of the world's fiercest football rivalries. Wylie was expressing his joy that Johnston had scored a last-minute winning goal against his old team in one of last season's *Old Firm* games, when the two men were joined by a visitor.

The football talk stopped when DS Alison Metcalfe popped her head through the door. 'I heard there was a handsome man in uniform visiting the office. Inspector Wylie, look at you, looking good. Congratulations.' She shook her former CID colleague's hand and followed up with a half hug. 'What's your posting, John?'

'Thanks, Alison. I'm coming here to head up the community policing team.' Wylie repeated most of his conversation with Stark for Metcalfe's benefit. The three colleagues chatted about the promotion parade and speculated about who was moving where and who the new Gorbals DI would be. Stark updated the latest news on the murder enquiry with Wylie looking forward to helping out with his new team.

'I need to dash,' Wylie announced. 'I'm bursting for a *Lillian Gish*.'

Metcalfe grimaced.

Stark laughed.

'And to think I'd heard he was a changed man.' Metcalfe

smiled as Wylie took his leave. 'Could he not just have said "pee"?'

Stark shook his head. 'You're lucky he wasn't away for a *Greyfriars Bobby*.'

'God, Gregor.' Metcalfe gave him a sour look. 'You're just as bad as he is.'

'You know John and his Glasgow rhyming slang,' Stark said with a big smile. 'I see a massive change in him, Alison. And not just physically. He's off the hard stuff and seems to have a different outlook in life.'

'All down to his new woman?' Metcalfe sounded sceptical.

'John's giving her a lot of the credit,' Stark began. 'You're not buying it?'

'This is the man who once described my tits as empire biscuits and when we worked together, asked me several times whether I thought I was suited to CID work.'

'Why was that?'

'Quite simple, Gregor. I'm a woman. This is the man who used to disappear to the pub and the bookies at lunchtime, regardless of how busy the rest of us were. She must be some woman if she can make this leopard change his spots.'

'On the plus side, Alison. John's a very experienced former detective. His community policing team will be helping us with door-to-door on the double murder. I'm sure the boss will be glad of any help he can offer.'

CHAPTER TWENTY-ONE

B y the time Kidston entered the briefing room everyone had got the news of his promotion. He saw Jimmy Gabriel glad-handing with colleagues. Trust Jimmy to be attired in an expensive-looking three-piece suit: a bold but tasteful mid-grey chalk stripe. As ever, his new DI cut his usual dashing figure with his handsome good looks, broad shoulders, and immaculately coiffed silver-blond hair – one former gaffer had unkindly tagged him the *Hitler Youth* candidate for CID. Kidston always felt that the thirty-seven-year-old detective looked more like a Nordic prince. But it wasn't Gabriel he was looking for. When he saw Gregor Stark arrive, Kidston beckoned him into the corridor.

'Congratulations, sir.' Stark shook his boss's hand warmly. 'Delighted to hear you've made DCI. It's well deserved.'

'Thanks, Gregor. Sorry I never got a chance to call you. It's been a hectic day since Joe Sawyers ambushed me with the news first thing this morning.'

'Who's my new DI at the Gorbals?'

'That's why I wanted to grab a quick word. Jimmy Gabriel's going to my old post, but I was thinking of transferring you to work with me here at DHQ. If you're up for it.'

Stark didn't attempt to hide his delight. 'I'm well up for it, sir.' The young DS beamed a wide smile. 'It's good continuity that you're staying with the Ferrier and Harrison cases.' He nodded his head sagely. 'Makes sense.'

'And, Gregor...'

'What, sir?'

'Away from settings like this one, it'll be Luc, or boss, never sir.'

———

The room was laid out with four rows of chairs and Kidston noticed that ACC Colquhoun had slipped in through the back door. Kidston had travelled back from force HQ with his assistant chief and was under instruction not to introduce him to the enlarged team of investigators drawn from both F and G divisions. Colquhoun wanted to observe proceedings from a discreet vantage point.

Kidston saw DI Ronnie Miller in the second row of the audience. Miller was the alpha male silverback whose formidable reputation thrived in the cut and thrust macho culture of CID. An impressive physical specimen, he carried his broad build and wide shoulders well due to his muscular six-foot one frame. With a ruggedly handsome face, a shock of wavy blond hair and a strong jaw, Miller could turn on the charm. He also carried an air of palpable menace; a fixed stare from his dark-brown eyes could unsettle anyone. Kidston had long considered Miller a bully who ruled his team by fear and coercion, too willing to bend the rules and take risky shortcuts in his enquiries.

Miller was chatting and laughing with G-Division

colleagues. Kidston was at a total loss to work out just how Miller could be in such a good humour. The launch of a joint investigation was about to highlight what a poor job Miller had done on his initial enquiry into the Adrian Harrison case. Miller had yet to congratulate him on his promotion and Kidston guessed that hell would freeze over before that happened.

Joe Sawyers opened the show. Standing tall and straight-backed behind a lectern, he covered the imminent move to his new role in the national team investigating the crimes of Robert Black. Sawyers announced that DCI Kidston would be taking over as SIO for what was now being officially treated as a double murder investigation. Outlining the links between the two murders and the fresh evidence for the Harrison case, Sawyers highlighted how the pathology team had altered their original view of death by hanging. All the available evidence now pointed to murder at the hands of the same suspect that killed Ryan Ferrier.

Sawyers was bringing his part to a close. 'We'll have a photofit of our suspect later today, based on the descriptions of three known witnesses who've seen our man in the company of both victims on the occasions that I've outlined.'

Kidston listened with interest. His departing boss had glossed over Miller's fuck-up at the Harrison scene. No criticism of the original investigating detectives – implied or otherwise. Kidston understood the need to build and maintain team harmony, but his old adversary was getting a free pass from the bosses. Kidston had argued for Miller to be removed from the joint investigation team, a view backed by Sawyers, but Colquhoun had insisted that he stay. 'He's a big boy', Colquhoun had said. 'He needs to suck it up'.

Sawyers handed over to Kidston and then took a seat beside Colquhoun at the back of the room. The newly appointed DCI stood at the lectern with a batch of papers and surveyed the room. Most of the faces were familiar. This would be an important briefing; a joint investigation team into a double murder was one thing but to have your assistant chief watching from the back of the room upped the ante considerably. He summarised the lab work completed on the two cases:

'As many of you are aware, the lab now has a small team trained by Cellmark on what's being referred to as *DNA fingerprinting*. Martin Reynolds' team has confirmed Adrian Harrison's DNA from skin-cell deposition on the cord from his dressing gown. We now believe that our victim was strangled by a method the pathologists described as a suspended strangulation. The scene was staged to make it look like death was due to a suspension hanging. The ligature marks were high up on the throat, under the victim's chin with the markings evident behind the jawline and ears. This contrasts with the neck circumference markings we'd expect to find in a normal garrotting. The cord is almost identical in thickness to the rope from the kitchen pulley.'

Kidston couldn't resist the opportunity. His gaze rested on Miller. 'We can see why the initial CID enquiry went wrong. However, with a bit more investigation, particularly around Mrs Harrison, we found several factors and inconsistencies that pointed to murder.'

Miller stared back, looking right through the newly promoted DCI.

If looks could kill.

'We have a viable DNA sample from the semen deposition on Adrian Harrison's robe. That same DNA was found on the dressing-gown cord, where the suspect had gripped it to compress the victim's neck and apply the strangulation force required to murder him.

'Analysis confirmed that it is a male profile, but not from the deceased Harrison. We got this negative result by cross-referencing his post-mortem samples taken at the city mortuary. We have a DNA profile, but we don't have a matching suspect. With good detective work we can build a list of possible suspects close to Nicky's profile, and we'll get a match through this method. We can also look at forensic materials left at the scenes of other serious crimes.'

'Can you expand on that thinking, boss?' It was one of the G-Division detectives, a grizzled veteran with a sceptical look on his face. 'DNA wasn't invented when I did my detective training at Tulliallan.'

'Fingerprints hadn't been invented yet, when you were at Tulliallan, Soapy.' A wag colleague got a laugh from the audience.

Kidston wasn't surprised by the question. The use of deoxyribonucleic acid or DNA was a recent development in support of criminal investigations. Detectives were still coming to terms with the most significant advance in forensic science since the introduction of fingerprinting in the nineteenth century. Strathclyde Police had achieved its first DNA conviction just nine months earlier, in November 1989, and its application to police investigations and crime-scene management was now a total game changer.

'I'm happy to explain my rationale here,' Kidston responded to the questioner. 'For those of you new to DNA, and let's face it we're all a bit new to DNA, scene-to-scene comparison would include any serious crimes – detected or undetected – that we have a sample for. Basically, any blood, semen, or saliva... anything we recovered from a crime scene, maybe the crime was detected, and we didn't have to use the sample, or it was undetected, and we may have had a suspect in the frame. We can look at that suspect, take a new sample and check for a match.'

'Sounds like a lot of work for the lab, boss,' the veteran detective said.

'It is a lot of work for the lab,' Kidston continued. 'Especially as we have to outsource much of the analysis and profiling to accredited laboratories like Cellmark. But given the nature of this investigation, the police board and the force executive have allocated funding for additional work, including reaching out to other forces and laboratories to compare our profile with all existing files.'

Kidston was on a bit of a roll now, but he was close to exhausting his full knowledge about the force's DNA strategy. He was momentarily grateful that he'd paid attention to a recent presentation Martin Reynolds had given on the subject.

'The longer-term vision is that, as DNA practice becomes more widespread and embedded, we will have our own accredited lab. Crime-scene capture techniques will improve and cops and detectives will become much more DNA aware. We'll have permanent records of the genetic profiles of all convicted persons in Scotland.' Kidston was conscious that he'd slipped into *wankspeak* – he could see the puzzled expressions on the faces of some of his audience. More change in the wind and many would be frightened by the new procedures. He wondered if he'd used the *vision* word to impress ACC Colquhoun, still sitting at the back, discreetly observing proceedings. 'Setting forensics aside, we will still require the bulk of the work to be done by investigators, boots on the ground, detectives conducting their normal enquiries.'

'What about fingerprints, boss?' a young detective in the front row asked and Kidston was glad of a return to more familiar forensic matters.

'There is a palm-print impression lifted from the inside door of the en suite bathroom where the robe was hanging. Again, this was not from Adrian Harrison. This lift was prioritised by the fingerprints section over the weekend, but we have no ident, no suspect.' Kidston leaned on the lectern and shuffled through his paperwork. He hesitated before reading the next section. 'As things stand, we have no forensics linking the Ferrier scene to the Harrison scene. For Ryan Ferrier, we didn't find any foreign blood, hair or saliva and no DNA other than that of the victim. Anal swabs were negative as was the severed penis. The only other lifts we got from the Ferrier house matched the elims taken from his cleaner, who clearly does a very good job cleaning the rest of the house.'

There was laughter from the group. The slightest release from the grim details of the case.

'One absolutely crucial point on both these murders; we have two unusual modi operandi. The media know nothing about Adrian Harrison's bisexuality or his staged hanging, or Ryan Ferrier's severed penis and it's vital that we keep it that way. There can be no compromising the integrity of the information around the crime scenes, or the MOs used, and it's vital... fundamental that we protect that evidence. I don't want us interviewing a suspect who tells us he got his *special knowledge* from a story in the *Evening Times*.' Kidston held up two A5 spiral-bound, blue-covered books of crime-scene pictures. 'Please familiarise yourselves with the contents of these books, but they don't leave this room. If anyone needs to reference them, they're locked in DS Alison Metcalfe's desk. Also check out the steak knife and wine glass that we're missing from the Ferrier crime scene. A4 copies of these are available but the same rules apply.

'Before I get to the assignments, I'd like to introduce the team to our newly promoted DI, Jimmy Gabriel, who will lead enquiries in and around the club scene and liaise with the city council and the police board.'

Gabriel stood up and smoothed down his suit jacket, preparing to speak.

'Oh, what a gay day. Shut that door!' It was Ronnie Miller in a comical high-camp accent. He'd uttered the two best-known catchphrases of popular gay comedian, Larry Grayson. Under his breath, a low voice dripping with contempt, he followed up with, 'Fuckin' homo.' He had a big stupid grin on his face.

There was a mix of shocked silence and muted tittering.

Gabriel fixed Miller with a livid stare.

'What did you say?' Kidston stepped out in front of the lectern. He glared at Miller. 'Say that again.'

'Oh, come on, Luc.' Miller squirmed in his seat. 'Jimmy knows I'm just kidding around.'

'I've had enough of you, Miller,' Kidston said with a look of disgust. 'There's no way I can trust you on an investigation as sensitive as this. You're off this team – get yourself back to Govan.'

'Do you not think you're overreacting, Luc?'

'That'll be Detective Chief Inspector Kidston to you, Inspector Miller.' It was Joe Sawyers, from the back of the room, now on his feet.

The room fell silent.

Then a new voice. Most of the room were unaware of his presence but when he spoke there was no doubting the commanding tone. 'Detective Inspector Miller. See me in Mr Sawyers' office this minute.' A furious Colquhoun rose from his seat, a look of cold-eyed utter contempt on his face. 'By the time I've spoken to your divisional commander, you'll be walking a beat again as a uniform sergeant.'

Miller's face flushed pink and then turned ashen white as he struggled to manoeuvre his burly frame out of his seat and slowly edged his way along the line, waiting for seated colleagues to pull their legs in. His head was bowed, avoiding eye contact with everyone.

Kidston surveyed his former colleague's dramatic exit. A strange thought slid into his head; *decapitated cockroaches can survive for weeks but will eventually starve to death.*

Miller's CID career looked to be over.

CHAPTER TWENTY-TWO

'I can fight my own battles, but thank you all for that,' Gabriel said. 'It's good to know that my bosses have my back.' Kidston momentarily imagined Gabriel and Miller going toe to toe. The bout wouldn't be the foregone conclusion that many would expect. Yes, Miller was a bruiser, broader and burlier than his would-be opponent with a very slight height advantage, but Jimmy Gabriel had the physique of a middleweight boxer, honed by strenuous workouts in the Kelvin Amateur Boxing Club gymnasium. With his hand-tailored suits and immaculately coiffured style, Gabriel may look as if he'd just walked out from the pages of *Vogue* magazine, but he could handle himself. 'I've been putting up with that type of nonsense for most of my career.'

'But that's the point, Jimmy,' Colquhoun said. 'You shouldn't have to put up with it. DCI Kidston is right; we can't have someone like Miller working on a case like this. I've just spoken to his commander. He'll be office-bound until the chief decides what to do about him in the longer term. I want him disciplined for that comment, so there'll need to be a formal hearing.' Colquhoun was sitting in Sawyers' office chair, sipping a glass of water, clearly still very angry at the outburst he'd witnessed. Sawyers, Kidston, and Gabriel were in attendance.

'Gentlemen, I apologise,' Colquhoun said. 'I wanted to keep Miller in the investigation team as a sort of penance for his mistakes, but I see now that was an error of judgement on my part. I didn't realise he was a blatant homophobe.'

'I think it was too good an opportunity to undermine me on my first day as DCI,' Kidston said. 'Ronnie's like a shark detecting blood in the water.'

'There's a dangerous air of indifference about Ronnie, these days,' Sawyers said. 'I'm angry that he pulled a stunt like that when I was in the room, but he really doesn't give a fuck anymore. Luc, you were totally right to pull him off the case but I'm afraid he's now likely to go off like a hand grenade.'

'Character is fate, that's what the Greeks said,' mused Colquhoun.

'True.' Sawyers nodded. 'Too many shortcuts, not investigating cases properly and looking for quick results. Ronnie's always been prone to that. It's the path of least resistance that makes rivers run crooked.'

Kidston was relieved when Gabriel interrupted the two senior managers philosophising. 'It means my promotion will be memorable for a colleague being disciplined.'

'Welcome to the South, Jimmy,' Kidston said with a rueful smile.

'I'm happy to be here... help you catch your Gay Ripper.'

Colquhoun spluttered a mouthful of water into his glass. 'Wash your mouth out with soap and water, Detective Inspector Gabriel, and never let me hear you use that term again. Seriously!' The assistant chief looked, stern-faced, across the group. 'Imagine if the journalists picked that up, they'd have a field day.'

'A gay detective, investigating a double gay murder,' Gabriel said with a sarcastic air. 'There's no way someone like Miller isn't going to use his media contacts to drop that line into a conversation. There's a media splash, right there.' Kidston was surprised at Gabriel's sarcastic tone but remembered that as part of Colquhoun's policy unit the two men would have formed a close working relationship.

'Jimmy, if you want to come off this case and start with something less high profile, less controversial, I'm sure Joe and Luc can work around the staffing.'

'Not at all, sir,' Gabriel said sheepishly. 'The original plan to involve me in the club enquiries and to liaise with Councillor Brodie is a sound one and that's where I can be most effective.' Matthew Brodie was the openly gay, young maverick councillor for the King's Park ward, who'd navigated the stormy waters of the police board to end up as committee chair. A vocal champion and lobbyist for gay rights, Brodie was said to be close to Gabriel. Now their link was to be official.

'Jimmy,' Colquhoun began. 'A key aspect of your liaison role with the city council and the police board will be to reassure some very nervous councillors that there'll be no return to our "No Mean City" reputation of the past. That reassurance starts with Matthew Brodie. It's a vital role; over and above your part in the investigation. No one understands public relations and media marketing better than Brodie. It's your job to keep him and the police board on side.'

Kidston fully understood where his ACC was coming from. Despite the astonishment of many observers, Glasgow had been selected as the 1990 European Capital of Culture. The city had enthusiastically embraced its new status as a cultural mecca with a veritable blitzkrieg of star attractions in its art galleries, theatres, and music venues: Pavarotti, Sinatra, Miles Davis, The Rolling Stones, the Bolshoi Ballet, the Berlin Philharmonic, and the works of Van Gogh, and Degas had challenged negative perceptions of the old Second City of the Empire and showcased Glasgow's cultural renaissance. Glasgow had stepped up to join major world cities like Athens, Amsterdam, Florence, Paris, and Berlin to be a worthy choice as European cultural capital. Glasgow, a city never afraid to take one on the chin, was punching above its weight.

A thoughtful Gabriel responded to his ACC's observations. 'I'm sorry, sir, I've let Miller's comments get to me. Disappointed that my promotion to DI will be remembered for all the wrong reasons.'

'Another casualty of much needed change, I'm afraid,' Colquhoun said. 'You've all heard me on this topic before, many times. We've done well on female recruitment, numbers for women in CID are increasing. We're getting women into senior ranks... my God, it's long overdue.' Colquhoun was on a familiar soapbox now. 'Tenure in CID is working, we're clearing out the deadwood, bringing in younger, more capable detectives, more women.

'I was in detective training at Tulliallan last week and I had a look at all of the course photographs on the wall. Have you noticed the clear theme on all the senior course pictures? They're all middle-aged men. There's hardly a female face to be found in any of them. There are no black faces... none! You know that old Greek proverb, "Society grows great when old men plant trees whose shade they know they'll never sit in"? Well, that's us, gentlemen.' Colquhoun pointed at all three colleagues. 'In case you haven't realised it by now you're all agents of change. This job needs to change, we should be better, even just to be relevant we need to transform our workforce. It's 1990, I swear I'll drag this job into the twentieth century before the next one is upon us. Sexuality will be the next breakthrough. We all know the job has many gay officers; why should they be expected to hide their sexuality?'

'Change is slow, sir,' Sawyers said. 'It's resisted and, to be fair, some of your colleagues in the executive corridor are among the very best at preserving the status quo.'

Kidston smiled and nodded at his boss's remarks. ACC Farquhar Colquhoun, the youngest ACC in the country, had a background in the Metropolitan Police. His appetite for reorganisation and change had scared the bejesus out of his fellow chief officers but he was effecting changes in policing that were long overdue. The politicians loved him, and he was tipped to be a future chief constable.

'What is it you always say, Joe?' Colquhoun pointed to the framed drawing of Charlie Brown on Sawyers' office wall. Charles M. Schulz's cartoon character was depicted missing the football moments after Lucy had snatched it away from his attempted kick. The little boy's exasperation at this repeated failure was evidenced by his familiar crumpled and downturned mouth.

'You Could Always Give Up'. Sawyers smiled and read the slogan from the drawing. He'd overprinted the original caption: 'GOOD GRIEF!'. He saw it as a universal, sad cosmic joke. Charlie Brown never gets to kick the football, but he never gives up. He never stops trying.

Kidston looked at his three colleagues. None of them were short of the resilience and persistence required for tough and challenging policework. His assistant chief was fond of his Greek proverbs, but he was no phoney when it came to driving change. Kidston liked the thought of being an agent of change for Colquhoun and was reassured that such a senior officer was willing to discuss high-level topics like this with him. But he was mostly relieved that Sawyers and Colquhoun had backed him up in how he dealt with Ronnie Miller's unacceptable behaviour. Sawyers had once told him that when you achieve senior ranks, the people issues start to take up as much of your time as police work. While he'd rather get on with murder investigations and high-level criminal enquiries, he wondered if, in his very first day as DCI, this was a taste of things to come.

At least he'd wiped that big stupid grin from Ronnie Miller's face.

CHAPTER TWENTY-THREE

D S Gregor Stark joined the group after Colquhoun had departed for force headquarters around 5pm. He went through the assignments that Kidston had allocated to the enquiry teams and handed over copies of the photofit. Pairs of detectives would be visiting Titwood Tennis Club, Bennets, and Goodnights to show members and punters what the photofit artist had come up with based on the descriptions offered by Amanda Devlin, Tricia Mathieson, and Marc 'Dusty' Monaghan. Other nightclubs and tennis clubs in the city had been added to a growing list of action logs as the investigation began to focus on the known behaviours of the mysterious Nicky. Door-to-door enquiries were scheduled for the Toryglen and Rutherglen areas. Stark had added a line on builders' merchants' premises to tie with the work carried out in the Harrison house. A total of twenty-six detectives supplemented by ten community cops were part of the joint investigation team – it was a major enquiry.

'What do you think?' Stark asked his three bosses who were inspecting the pictures.

'I never like these images,' Kidston said. 'They're never

human enough for me, but it matches how all three witnesses described him.'

'Have you circulated the image to all the divisional collators?' Sawyers asked.

'It's in today's despatches, boss,' Stark replied, 'with a dedicated intelligence bulletin requesting possible identities.'

'Good work.' Sawyers waved the picture in his hand. 'Hopefully we're closing in on this monster before he strikes again.'

'What about you, Jimmy?' Kidston asked. 'Anyone you might know from the Glasgow scene?'

'I'm a bit like you, Luc,' Gabriel replied. 'I often see these photofits as too one-dimensional.' He scrutinised the picture. 'The face is not calling anyone to mind but I'm not the clubber I used to be.'

Gregor Stark had assigned himself door-to-door duties with Zorba Quinn. Kidston and Gabriel were scheduled to deliver a personal briefing at the King's Park home of councillor Matthew Brodie.

————

Brodie invited the detectives into the tidy, well-appointed lounge of his semi-detached home. The police board chair was dressed in a black Adidas tracksuit, explaining that he'd just returned from a game of badminton at the local leisure centre. Brodie was a slim and fit-looking forty-one with short brown hair, piercing blue eyes and an engaging smile. Away from politics, Brodie ran a successful media marketing company and was tipped as a Labour candidate in the next Westminster elections. The three men sat around Brodie's dining table and the host produced tea and Jaffa Cakes for his visitors.

'Congratulations to both of you on your promotions.' The

politician was well informed, and Kidston wouldn't expect anything less from the chair of the police board.

'Congratulations to you too,' Kidston said. 'And to the entire city council. You must be very pleased with how the City of Culture year is going.'

'Yes,' Brodie replied. 'It's exceeded all our expectations; visitor numbers for tourism and audiences at events are all excellent. Have you caught anything?'

'I took my wife to see Luciano Pavarotti back in May, we did Sinatra at Ibrox last month. Sensational shows and two names I didn't ever expect to be playing my home city. Jimmy did Miles Davis in June, he's the jazz man.'

Gabriel nodded. 'Another name I didn't think I'd see performing in Glasgow.'

'Brilliant,' Brodie said. 'I was fortunate to see all three. I've never been so proud to be a Glaswegian.'

Kidston shared that pride for his city and had embraced as many of the cultural events that he could. 'As a former shipbuilder, I'm looking forward to Bill Bryden's *The Ship* next month.'

'You won't be disappointed,' Brodie said. 'I caught a snatch of rehearsals. They've created a sixty-seven feet wide model of a ship inside Harland & Wolff's old engine shed at Govan. They're recreating a launch at the end of each performance. It's going to be spectacular.'

'That does sound like something to see,' Kidston said.

Brodie changed tack. 'How's the investigation coming along?'

'Not as quickly as I'd like,' Kidston admitted. 'But there is a suspect coming into focus.'

'Do you believe he's targeting gay men?' Brodie asked. 'I know you're here for a board liaison visit and to discuss the additional DNA monies but in Glasgow's year as City of

Culture we can't have headlines about serial killers hunting gay men.'

'You're right, Councillor Brodie–' Kidston was interrupted.

'Matthew, please. Jimmy and I are well acquainted and there's no need for formality.'

'You're right, Matthew. My brief from ACC Colquhoun is to reassure you about the size of the team working this investigation and to confirm the additional DNA spend is being well targeted... and it is. But there's no harm including you in this part of the enquiry. In the strictest confidence.' Kidston nodded to Gabriel who flipped open his folder to display the photofit picture of their suspect.

'What about this guy?' Gabriel asked. 'May go by the name Nicky.'

'I think I've been with him.' Brodie put his mug of tea down with a start and took hold of the photofit. The worried expression on his face caused the two detectives to exchange a quizzical glance.

'With him, how?' Gabriel asked.

'I gave him a lift home from Goodnights around five or six weeks ago.' Brodie gave both detectives a solemn, confirmatory glance, a look of fear forming in his bright blue eyes. 'Yes, I'm sure it was him. Nicky.'

'You can recognise him from this image?' Kidston asked.

'Yes... I think so and the name... Nicky, of course.' The politician looked dazed. 'Am I in any danger?'

'Did he come back to this house?' Kidston asked.

'No, I dropped him off near where he lives.'

'You didn't go to his place or see his house?' Kidston asked.

'I met him at Goodnights and offered him a lift home,' Brodie explained. 'He asked to be dropped off in Curtis Avenue, at a path linking King's Park to Toryglen. I got the impression that Nicky was ashamed of living in a council flat.'

'I need to ask, Matthew,' Gabriel looked intently at Brodie, 'was it a romantic encounter... a sexual liaison?'

'It looked like that at the outset. My plan was to bring him back here, but something made me change my mind and I said I'd drop him off.'

'What changed your mind?' Kidston asked.

'I got a really strange vibe off the guy, a sense that he was going to hustle me for money. He kept asking if I needed any landscaping work done.'

'But you declined the offer,' Kidston said. 'Did he have a business card? How did you leave it with him?'

'I told him my brother-in-law did all my gardening work. You think this man killed Ryan Ferrier and Adrian Harrison. I knew Ryan Ferrier.' Brodie's speech was nervy and racing, a fearful expression on his face. 'Is this guy going to come after me – he had very dark, unsettling eyes. Was I sitting in my car with a double murderer?'

'Slow down... please think,' Kidston said in his most comforting voice. The councillor was now less anxious about the city's reputation and more concerned about his personal safety and maybe his own standing. 'He's never been to your house. You two never started anything and if he was going to follow it up it would have been before now.'

'He did give me a cheap tacky business card, one of those ones from a printing machine but I threw it straight in the bin. Sometimes I remember that I'm chair of the police board and question whether I should be associating with people like him.'

'Can you remember anything that was on the card?' Kidston asked. 'A business name or a dialling code?'

'I hardly glanced at it, I'm sorry.'

'Did you see his name on the card?' Kidston asked. 'Does "Nicky" come from a nickname or a first name?'

'I'm not sure. He was introduced as Nicky, and I called him that when he was in my company.'

'Had you met him before that night?' Kidston asked.

'I'd seen him around Bennets and Goodnights on a few occasions but that was the first time we spoke to each other. I haven't seen him since.'

'DI Gabriel will note a full statement from you,' Kidston said. 'Take your time and try and remember everything you can about the whole encounter. We'll need to arrange a full forensic examination of your car.'

'It was valeted around two weeks ago.'

'That's unfortunate,' Kidston said, unable to hide his disappointment. 'We'll still need to check it out.'

'Will you need to inform Colquhoun and the chief?' Brodie asked, his face tightening into a disagreeable frown.

'We'll brief ACC Colquhoun and he'll brief the chief, but we'll keep it tight,' Kidston said. 'I'll file your statement under a pseudonym to avoid any scuttlebutt.'

'That's very much appreciated,' Brodie said. 'My name and my position on the council is a matter of public record. I must ask again, am I in danger from this person?'

'Did you reveal those details about yourself?' Kidston asked.

'Never mentioned anything about my council work.'

'You'll be okay then.' Kidston spoke reassuringly. 'As I said earlier, it was five weeks ago, and he hasn't attempted any follow-up contact.'

The next forty-five minutes were spent going through Brodie's statement in detail. Kidston thought about the councillor's actions and the potential clue that had eluded them. If only he'd held on to that business card.

———

The two detectives decided on one more action before they called it a night. Checking out the lie of the land where Nicky was dropped off could give them a better idea of where he might be found. There was talk about grabbing a beer and a bite to eat to celebrate their joint promotions, but they would do something the following evening. Gabriel had a prior engagement at his boxing club, where he was coaching a couple of teenage boys. Kidston had planned a celebratory meal at L'Ariosto with Grace for Saturday night.

'You could join me at the club.' Gabriel smiled mischievously.

'No thanks.' Kidston laughed, remembering his one and only visit to the Kelvin ABC, where Gabriel had tortured him with punishing circuits of burpees and sessions on the punch bags. Kidston had ended the evening vomiting over a sink. He'd failed to persuade Gabriel to take him on at tennis but had evened things up by beating him on a competitive run at Tulliallan. Gabriel had agreed to give him a game of tennis if Kidston was willing to step into the boxing ring for three rounds. It would never happen – neither man wanted to take a beating.

They parked their car halfway up Curtis Avenue, where Brodie had dropped Nicky. A pedestrian path led between two four-in-a-block cottage flats on the very edge of the King's Park estate. They walked the route, emerging into Lubas Avenue, then Ardmory Avenue and saw the dramatic change in housing styles. Now they were surrounded by flats and maisonettes. The next street across was Ardnahoe Avenue, where the flats were built higher, and they could spy the multi-storey tower blocks and the promised lands of Prospecthill in the distance. They were now in the midst of the vast Toryglen housing scheme.

'Look at the scale of this place,' Gabriel announced. 'Where do you start?'

'We knock one door at a time, Jimmy,' Kidston replied. 'The chair of the police board had him in his car. We're close. He'll come again.'

Gabriel didn't share his DCI's confidence. 'If Nicky's not on the voters' roll, it'll be like looking for a needle in a haystack.'

CHAPTER TWENTY-FOUR

G abriel started by working the speed bag, building up a rapid pace and feeling the blood begin to rush through his arms and shoulders. Ronnie Miller had riled him, and he needed to work out some of his aggression. He pulled a skipping rope off the wall hook. When he jumped rope, the soles of his feet tapped out a steady rhythm matching his breathing. Skipping was the first thing that he'd mastered when he tried boxing training as a kid. His old man, Jimmy Senior, had taken him to boxing lessons as a twelve-year-old. Gabriel suspected that it was when his father had started to fear that his son may be a bit of a 'pansy' – a delicate flower. His dad had been a keen amateur boxer in his youth and encouraged his son to get involved. Gabriel loved it and threw himself into all the training routines. There was one stipulation: he never sparred without a headguard. Gabriel's good looks and vanity were non-negotiable and shots to the nose were bloody sore. His old man carried the legacy of his boxing years with a badly deformed cauliflower ear. Gabriel could hardly bear to look at it as a child.

The Kelvin Amateur Boxing Club was in Belleisle Street, a little-known corner of Glasgow's south side, tucked behind the imposing red sandstone of the Holy Cross church. The gritty old gym had originally formed part of Govanhill police station and dated back to the ancient burgh police era of the late nineteenth century. The interior was dominated by a full-size boxing ring, surrounded by various gym and boxing equipment. The exposed brick walls, painted a light blue, were adorned by pictures of some of the boxing greats: Ali, Marciano, Tyson, Hearns, Leonard, Hagler, and Durán. Scottish faces too, Jackie Paterson, Ken Buchanan, John 'Cowboy' McCormack, Dick McTaggart, Walter McGowan, Jim Watt and Kelvin ABC legend, Donnie Hood. A huge painting of the legendary Gorbals flyweight, Benny Lynch took pride of place. This Scottish contingent, between them, could boast world, Olympic, European and Commonwealth titles as well as numerous Lonsdale Belts; it was like a boxing hall of fame. Gabriel had been training there on and off for around ten years and loved the honest toil of the place. The club's twin mantras were discipline and respect. No posing and no machismo suited him fine. No one at the club had ever questioned his sexuality; given his boxing prowess, it was unlikely to ever come up, but it was something he'd had to contend with at work since coming out.

Gabriel had come out to colleagues in 1988, after three years as a detective sergeant. Family and close friends already knew. The AIDS hysteria was beginning to die down, but his main motivation was to be true to himself. He was sick and tired of pretending to be something he was not. Bosses and senior managers were very supportive; Kidston, who he'd met on a detective training programme at Tulliallan was particularly supportive and was one of the first people he'd come out to. He'd gotten the occasional snide remark from colleagues, often passed off as banter but he always challenged anything that crossed the line. Homophobic cartoons – anonymous and unattributed – posted on the canteen wall to see whether he'd rise to the bait. He never did. Most colleagues were fine with it, especially the younger ones. The ex-military guys were the most resentful. Some colleagues thought he was joking; he didn't fit their preconceptions of gay men and was challenging traditional stereotypes of masculinity.

There was a period when he wondered if policing was the right career choice – wondered if he'd ever truly fit in. Gabriel wasn't sure how many rounds he had left in him; how many knockdowns he could take before he stayed down. Miller was just the latest in a series of cheap shots and the most frustrating thing was that all the bosses had quickly jumped to his defence, making him look weak. He was confident he could handle Miller, verbally and physically, but that would have to wait. It was a tough decision to come out in the macho world of CID, but it was the right one. The despair and anxiety of leading a double life was over. He wouldn't be falling victim to a bully like Ronnie Miller.

Tonight, the club was busy with the chatter and banter of its members and the sounds of speed bags being pummelled, punch bags being thumped, the rhythm of skipping ropes and the voices of the trainers urging more effort. Gabriel looked around at the familiar faces; there were two recovering addicts, a fireman and a guy who played in a local rock band. Gabriel had supervised a bout between two fifteen-year-old boys he was helping to coach. They'd gone at it hammer and tongs without inflicting too much damage on each other. The padded equipment made sure of that. One of the kids was battling hard to overcome an asthma condition and his determination was evident. And it was two less teenage boys hanging around street corners, not chasing a drugs hit or screwing motors. Gabriel saw it as a worthwhile endeavour and good use of his time. When he was coaching kids, he always got the feeling that his own inner child still accompanied him into the boxing ring – it had all started in an effort to impress his father.

Colquhoun and Kidston were the men to impress now. He'd been promoted to an operational posting after a long stint in policy work and some would question his suitability – some like Ronnie Miller – but Gabriel had silenced many doubters in the past. There was a gay element to this investigation, and he was confident he could make the difference.

Now he was focusing on his own workout and had moved on to the heavy bag. He started with some shadow-boxing, throwing punches at the unstoppable air, some nimble footwork as he danced around the bag, throwing jabs, hooks, and uppercuts; some of the ringcraft he'd taught the youths earlier in the session. Then he set about the big, hefty bag with violent intent. Filled with sawdust, sand, and old rags, he imagined it to be Ronnie Miller. He threw a series of combination punches, thudding hard into the faded and patched leather. He wiped the sweat from his brow with the back of a glove and kept the sequence going, leaning in, steadying the bag with his shoulder, and driving more body punches, attacking with vital force, cracking ribs, and smashing into the solar plexus. Miller had humiliated him, had tarnished his greatest achievement as a police officer. There is great violence in boxing; it's converted and elevated to a special skill, but nonetheless, Gabriel had the weapons he needed to inflict considerable damage. He would store up some violence for Ronnie Miller; one way or another, there would be a reckoning.

CHAPTER TWENTY-FIVE

TUESDAY, 21 AUGUST 1990

A full day of enquiries and investigation produced nothing. The enquiry team was hitting its stride; tasking and work streams were well delineated; intelligence bulletins were being religiously updated and door-to-door enquiries in the sprawling Toryglen housing estate were being routinely checked off on the master control sheet. As Kidston suspected, a forensic exam of councillor Brodie's car produced nothing. Following the councillor's revelations, the door-to-door house calls were focused on the south side of Toryglen, where it borders King's Park. Residents were shown the photofit and asked for information on anyone who went by the numerous variations of surnames or forenames that might produce the moniker 'Nicky'. There were far too many for Kidston's liking. Similar enquiries were ongoing with the Department of Social Security. DSS checks could confirm whether their suspect was picking up unemployment benefit, known colloquially as 'buroo money', and provide a current address for where his giro cheque was delivered.

The police laboratory had prioritised Kidston's double murder investigation and was processing the samples he'd referred to at the briefing as 'scene-to-scene' comparisons. Working their way through any blood, semen, or saliva samples, starting with the more serious crime categories, and including both detected and undetected cases. Martin Reynolds was co-ordinating a national response with other police labs across the UK, who, armed with the Strathclyde 'Nicky' sample, were conducting the same analyses. ACC Colquhoun with the support of councillor Brodie and the police board had secured additional funds to finance the DNA strand of the investigation. The fingerprints section were committing resources to identify the palm print found in the Harrison en suite but had so far drawn a blank.

Frustratingly for Kidston, his first big case as a DCI was badly in need of a break but he wasn't a man known for quitting. Like the little cartoon character on Joe Sawyers' office wall, Kidston would never give up attempting to kick the football. He would persevere. Tennis clubs in the city, including municipal courts run by the city's parks department were all being visited by detectives. Likewise, building merchants were receiving similar visits. Late-shift teams continued to visit nightclubs and gay-friendly bars in the Merchant City district.

At the morning round table briefing, he'd challenged his team to identify new avenues of enquiry. It was Gregor Stark who'd suggested the latest line. Based on the testimony of the witness 'Murdo Bissett' (Gabriel's pseudonym for Matthew Brodie and known to Stark as part of Kidston's inner circle) about a lost business card offering landscape gardening services, Stark suggested checking with all the newsagents, supermarkets, minimarts, and corner shops who display advertising boards offering local services. Kidston was becoming more and more impressed by his young DS, who was a lateral thinker and someone who offered up new ideas and fresh approaches. Stark had very good detective instincts and had proved an effective sounding board on numerous occasions. Importantly, the younger man was willing to offer a contrary view to his boss and back it up with reasoned, rational argument. Kidston didn't believe in the notion of a genius detective who magically uncovers the invisible thread that connects the various strands of big investigations, but he did believe in putting in the hard yards and in an investigator's instinct. Stark was demonstrating a keen instinct to go with his serious work ethic.

―――――

The day's wash-up briefing concluded at 7.15pm. The day shift teams had worked a straight twelve hours. The map of completed house-to-house enquiries in Toryglen was updated in yellow highlighter. Householder statements were added to a wall of box files and drawers full of alphabetised index cards were filed by detectives and administrative assistants. The lists of shops and builders' merchants were checked off to show the considerable levels of enquiry carried out.

'Thanks, everyone, for the massive amount of work covered today,' Kidston began. 'I know it doesn't look like we're making progress, but we are. I can see all those streets in Toryglen turning yellow on the control sheet. We're getting there. Well done on a great all-round effort. The late shift are out again tonight in the pubs and clubs – one of you is going to get the break we need in this case. Thank you all. We go again tomorrow.' As the detectives filed out of the briefing room, Kidston and Gabriel headed off in their individual cars to their prearranged dinner meeting at the Orchard Park Hotel in Giffnock.

―――――

The Orchard Park diner was quiet, and the service was quick. Kidston ordered burger and chips; Gabriel ordered a spicy sausage and penne pasta. Both men opted for a glass of the house red and a jug of iced water.

'Did you get into that jazz tape I sent you?' Gabriel asked as he forked up some spicy penne.

'I did thanks, I preferred the side with the female jazz singers, Sarah Vaughan, Peggy Lee, and Ella Fitzgerald. Great singers.' After doing a residential detective training programme at Tulliallan, the two detectives, who shared a love of soul music, had taken to exchanging music tapes.

'What about the Coltrane stuff? Miles Davis, and Wynton Marsalis?'

'Yeah, all good but I prefer a nice vocal,' Kidston replied. 'What about that country tape I sent you?'

'Hmm... I'm gay, Luc, not tragic.' Both men laughed. Kidston's attempts at turning his colleague on to Grace's preferred music genre had fallen on deaf ears.

Beyond a celebratory dinner for their promotions, the main purpose of the night was to afford Kidston a chance to run down the set-up at Gorbals police office. Kidston gave everyone in his old CID team a positive report card but urged Gabriel that they were his people now. He could make his own assessment. Kidston covered the strengths and weaknesses of the four uniform patrol group inspectors that ran the shifts and highlighted some of the great *thief catchers*, plain-clothed cops and the many and various characters that worked at the Gorbals. Gorbals would still come under his divisional wide expanded remit, but he would miss his old station. Promotion to DCI would locate him at divisional headquarters and he would let Gabriel get on with it.

'No Ronnie Miller types to contend with,' Kidston

reassured his successor. 'You shouldn't have any problems on that front.'

'Other people will have the problem, Luc, not me. My days of pretending to be someone else are long done. I used to go around kissing girls, running in gangs, and chasing footballs just to fit in but nowadays I prefer to be me.'

'I'll drink to that, Jimmy.' Kidston raised his wine glass to toast his friend.

'Cheers, Luc.' Gabriel clinked glasses.

With the Gorbals personnel issues covered, inevitably the discussion turned to their current investigation.

'We need to catch a break on this case, Jimmy,' Kidston said. 'Where is this guy?'

Gabriel took a sip of his wine. 'We need to believe that the net's closing in. Someone will point us to him.'

'Nicky, Nicky, Nicky.' Kidston drummed his fingers on the table. 'Where the hell are you? Sometimes I think I've made you up.'

'He's real enough, Luc,' Gabriel reassured him. 'Don't worry, you're doing all the right things with our investigation. It's only a matter of time.'

'But how much time, Jimmy? How long before Q sends in a review team to go over everything we've done – tells me where I've gone wrong.'

'Not before the twenty-eight-day mark.' Gabriel dabbed the corner of his mouth with his napkin. 'You know Farquhar's got absolute faith in you as SIO, otherwise he wouldn't have approved you leading the investigation.'

Kidston footered with his cufflinks. 'As part of Q's staff, you saw those review reports coming in from across the divisions. Is there anything we're missing for our enquiry?'

'Trust me, Luc. I'm steeped in those reports and if there was any other so-called "sound investigatory practice", I'd alert you to it.'

'That's reassuring.' Gabriel's response had eased Kidston's anxiety. As a long-serving DI, he'd led a sizeable number of murder investigations and had always managed to secure detections and arrests prior to any headquarters review being instigated. In this, his first big case as a newly promoted DCI, he badly wanted to maintain that record.

Sweet course options were declined and both men made their way along Fenwick Road, towards where their cars were parked in a nearby side street.

'Promise me one thing, Jimmy.'

'What's that?'

'If you see me going wrong or feel I'm missing something you need to flag it up,' Kidston began. 'I started out as deputy SIO to Joe Sawyers on this investigation and it's an undertaking I always give him. You're technically my deputy SIO, the investigation is now a double murder and we're both newly promoted. If I fail, people will say it was a recipe for disaster.'

'If *we* fail, Luc, but we won't fail. Stop overthinking it. Trust me, you've got this.'

CHAPTER TWENTY-SIX

C anavan was enjoying a large Laphroaig in his office with fellow whisky drinker, Cassandra. They were seated together on the large brown leather couch. He was in shirtsleeves, and she was wearing her hostess's uniform; a halter-neck formal evening gown in midnight navy with silver brocade trim and slashed to the thigh. The cut of the dress showed off her long legs, elegant shoulders, and toned arms. It was that quiet period in the club, a few hours before the deejays took to their decks at the main dance floors. The VIP lounges were quiet, and the hostesses were milling around waiting for the music to start up and the evening's entertainment to begin. He'd dabbled with a few of the girls that worked the club, but Cassandra was his favourite. She wasn't afraid of his prosthetic – on the contrary, she was comfortable with it, curious even. He'd told her the story of how he lost his hand and that had piqued her interest further.

'This bad police detective,' Cassandra began in her soft Caribbean lilt, 'he never stopped the man attacking you? But he could have?'

'He could have, and he should have, Cassie. If he had, I'd

still have two hands.' Canavan rested his whisky glass on the large mahogany coffee table.

Her dark eyes shone with sympathy. 'Poor baby.' She reached across and gently stroked Canavan's arm, through his shirtsleeve, at the part where the rubber prosthetic sheathed over his forearm. 'And you tell me that the police bosses ignored your complaints and your lawyer's legal claim?'

'They don't care, Cassie. They said he's a hero. He took my money, he took my hand, but I'll get even with him.' Canavan caressed her arm with his good hand. She was beautiful, the standout in a line-up of lovely hostesses that Sarah had recruited. 'I'll take something from him.' Canavan felt a sudden seizure of lust. 'Do you fancy a wee line of coke, Cassie?'

She leaned across and kissed him full on the mouth. 'Yes, Philip... a wee line.' She mocked his Glasgow accent. It was code for sex; they'd been enjoying coke-fuelled intercourse for over a month.

Canavan pulled a small bag of white powder from a coffee table drawer and handed it to Cassandra. 'Ladies first,' he said. She expertly spread four neat lines of cocaine on the tabletop and used a rolled-up ten-pound note to snort the first of them in quick time.

'Ooh, baby, sweet lord Jesus, that's great cocaine.' Cassandra threw her arms up and squealed her seal of approval.

Canavan followed suit; the second line gone in an instant. He jolted his head back. 'Oh mammy, daddy! Get some of that up your nostrils, Cassie.'

The final two lines went the same way. Cassandra unhooked the clasp of her halter-neck, revealing her naked breasts. Canavan sprinkled the last of the cocaine down her cleavage. The sight of white powder on black skin fired him up and he buried his head between her breasts, sniffing and licking the remnants of coke from her torso. She unbuttoned his shirt and pulled it off over his head. He struggled with his belt and flies, but she helped to undo his trousers. Cassandra stepped fully out of her dress, slipped off her panties, and sat astride him on the sofa, kissing his face, neck, and shoulders. Canavan moaned as she slowly, expertly manoeuvred herself onto him.

'Fuck me, Philip, fuck me.'

Nobody ever called him Philip, but he loved it when she did. Cocaine, sex, and Cassandra were like a tiny glimpse of joy. These recent sessions with her were the closest thing he'd experienced to happiness since losing his hand; the closest he'd come to escaping his current life, the closest he'd come to living in a very long time. He was damaged; Kidston had broken him, ruined his reputation. But this seemed more like a life. Maybe he should give up on his plan for vengeance, let the Kidston thing go. He could try for a normal life with Cassie. *Was this the cocaine talking? It did some strange things to his mind.*

He flipped her over. Cassandra loved it doggie style and she moaned, screamed, and shouted her encouragement as Canavan, completely wired into a hyper-alert coke-sex high, powered into her with an energy that he could never find anywhere else. He caught sight of himself in the big wall mirror and smiled. A maniacal grin spread across his face as he thought about *Cowboy Phil, riding the bucking bronco.* Watching himself thrusting hard into Cassandra, enjoying the show, he raised his good hand, swirled an imaginary lariat in the air, and yelled a mighty 'Yee-ha!'

'What the fuck?' It was a rude awakening for the drug-fuelled lovemakers as Sarah Canavan burst into her brother's office. 'Cassandra, you're finished here, get your clothes, and get out. As for you, Phil, this is not why I gave you this job.' She picked his shirt up from the floor and threw it at him. 'Sort yourself out.'

'C'mon, sis,' a dazed Canavan implored his sister as

Cassandra rushed out of the office clutching her clothes to her chest. 'We were only having a bit of fun. Don't take it out on Cassandra.'

'Fun? Is that what you call it?' Sarah Canavan knew what a coke high looked like. The dilated pupils were a dead giveaway but the discarded empty polythene bag on the coffee table had enough residual white powder to confirm her fears. 'How long have you been doing coke, Phil?'

'A few months, Sarah, but it's not what it looks like.' Canavan's vanishing euphoria was evident as he pleaded his case while adjusting his trouser belt one-handed. 'I took it for the pain in my stump, but I'm not addicted, honest, it's just something that helps with my pain and my mood.'

'Oh, c'mon, Phil, don't kid yourself. You know better than anybody how addiction works. You need to get off this shit and you'd better not be allowing anyone to deal coke at my club... and I mean anyone, or you're finished. Is that understood?'

Canavan lowered his head and averted his eyes. Sarah was the only person who could give him a rollicking like that with impunity. 'Understood.' He was bowed, broken, and humiliated by his young sister.

Sarah stormed out of his office.

———

Canavan slumped back on his office sofa. His stump was louping and his head was spinning. The cocaine he'd just snorted was having little effect. Sarah's outrage had been a shock to his system and his comedown was descending at an alarming pace. He'd let her down badly and fucked up his chances. He knew how protective Sarah was about her liquor licence – she'd replace him as manager and bring in somebody with proper nightclub experience.

Canavan's life seemed to be unravelling.

Again.

He was a man with nothing to lose.

It was time to move on Kidston.

It was time for payback.

CHAPTER TWENTY-SEVEN

The first strike hit Kidston on the back of his neck, and he lurched forward. The suddenness of the attack broke his stride. As he felt his neck, the second strike hit him square between the shoulders. He inspected his hand – egg yolk! It became immediately clear who the culprits were. As he and Gabriel walked back to their cars after dinner, they'd been ambushed by three teenage boy racers in a souped-up silver Astra. The car, with both passenger side windows open, sped past them.

'Ya fannies!' shouted one of the occupants as the driver gunned the accelerator.

Kidston wiped his hand on his shirt and broke into a sprint. It looked like a hopeless pursuit as the car raced into the distance. But he knew the area and the next two junctions were notoriously slow for getting through the traffic lights. He burned the car's registration number into his brain; there would be repercussions whether he caught up or not. A new Hugo Boss suit was ruined. He wasn't dressed for running but was surprised by the pace and rhythm he was getting as he punched his arms into each stride. His breathing was sound, but he felt the burger and chips in his stomach – he never ran after a meal; always before. The driver slowed as he approached the first set of traffic lights on Fenwick Road. Kidston gained on the silver car, but he was still a block back. Then a stroke of good fortune as the lights of the pedestrian crossing turned red and the Astra slowed to a stop. If the next junction was a red light, Kidston had a chance.

Red light spells danger. The silver Astra was caught in a queue of traffic at the big, busy junction at Braidholm Road, right beside Giffnock police office. Kidston ran to the front of the vehicle and straddled the bonnet. Other motorists looked on, alarmed by the incursion of a pedestrian onto the roadway. With other cars front and rear and on either side of him the driver was boxed in. Kidston pressed his warrant card onto the windscreen and gestured for the driver to switch off the engine.

The chaos was increased by the arrival of a marked police van, sirens wailing, blue lights flashing. Gabriel arrived on the scene with two uniformed cops. Kidston did a double take as he recognised Costello and McCartney. 'What are you two doing in this neck of the woods?'

'One of my complainers for the stolen radio cassette players you helped me with the other day, lives around the corner,' McCartney said. 'We were out getting some witness statements.'

Kidston took great satisfaction from the defeated look on the spotty faces of the three youths, dressed in hoodies, sweatshirts, and designer trainers, who were suddenly caught up in an episode of *The Bill.*

'I was wondering where you'd got to, neighbour,' Kidston said to Gabriel, recovering his breath from his mighty sprint.

'I thought I'd make use of the local constabulary.' Gabriel laughed. 'There was no way I was going to keep up with your

Allan Wells impersonation. I waved these guys down after you sprinted off.'

'Have you guys met your new DI for the Gorbals yet?' Kidston did quick introductions.

'Congratulations on your promotion, sir,' McCartney said to Kidston. 'We're all sorry to lose you at the Gorbals.'

'But we're equally looking forward to working with DI Gabriel.' Costello smiled at his neighbour. He'd already congratulated Kidston, his former probationer, on his latest achievement.

The three teenagers were escorted to Giffnock office. A search of the Astra, by Costello and McCartney, found a small bag of weed as well as a half-used carton of eggs. Costello agreed to write up the case and offered to return the youths to their homes, but Kidston had other ideas.

'If you take us to their houses, I'll confirm their addresses and speak to the parents.' Kidston's ruined suit jacket was folded across his knees in the police van.

The first two boys were suitably chastened in front of their parents as Kidston related what they'd been up to. Mention of cannabis sent the parents into genuine shock and concern for their sons. Residing in leafy Giffnock, not too far from the police office, meant that these were middle-class, law-abiding families. Kidston held his ruined jacket up as an exhibit in both houses. The father of the Astra driver was apoplectic, and it was clear that the boy would face a degree of parental summary justice.

It was at the home of the third and final teen, the chief egg thrower, that things became more interesting. An architect father and a doctor mother were keen to emphasise that this was just youthful high spirits and there would be no need to damage the prospects of a young man who'd secured a place to study law at Glasgow University. *Just a suburban version of teenage wildlife*, thought Kidston. The main difference between the suburbs and the housing schemes of Glasgow was that very few schemies would have access to a sporty Vauxhall Astra, barely three years old.

'Please, Detective Chief Inspector, let me reimburse you for the cost of a new suit,' the architect said. 'I don't think dry cleaning will remedy that and it looks expensive.'

'That won't be necessary, thank you,' Kidston said. 'The courts will take care of that aspect with a compensation order.'

'Courts,' said the doctor with a note of alarm. 'Surely there's no need for this to go to court. It's just some youthful high jinks.'

'It's actually more than that,' Kidston said. 'The boys had a bag of weed in the car. As a doctor, I'm sure you're aware of the risks of cannabis as a gateway drug and all the other factors.'

Gabriel produced the weed from his inside pocket and held it up triumphantly – exhibit 'B'.

'The weed isn't mine, Mum,' the egg thrower piped up.

'You've heard him, Ewan doesn't even smoke,' said the doctor.

'That will be a matter for a defence lawyer and the procurator fiscal,' Kidston said.

'Lawyers, fiscals?' the architect bristled. 'Surely it won't come to that. Can we not come to some agreement that will keep it out of the courts? I'm more than willing to compensate you for the suit.'

'I'll caution you to avoid any further offers of compensation.' Kidston drew the architect a steely look. 'In the future, young Ewan here might think about the consequences of his actions.'

As they exited the large, detached house, Kidston and Gabriel heard the muffled sound of raised parental voices through the lounge window. There was quite a screaming match developing.

'I thought you'd just note the reg number and pick up an

enquiry on the PNC,' Gabriel said as they walked back to where they'd parked their cars.

'That was my backup,' Kidston said. 'But I know those lights on Fenwick Road and so long as the wee buggers didn't take a side street, I thought I'd have a chance. I nearly spewed up my burger and chips though.'

Gabriel laughed. 'Came a bit too close to bribery there with the architect fellah. I thought he was going to take you to Ralph Slater's and let you pick out a new suit.'

Kidston removed his jacket and held it up in the bright late-evening sunshine to further inspect the mess. 'This one's a goner. I'm sure they'll engage a good lawyer to sort it all out. I'll be getting a compensation order for the suit, one way or another. Typical middle-class parents – we'll sort it all out with cash. I'm not a fan of postcode policing; apply the rules fairly and consistently and there can be no complaints.'

———

As they returned to the side street where both cars were parked, Kidston caught the glare of the late-evening sun reflecting off windscreens. He screwed his eyes as he noticed the lack of glare on the rear window of his BMW – there was no glass. Both detectives hastened their pace and Kidston peered into his car's interior, the back seats littered with broken glass. Gabriel's car was undamaged as were all the other vehicles in the side street. Kidston opened his back door for a closer inspection. 'What the hell?'

'Seems to be just your car, Luc,' Gabriel said. 'Somebody who doesn't like Beamers or more targeted than that?'

'I've no idea,' Kidston replied. 'Looks like a pickaxe, a crowbar or a baseball bat, there's no bricks or boulders and my radio cassette is untouched.'

'What about the boy racers we just lifted?' Gabriel posed the question and his initial theory. 'Or one of their mates?'

'Seems unlikely.'

'Ronnie Miller's revenge?'

'Nah, Ronnie's more likely to be in your face for a square go, this isn't his style.'

'You know him better than I do,' Gabriel said. 'Talk about having the shine taken off our promotion celebrations. Me yesterday, you today. Might be just a random act of vandalism.'

'I don't believe in coincidences, Jimmy, or random occurrences. This is worrying. Has someone targeted my car?'

CHAPTER TWENTY-EIGHT

WEDNESDAY, 22 AUGUST 1990

'Are you sure you're not overreacting?' Grace was responding to her husband's breakfast table request that she and Florrie stay at her sister Veronica's house for a few nights until he bottomed out the troubling attack on his car.

'I might be,' Kidston began, 'but as long as I've got that niggly feeling in the back of my head, I'd rather you were both safe. It's what Gregor would refer to as his *Spidey-Sense*.'

'Might it just be a coincidence?'

'Of course, it might be, but I don't believe in coincidences. Plus, I've got this big case on, and it'll be company for you and Florrie.'

'Okay,' Grace said. 'You know I'll always trust your judgement but we'll both miss you.'

'When this all dies down a bit, we can take up Veronica on her offer of the cottage.' Veronica's seaside getaway in St Monans was becoming a favoured destination for short family breaks. 'I'll try and pop in this evening depending on what time I get back from the office.'

And he meant it. He enjoyed the company of his wife and toddler daughter and didn't want to be apart from them any longer than necessary. Having recently celebrated his third wedding anniversary, he'd worked hard to ensure that the demands of his job didn't affect family life. For Kidston, policing had been a very harsh mistress in the past. His ex-wife, Melanie, had battled constantly for his time and attention. He'd put the job first. And it had happened too often. Nights out, parties, weddings and ultimately a family holiday all lost out to ongoing investigations or a requirement to attend court. And memorably, a family Christmas dinner ruined. Random call-outs for hostage situations. Thinking back, he should have seen it coming, but he'd been so absorbed in his work that it had been a shock when Melanie asked him for a divorce.

He sensed that Grace could handle his absences better than Melanie, but he didn't want to push that line or take advantage. Grace had Florrie. They both did. His absences were fewer now; the new Kidston took all the leave and days off he was due. The office wouldn't fall apart when he wasn't there. Investigations wouldn't crash and burn just because he wanted to be home in time to bath his daughter and read her a bedtime story.

But this was different. This was about protecting his family.

———

Kidston and Gabriel attended Goodnights for a prearranged afternoon meeting with Sarah Canavan, who invited them into her plush basement office, all dark wood, maroon leather sofas and expensive art prints. Kidston hadn't seen her for over two years, since after her brother's trial. Sarah had first crossed his orbit during the Ellie Hunter investigation when she'd offered up information to help the enquiry, although Kidston realised that she was pursuing her own agenda at the time. He recalled a slightly anxious visit to her home for an interview when she'd flirted outrageously with him. She was as stunning as he remembered her. Her light-brown hair was cut shorter with blonde tints, scraped back in a slicked wet-look style. It showed off her strong cheekbones and large expressive blue eyes. She was wearing a three-quarter length black leather coat over a white silk blouse and white jeans.

'Detective Chief Inspector Kidston,' Sarah greeted him with a broad smile. 'Congratulations, Luc. And this must be your replacement, Detective Inspector Gabriel. Is that right?'

'Thanks, Sarah,' Kidston said. 'Yes, this is Jimmy Gabriel, who's taking over from me at the Gorbals.' He wasn't surprised at her being up to speed with their promotions – she'd previously demonstrated access to an intelligence network that could rival anything the police had. 'You're well informed, as usual.'

'You know me and my sources.' She smiled.

Sarah Canavan had been the brains behind her family's criminal enterprises long before her parents passed away. A family consigliere to her late father, Big Davie, who'd taken her advice on property deals and other investments as she worked to legitimise her part of the family business. It was no surprise to Kidston that she'd traded up her chain of tanning salons and was now running a successful nightclub.

'Congratulations to you too, Sarah,' Kidston said. 'This is quite the operation you've built up here.'

'What can I do for you, gentlemen? I know you've had your colleagues visit the club during opening hours for your murder investigation. Any leads?'

'Sadly, not as many as we'd have liked,' Kidston said. 'In some respects, that's why we're here. Your head bouncer: where did you get him?'

'Chief steward, tut tut, Luc. You're bringing down the tone of my club already with comments like that. Billy

Bannerman's very experienced, worked all the major clubs in the city.'

'He's got convictions for drug dealing, I'm not sure you'd be aware.'

'I wasn't aware. There'll be no dealing here, I can assure you,' Sarah said indignantly. 'If I catch any of them dealing, including Bannerman, then their feet won't touch the ground.'

'My sources tell me that cocaine, poppers, and ecstasy are freely available here any night of the week,' Kidston said. 'While I've no *prima facie* evidence that your stewards are dealing, I suspect that to be the case.'

'That's news to me,' Sarah said, her expression changing to a look of grave concern. 'What can I do about it?'

'Sarah, I could blitz your club with undercover cops, with the drugs search dogs and the ultraviolet lights and there would be plenty of evidence to close you down. But I don't want to do that.'

'Why not?'

'Because this double murder is my number one priority, and your staff weren't very co-operative when I made enquiries about one of your punters.'

'I thought he was a Bennets punter.'

'Comes here too.'

Sarah fished in her desk drawer and pulled out the familiar photofit picture of the evasive Nicky. 'This is your guy?'

'Yes, and I think Bannerman knows who it is. If you lean on him for a name and address, then I'll allow you a few weeks to tidy up your operation here. I know you don't want to lose your licence.'

'Leave it with me. I'll try and get more information about your suspect.' Sarah Canavan's expression darkened, and Kidston saw her beautiful features harden. 'I swear if I find out these chancers are dealing drugs, I'll be letting you know.'

———

Sarah Canavan sat in her plush office and contemplated everything she had achieved and everything her big brother may be putting at risk. *Everything!* Especially if he was now succumbing to a cocaine addiction and was dealing drugs in her club. Selling off her chain of tanning salons had allowed her to buy a nice bungalow in Kissimmee, Florida, and start up Goodnights. Phil had run the heroin trade in Glasgow's south side for ten years and had never gone near any drugs. He knew the carnage and devastation caused by the deadly light-brown powder and how easy it was to become addicted. Sarah had never been a user; her drug of choice was champagne or a good vodka martini. She wasn't naïve – a girl from the housing schemes doesn't become a woman of the world without understanding how things work. Her club clientele was a well-heeled crowd, and many would crave more than alcohol on a night out. Punters bringing coke, speed, ecstasy, or poppers to her club for personal use was to be expected but she would not tolerate any dealing.

She'd suspected Phil had been using for some time but assumed it was restricted to strong pain medication. The mood swings were getting more marked recently, another clue that he'd moved on to coke. How did she miss it? Phil's behaviour yesterday was troubling, it was reckless. How much coke was he doing? She had some sympathy for his pain management explanation. He was still experiencing physical and phantom pain three years after the amputation, and she knew that he'd tried various painkillers without long-term success. Her long-suffering brother had moved on to harder illegal substances and in some dark vale she was terrified that he might turn to heroin. She'd witnessed the psychological trauma; the change in his personality had been marked. Before the attack, Phil was upbeat, outgoing, and always wisecracking. After the incident, he'd become withdrawn, less talkative, his mood was darker, and he'd lost confidence. It was almost like his mighty reputation as a hardman, and a blade artist had been diminished by the loss of his right hand.

She wouldn't be grassing him up to Detective Chief Inspector Kidston; her family code forbade that. She would help get him clean and she would sack Bannerman based on what Kidston had told her. Her brother had an unhealthy obsession with the handsome detective who'd just visited her.

He hated Kidston and blamed the detective for all the ills that had befallen him.

Kidston's visit to the club on Saturday had really spooked Phil, now more convinced than ever that the detective was gunning for him and trying to send him back to jail. She would make some enquiries about getting him into a drugs rehab, take him out of the firing line, let him get his head straight. Somewhere upmarket. She could afford it.

CHAPTER TWENTY-NINE

THURSDAY, 23 AUGUST 1990

I t wasn't a completely new experience for Grace Kidston to worry about her husband. After all, he was a police officer, who in addition to being a senior detective, was a specialist negotiator and called upon to intercede in armed sieges, hostage incidents and suicide interventions. But this was different. Luc was always honest with her around the levels of risk and threat he faced at work. The attack on his car might have been random; it was parked in a side street in a quiet, residential area. No other cars were targeted, and that's what was worrying Luc. He might have been overcautious but if he was taking the extreme step of moving his wife and daughter out of the family home for a few nights, she would just have to trust him.

'You promise me everything's okay with you and Luc,' Veronica said.

'It's a work thing, honestly,' Grace replied. 'Luc's taking precautions around an ongoing investigation.'

Grace was pleased to stay with her big sister, even if it was taking a bit of time to reassure her that their marriage was not in trouble. They were seated on a large grey leather sofa in Veronica's spacious lounge sharing a pot of coffee and some almond cake. Florrie played with her two cousins like it was one of her regular visits. The three kids fussed around Tallulah, who was enjoying the attention.

'Besides,' Grace said, 'there can't be any marital problems between Luc and I because I think I'm pregnant.' She patted her tummy and beamed a wide smile at her sister.

'Does Luc know yet?' Veronica asked.

'I'm to phone the surgery today to confirm. I was waiting to tell Luc when I knew for sure. Can I use your phone?'

'Of course. Use the one in the bedroom for privacy.'

When Grace emerged from the bedroom two minutes later, her smile was even wider. 'You're going to be an auntie again. Another one for our growing little kindergarten here. Doctor Hendricks reckons I'm ten weeks gone.'

'That's brilliant news, baby sister.' Veronica got to her feet and hugged Grace. 'I'm so happy for you. And for Luc; I'm so glad you two found each other again.'

'I'm so happy, Veronica.' Grace waved a hand in front of her face to stop the tears coming but only partly succeeded. 'Three years ago, I could never have dreamed of this life that I'm living now.'

'Bring it in, baby sister.' Veronica wrapped her arms around Grace, who sobbed gently on her shoulder. 'Are you worried about Luc?'

'Not really, but there must be something or why would he move us out of the house?' Grace dried her tears with the back of her hand. 'These are happy, baby tears.'

Once the happy tears had subsided, the coffee was finished and the almond cake had been devoured, Grace asked Veronica to watch the children while she took Tallulah for her morning walk. It was a fine, sunny day. Veronica spread the large activity mat in the back garden for the kids, while Grace prepared an eager husky.

Veronica's house was a fifteen-minute walk from Grace's home. She was wearing her favourite walking shoes; a pair of snazzy white trainers that went nicely with her pale-blue, front-buttoning, light cotton dress with its oversize daisy print. Walking Tallulah in a neighbourhood she was so familiar with on such a fine, sunny day seemed such a good fit for her current mood. She couldn't wait to tell Luc her news. He would be delighted.

Just over three years ago, Luc had been going through a challenging time, personally and professionally, with the Gorbals Samurai case and the overlapping Ellie Hunter investigation. The two divorcees had realised that life was offering them a second chance and they reconnected romantically, after a seventeen-year gap. Suddenly, there was a wedding, a wonderful honeymoon in Nashville, and then their baby daughter, Florence had come along. Now their little family was about to grow, and she couldn't be happier.

Tallulah pulled on her lead. Grace knew she'd much rather be running through Rouken Glen Park with Luc, but she loved walking her, especially when they were accompanied by Florence in her pushchair. Her daughter adored the dog, and the feeling was mutual as the fiercely loyal, protective, and affectionate Tallulah doted on the toddler. The husky hadn't seemed in the least bit slighted that Florrie had stayed behind to play with her cousins.

It dawned on Grace that she'd forgotten to bring any of Tallulah's dog food to Veronica's and she'd have one very hungry husky on her hands after their walk. She made a spur-of-the-moment decision to change her route and go by her own house to pick up a bag of Tallulah's dried dog food. She had a quick check around the house, made sure the patio doors to the back garden were secure and grabbed a pack of dog food from the kitchen cupboard. Whatever was troubling Luc, whoever smashed in his car windscreen, everything was fine with the house. When she'd pressed him on his reasons for moving her out, he was unable to offer any specifics; just a nasty hunch that someone, somewhere was going to take things to a personal level. 'Better to be safe than sorry,' he'd said.

As she exited the garden gate, she was very disappointed to notice that one of her favourite rose bushes was blighted by Botrytis. The tallest, largest-headed flower in an abundant bush of yellow roses was covered in fungus. Such a shame. Grace never noticed the white Ford Transit parked some way back from her house. She never noticed that its engine started up just as she closed her garden gate and she never saw it tailing her at a discreet distance as she started out on her walk back to Veronica's.

CHAPTER THIRTY

With no break in the case, Kidston began to feel the grind and the anxiety that came with an undetected double murder. He often wondered where the public got their perception that police work was cool and exciting. It could be the dullest most mundane stuff imaginable. *Shoe leather*, Sawyers called it. Boots on the ground. Knocking on doors, speaking to people, checking then double-checking details. And lots of tea. If you declined a cuppa, your interview gets off on the wrong foot. People take offence – *you think my house is too dirty to take a cup of tea?* That initial rapport over shared tea and biscuits was golden, even if your kidneys were floating.

Nicky was in the wind. The level of police activity on this case would have spooked anyone. Kidston was beginning to wonder if Nicky really existed at all. He wasn't much more than a police construct – a composite created by Stark and him – built on the flimsiest info; a name or a nickname that they couldn't be certain about, a tennis story, nightclubs, and a possible landscaping business. Kidston was beginning to believe Nicky was a phantom. He would need to be a phantom made flesh – and soon – if this investigation was to be a success.

Adrian Harrison was three weeks ago; Ryan Ferrier was seven days and counting. He had to admit to himself, his first major case as a DCI was going cold.

———

The van was alongside Grace before she reached the main road. Brakes screeching, a white Ford Transit skidded to a halt at the kerb. The side door panel slid open, and she was bundled inside before she or Tallulah had a chance to react. The good-natured husky probably thought it was all a game as Grace's captor ripped the lead from her hand and her favourite dog food scattered all over the pavement. Tallulah knew better when a kick was aimed at her, and Grace screamed in alarm before a sweaty hand covered her mouth and a filthy sack was pulled over her head as she was hauled onto the floor of the van. Tallulah produced an alarming full-throated howl and bravely tried to jump into the van beside Grace. Only a swinging boot in her face and the door being violently slid shut prevented her from doing so as the van sped away.

As the white van turned on to Fenwick Road and raced towards Shawlands, Tallulah kept pace, running alongside, trailing her lead behind her, and ignoring the heavy daytime traffic. As the van slowed to comply with the Kilmarnock Road traffic lights at the Tinto Firs Hotel, Tallulah drew level, then overtook the stopping vehicle. The husky howled and jumped wildly at the driver's door; her ice-blue eyes fixed on the van that held her mistress captive. The driver's path was blocked by the queue of traffic. Desperate to shake off the crazy wolflike dog that was stalking them, the driver saw his chance when the lights turned green. The dog was running in front of the van as it accelerated away from the lights, turning her head, howling alarmingly, and drawing the attention of other motorists and pedestrians. A quick pull on the wheel, a slight deviation towards the white centre lines was enough to strike the husky and run her down.

As the van sped away from the scene, the stricken husky lay motionless in the middle of the road.

CHAPTER THIRTY-ONE

Detections can come from the most unexpected places. For Kidston, Yates's Wine Lodge in Blackpool was one of the most surprising. After days of door-to-door enquiries, tennis club and nightclub visits, and checks with builders' merchants – all of which proved fruitless, it was police colleagues in England who came up with the matched DNA profile that broke the case.

Lancashire Constabulary's had been notified by their accredited laboratory supplier and had alerted their Strathclyde counterparts to the DNA match. Kidston nearly swallowed the receiver when he took the call from Martin Reynolds.

'Who is it?' Kidston asked.

'Richard Nicolson, twenty, born 12 April 1970, and residing in Bankhead Road, Rutherglen.'

'What's he charged with?' asked Kidston.

'That's the strange thing,' Reynolds replied. 'He's not an accused. He was the victim of a mass brawl in a Blackpool pub six months ago. It all kicked off when a stag night got violent. He was glassed in the neck with a tumbler and his blood was sampled and matched to stains on the sleeve of the guy who assaulted him.'

'So Lancashire wouldn't have photographed or fingerprinted him as a victim?'

'No, there'll be photos of the injury, probably showing his face, but no classic mugshot picture. I've asked them to fax any pictures and I'll pass them on.'

'No matter, we'll go and get him based on the DNA hit.' Kidston's mind raced through the information he'd just been given. Richard Nicolson is the mysterious Nicky. His DNA was on Adrian Harrison's bathrobe – they'd be able to back that up with an evidential blood sample from Nicolson. An interview would get more of the story and probe the circumstances around Ryan Ferrier's murder. They'd turn Nicolson's house over and see what they could find.

———

Kidston, Gabriel, Stark, and Metcalfe attended at the Bankhead Road flat in two CID cars. Richard 'Nicky' Nicolson answered the door and was immediately handcuffed by Stark who cautioned him in terms of a *Section 2* detention. The relevant legislation gave police the powers to detain a suspect for a period of up to six hours. Nicky closely matched the description given by the witnesses Monaghan, Devlin, and Mathieson. The ugly scar on the left side of Nicolson's neck corroborated the information from Lancashire police.

Kidston continued with the legal formalities. 'Richard Nicolson, I am detaining you on suspicion of the murder of Adrian Harrison. You are not obliged to say anything but anything you say may be given in evidence.'

'Whoa, big man. I don't know who you're talking about. I haven't murdered anyone. I want to speak to a lawyer.'

Kidston and Stark led their prisoner out to the CID car, while Gabriel and Metcalfe remained to search through Nicolson's flat.

The six-hour clock was ticking.

Back at the station, Kidston and Stark presented their detainee to the duty officer, who noted Nicolson's full particulars. He gave his occupation as electrician. Stark completed the requisite written forms, recording the reasons for Richard Nicolson's detention. Kidston disliked the bureaucracy and paperwork associated with the ten-year-old legislation. Back in the day, detectives would use the powers conferred by common law to detain a suspect, but the pendulum had swung in favour of the rights of an accused person. With a six-hour limit – a time period that could pass surprisingly quickly – investigators now favoured securing sufficient evidence prior to detaining a suspect. In this particular case, there was the DNA hit secured by police colleagues in Lancashire, so they were on solid enough ground. But they had little else to go on.

When the duty officer afforded Richard Nicolson an opportunity to comment on the grounds for his detention, his reply was straightforward:

'Not guilty.'

Nicolson was searched by a turnkey and possessions were carefully placed on the uniform bar counter. Cigarettes, lighter, wallet, belt, and some loose change. The turnkey counted the money and logged the amount onto the property sheet, which he presented to Nicolson for signing.

'When do I see a lawyer?' Nicolson said as he signed the document.

'We'll get to that,' Stark said as he took hold of his prisoner's arm to escort him to the interview room.

What's wrong with this picture? Kidston thought as he walked behind Stark and their detainee. Something was troubling him.

As Nicolson sat in the interview room, Kidston beckoned Stark back out into the corridor. 'Have you still got your notes from the interviews with Amanda Devlin and Patricia Mathieson?'

'Yes.' Stark flicked through his folder to the relevant pages. 'What are you looking for?'

'Amanda Devlin described Nicky as a "lefty with a ferocious serve". Is that correct?'

'Yes, here it is,' Stark said as he found the page. '"A lefty with a ferocious serve".'

'He signed his property sheet right-handed, which would be highly unusual for anyone who plays tennis left-handed.'

'But the DNA...' said a bewildered Stark. 'Maybe the lab's fucked it up.'

Both detectives re-entered the interview room and Stark started the tape recording. 'Mr Nicolson,' Kidston began after repeating the caution, 'I need to confirm that you were the victim of a glass attack six months ago. That wound on your neck, you got that in Blackpool?'

'Aye.' Nicolson pulled his shirt collar open to better show his scar.

Both detectives leaned in for a closer inspection. Kidston saw that the gash was below the collar line, which might explain why no witnesses had made any reference to it. 'That's nasty,' Stark said. 'How many stitches?'

'Fourteen or something.' Nicolson ran a finger over his scar. 'Some internal.' Stark grimaced at the thought.

'Blackpool police have charged a man based on the blood from your neck wound,' Kidston said. 'Is that right?'

'Aye, but it hasn't been to court yet.'

'How often do you go to Blackpool, Richard?' Kidston asked.

'I go quite a lot; I've got lots of family there. Two older sisters, an auntie, cousins, and that.'

'What do people call you, Richard?' Kidston asked. 'Do you get Ricky or Nicky?'

'I get both depending what company I'm in, but mostly I'm Ritchie or Ricky.'

'What other family members are there?' Kidston asked. 'You mentioned older sisters in Blackpool, who else is there? Any brothers?'

'No brothers, just five big sisters,' Nicolson replied. 'I'm the youngest of six. My mum and dad live near me in Bankhead, Rutherglen.' Stark noted the parents' details and home address in his folder.

Kidston's brain circuitry started to frazzle as he frantically calculated the various permutations on how this detention could have gone wrong. Had the Lancashire cops got their blood samples mixed up? 'But you sometimes get called Nicky?'

'Aye, some people call me that at work but mostly Ritchie or Ricky.'

'What about cousins your age?' Kidston asked, his mind desperately reaching towards the unacquainted territory of familial DNA.

'My cousin on my dad's side is Michael... Michael Nicolson.'

'Where does Michael live?'

'He lives in Toryglen. Prospecthill Circus.'

'What does he get called?' Kidston asked.

'He gets Micky or Nicky.'

'How old is Michael?'

'Born a week after me; 19th April 1970. We used to have joint birthday parties when we were kids.'

'Does Michael have any siblings... brothers or sisters?' Kidston asked.

'He's an only child.'

'Are you close to Michael?' Kidston asked. 'Do you hang around together?'

'Pretty close, aye,' Nicolson replied. 'Our dads are brothers, and our mums are best pals. We used to hang around a lot but not so much now. I've been living with my girlfriend for two years.'

'Do both your dad and your cousin visit Blackpool?'

'We go down two or three times a year but not always together.'

'Was your cousin or your father involved in the Yates's pub brawl when you were glassed?'

'They were at the stag night, but they weren't involved in the fight.'

'Are you sure?' Kidston asked.

'Positive.'

'How would you explain your DNA being found on an item of clothing belonging to a murder victim from over three weeks ago?'

Nicolson offered a blank stare. 'What's DNA?'

'The DNA from your blood that was found on the clothing of the guy who's been charged with assaulting you.' Kidston spoke slowly, more measured tones – he wanted Nicolson to understand him fully. 'Genetic materials, Richard, from your blood. The same genetic materials we found at a murder scene. Did you kill Adrian Harrison?'

Nicolson looked shocked. 'Not me. I don't know anyone by that name.'

Kidston signalled Stark to pause the tapes and left the room to make a call. When the duty officer saw him, he handed him a note with a phone number. 'Call DI Gabriel on this number. I didn't want to interrupt your interview, but I think it's urgent.'

Kidston dialled the number. Gabriel picked up. 'Luc, the girlfriend is here with their passports showing that they were both in Benidorm at the time of the Harrison murder. There's nothing in this flat tying him to that attack.'

'Shit, it's all blown up at our end as well,' Kidston said. 'Richard Nicolson's not looking like our man. He's got the gash on his neck but he's right-handed.'

'Eh?'

'Our Nicky's a lefty. I hate playing lefties. What you'd call a southpaw, Jimmy. Vicious spin serves out wide like McEnroe. I'm just about to phone Martin Reynolds and get a tutorial about familial DNA. Come back to the station, we'll see where we are with this.'

Kidston phoned Reynolds at the lab. 'Martin, my murder suspect from the Blackpool DNA hit. Can he have the same DNA as his father or cousin?'

'Monozygotic but not dizygotic twins,' Reynolds reminded him. 'I thought you were at the DNA presentation I did at Tulliallan.'

'So identical twins share the same DNA but not any of the other familial relationships?'

'Correct,' Reynolds confirmed.

'What about a cousin?' Kidston asked.

'Sorry, no. But remember back in the day large Glasgow families used to split up their kids to be raised by aunts, grannies, and such. Died out a bit in recent times with the expanded welfare state but it used to be commonplace. Might be the twins were brought up separately.'

'Hmm.' Kidston pondered the scientist's theory. 'That fits

with the family size... it could be that cousin Michael and Richard Nicolson are twins. Their dates of birth are only one week apart. Easy enough to doctor the birth certificates.'

'I'm telling you, Luc,' Reynolds said. 'Either Richard Nicolson's an identical twin of your killer or Lancashire police have made a massive error with the DNA.'

CHAPTER THIRTY-TWO

With the interview suspended Richard Nicolson was placed in a detention room so the detectives could make further enquiries. Gabriel and Metcalfe returned to the police station. They'd brought documentation supplied by Nicolson's girlfriend to help exonerate him from any charges. Kidston examined the passport, which confirmed the date of birth supplied by his suspect and cemented his alibi.

'We thought this would be of interest,' Gabriel said as he laid out a large group picture in a glass frame. 'Look at the faces in this photograph.'

Kidston and Stark leaned over the picture. It showed clan Nicolson, around a dozen strong, at a family wedding, everyone dressed in their finery. Two young men outfitted in identical morning suits were difficult to tell apart. 'The resemblance is uncanny,' Stark said. 'Which one is which?'

'Exactly,' Metcalfe said. 'I defy you to tell me which one of those boys is sitting in our detention room.'

'But they're cousins,' Stark said with deadpan scepticism.

'Aye, right,' Metcalfe said, mirroring her fellow sergeant's cynicism.

Kidston explained Martin Reynolds' theory about splitting up large families.

'I've heard about that happening,' Metcalfe said. 'Those boys have got to be twins. How is it they don't know?'

'Maybe their parents were waiting until they turned twenty-one.' Kidston held up the picture for closer inspection. 'Should we be the ones to tell him?'

'Do we interview the parents first?' Stark asked.

'No,' Gabriel replied. 'The less people who can alert Michael Nicolson that we're on his trail the better.'

'I agree,' Kidston said. 'I'll play it cagey with the DNA, familial links, and all that. The main thing is to locate Michael Nicolson and try to flesh out some of his background. We'll keep Richard here until we have our hands on Michael. Let's go.'

———

Stark fetched Richard Nicolson from the detention room and the interview was resumed.

'Richard, can you tell me who the two young men are in this photograph?' Kidston placed the picture in front of his suspect.

'That's me and Michael at my big sister's wedding two years ago.'

'Who's who?' Kidston asked.

'I'm on the right of the bridesmaids.'

'You look like twins,' Kidston said. 'How can people tell you apart?'

'Everybody says that,' Nicolson replied. 'Michael's slightly taller and the hair's a bit different.'

'The resemblance is uncanny,' Kidston said.

'Well, our two dads are brothers, and they look very alike.'

Kidston nodded in agreement. The two older men in the photograph could pass as twins. It would have made the lie more palatable, if indeed it was a lie. Kidston was still to convince himself. 'What does Michael do for a living?'

'He's on the buroo, used to work for the Parks Department as a landscape gardener. Does a wee bit of that when he can find work.'

'You and Michael grew up pretty close,' Kidston began, 'played together, socialised together, is that right?'

'Aye.'

'Did you play tennis together?'

'A bit when we were young. Michael's much better at tennis than me.'

'But Michael's left-handed and you're right-handed, is that right?'

'Aye. that's another way to tell us apart.'

'Richard, because you and your cousin Michael are related, you share similar DNA,' Kidston said. 'So you've been identified for a crime that was, in all probability, committed by Michael.'

'I don't understand any of this DNA stuff.' Richard Nicolson looked confused.

'Are you still close?' Kidston asked.

'We're still pretty close. I live with my girlfriend. He's got his own flat. He hangs with his own crowd.'

'Is he homosexual or bisexual?'

Richard Nicolson looked shocked by the question and took a while to answer. 'He's straight as far as I know.'

'Does he have sex with men for money?'

'Look, where's all this going?' Nicolson asked. 'What's he accused of? I can't believe he's involved in any murder.'

'Your cousin Michael hangs around gay nightclubs,' Kidston said. 'What do you think's going on there? He must be gay or bisexual. Do you go to gay clubs, Richard?'

'No. I do not. Look, when Michael was sixteen, he got

money for wanking off an older guy he met in a sauna. It happened again... a few times. The guy passed him around a few of his pals. One of them offered him more money for a blow job and he took it.'

'So he's gay,' Kidston said.

'He goes with women too,' Nicolson said. 'I don't think he's into any anal stuff, but he lets guys blow him off for money.'

'Like a male gigolo or a rent boy. I've heard Michael likes to hustle older guys for money.'

'What's he done?' Nicolson asked. 'What's this murder stuff all about? I haven't done anything wrong; I think you've made a big mistake. Do I need a lawyer?'

'We need to speak to Michael,' Kidston said. Richard Nicolson's description of his cousin's behaviour fitted with the suspect he'd formed in his mind. Now they were getting close. 'You're still a suspect in this until your cousin Michael exonerates you. I need to bring him in for interview, or I'm afraid I'll need to detain you much longer.'

'You're going to arrest Michael?'

'Correct, we're going to arrest him for the crime we've just detained you for. You share similar DNA to your cousin. We'll need to detain you a bit longer. One of my colleagues will take a full witness statement from you and then we'll get you back home.'

There was a look of incredulity on Richard Nicolson's face when he provided the address and flat number for Michael.

————

'So he's now a witness rather than a suspect, boss?' DC Mork Williams asked.

'For the moment, Mork. Until we know more.'

'Understood, boss.' With his short stocky body shape,

Williams was the exception to Kidston's team's sartorial standards. It wasn't that the little chubby-faced, ginger-haired detective didn't try, but his ill-fitting, *off the peg* jackets always hung loosely from his frame.

'Take a full statement from Richard Nicolson while we make further enquiries to trace his cousin,' Kidston directed. 'Make sure the statement covers everything Richard knows about Michael's behaviour with older men and take your time.' It was a convenient ploy to prevent one suspect alerting the other. Detaining 'cousin' Richard for an overlong period may be unwise – Kidston was already imagining a lawyer's letter complaining about an unlawful arrest – but was strictly necessary. Mork, whose lack of fine tailoring had zero effect on his abilities as a detective, was as tenacious as they come and would prolong taking the statement until he got the all-clear.

Kidston had a niggling worry that the entire exercise might prove academic. Michael Nicolson may be already in the wind.

CHAPTER THIRTY-THREE

With the sack removed from her head, Grace tried to take in her new surroundings but apart from the low glow from a single distant paraffin lamp, the room was in total darkness. The cool damp air and the earthy smell of clay hinted that she was underground. A faint stink of ammonia mixed with the odour of paraffin. Her hands were bound behind her back, and she'd been tied to an old wooden kitchen chair. She strained her eyes in the dim half-light and saw that the lamp was placed on a low side table situated by an old, battered leather sofa. Two men were seated there; one tall, one short, and the shimmering glint of the flickering lamplight on a metal hand told her immediately who her captors were.

Phil Canavan and Johnny Boy McManus.

So Luc's instincts had been correct; the threat to their family was real. Grace quickly calculated her odds of whether it would be better to make them think she didn't know who they were. Luc had often talked about his run-ins with Canavan and McManus. She knew the details of the Gorbals Samurai case and was aware that Canavan had instructed his lawyers to sue Strathclyde Police for damages. Was this some sort of twisted revenge? A crazy kidnapping scheme? Was he hoping to extort money from Luc? Grace's head ran through multiple possibilities, each scenario as scary as the next. What would revenge look like for Phil Canavan? Would she be maimed or raped? Would she be murdered? She'd heard many of Luc's negotiator stories and understood the importance of establishing rapport with perpetrators, knew all about Stockholm Syndrome. Would it help her case to tell them she was pregnant? What would Luc do in her situation? He'd start a conversation.

'Where am I?' Grace demanded. 'And why have you taken me?'

'All will become clear, Mrs Kidston,' Canavan said. He spoke calmly.

'You know me? Then you'll know who my husband is.'

'We know him all right,' Canavan said. 'He has something belonging to me and now I have something of his. You can go back to hubby once I have my property back.' Canavan's steel prosthetic caught the lamplight and glinted menacingly in the semi-darkness. 'As I say, all will become clear.'

'What property?'

'A bag of money was taken off an associate of mine, and I'd like it returned.'

'I don't know anything about that,' Grace lied. 'He never discusses his work with me.'

'You won't know us then.' Johnny Boy laughed. 'Let's just say we're acquaintances of your husband.'

'Who are you? What do I call you?' Grace continued with her lie and saw the shorter man look at his taller companion, who shook his head. 'What are you planning to do with me? I've got a two-year-old daughter waiting for me back home. She'll be frightened if I don't get back to her. Please let me go. I won't say anything to my husband.'

'You won't be going anywhere for a while, missy,' Canavan

said. 'You sit tight, behave yourself and nothing bad will happen to you.'

'What's this about?' Grace asked, unable to disguise the agitation in her voice. 'What's your plan?'

'You're a mouthy cow, Mrs Kidston.' Canavan rose from the sofa and walked over to her. 'Shut the fuck up, or I'll make you.' Grace felt the full force of Canavan's steel claw as it rattled her jaw. He stuffed a tennis sock in her mouth. Johnny Boy peeled off a length of gaffer tape to hold the gag in place. Her jaw was throbbing. Grace muted her sobs and bowed her head to hide her tears.

The sack remained off. She was thankful for that, but the reason was soon apparent. By the light of a small torch, Johnny Boy turned off the lamp, plunging the room momentarily into frightening total darkness. The torch flicked on and off as her two captors moved away from her location. She heard two sets of footsteps ascending a wooden staircase. A sudden shaft of daylight and a creaking sound that revealed a hatch cover being lifted, flooding more light into her prison. Briefly, she was able to glimpse a large underground cellar laid out with a battered old three-piece leather suite with some tables and chairs. Some kind of underground lair. A draught of cold air fanned the room as the hatch was dropped shut. She heard her two captors walking across the hatch and the scratching sound of items being placed on top.

Where the hell am I?

CHAPTER THIRTY-FOUR

Nicky drove the little Bedford van that he used for his landscaping work. He knew the CID had been asking around for him. Billy Bannerman at Goodnights and Scarlett Mascara at Bennets had tipped him off. It seemed like the cops were closing in on him. He knew there would be a reckoning, even though he'd never set out to murder anyone. Strangling Adrian Harrison was a spontaneous act; an angry reaction to the man pushing it too far. He'd warned him not to, but he'd treated him like a fuckin' rent boy. He couldn't deny there was an excitement in watching the light go out in Harrison's eyes as the cord tightened around his neck. Definitely some childhood trauma there. He was surprised when it all came flooding back. But he'd covered his tracks and staged the suicide scene pretty well – the cops wouldn't have that one.

Ryan Ferrier was different. He was lonely; a man who wanted sex and wouldn't take no for an answer. He'd gone there to price a landscaping job. Ferrier was finishing his dinner and had offered him a glass of wine. He preferred beer but it was pleasant enough and he had a second glass in that big swanky lounge. All his stuff looked expensive; a fancy sofa made from cowhide. The guy had a piano in his lounge, for fuck's sake! Nice stuff. *Oh, fuck!* He remembered that he'd taken a steak knife and a crystal glass from Ferrier's house. He knew his prints would be on them and it was easier than wiping them off. He'd intended to get rid of them, but it was nice stuff and he'd stashed them in a safe place. He'd get shot of them when he got back to the flat.

He badly needed some 'fuck off' money to get out of town. Maybe Blackpool; he'd family there. Maybe he could put the squeeze on Matthew Brodie. He knew he was some big shot in the city council. They'd fooled around in his car a wee bit before the councillor lost his nerve. Brodie would be good for some cash. He'd really like to sort out Dusty Monaghan before he left town. Dusty had ratted him out to the CID. Maybe Dusty could come up with some money for his travel fund. One way or another he needed to be on the move.

CHAPTER THIRTY-FIVE

Kidston and Stark piled into one CID car, Gabriel and Metcalfe took a second and the four detectives headed for Prospecthill, Toryglen. Kidston had alerted the Identification Branch and the group would rendezvous with an IB photographer at the locus.

'Mork will be ages taking that statement from Richard Nicolson,' Stark said as he drove to their destination. 'The boy can spin these things out when required.'

'I'm not worried,' Kidston said. 'I've told him to provide lunch if he has to.'

'Michael Nicolson's coming into clearer focus now,' Stark said. 'He's our killer but he seems a bit of a crazy mixed-up kid.'

'I hope he's not pissed off to Blackpool or gone to ground,' Kidston said. 'I really want to put this case to bed before it drifts further away from us. And we've been working silly hours, you could probably do with a break, some time off.'

'I'm good, boss, really. This is a massive case and I'm more than happy to put in the hours. I'm sorry, you know I'm always reluctant to take time off during big cases. Hate to miss out. I guess I'm just ambitious.' Stark hesitated. 'Although Marianne's complaining that she never sees me.'

'I'm sorry to hear that. The job cost me my first marriage – it won't claim my second. Gregor, this desire to live quickly, to wish your career and your life away. I'm going to give you the advice I'd like to have given to a younger version of myself.' Kidston gave his DS a thoughtful look. 'The race is not always to the swift. Take a break... pause for breath... enjoy the here and now and tomorrow will bring its own rewards. And, Gregor...'

'What?'

'Never apologise for being ambitious.'

———

The house was a second-floor maisonette flat in Prospecthill Circus, overlooking a fenced-off playground marked out for five-a-side football and basketball.

The entire flat would be treated as a crime scene; at the agreed rendezvous point the group picked up the IB photographer, who turned out to be the popular Suzanne, who'd been with the Branch for eight years and was dressed in her familiar garb of T-shirt, cargo pants and trainers. Kidston briefed Suzanne on the job, and everyone donned rubber gloves. Gregor Stark was posted in the common close to cover the back and front gardens just in case. There too many great escape stories, Kidston wasn't willing to risk another one. The other three detectives grouped at the door marked 'Nicolson' and Kidston gave the door a robust knock then rattled the letterbox.

No reply.

Alison Metcalfe wedged the letter box open and squatted on her hunkers to listen for signs of occupation. She shook her head. 'No TV, no music, it seems empty.'

Gabriel produced a folded search warrant from his inside pocket and nodded to Kidston before putting his shoulder on the door. A single Yale lock bust easily, and the three detectives filed in. The flat was manky; a complete tip, the entire three-apartment house resembling a teenage boy's bedroom. There were discarded clothes and training shoes strewn everywhere producing a pungent smell. Tin foil trays: the remnants of half-eaten Chinese takeaways, pizza boxes, fast food containers, and old fish and chip wrappers throughout the house, added to the stale odour. A Nintendo games console was plugged into a modern Sony Trinitron colour TV with a stack of video games and unboxed VHS cassette tapes piled on top.

Kidston pushed open the lounge window for some fresh air and shouted down to Stark for him to rejoin the group.

'Let's give this place a good turn,' Kidston said, impressed that Gabriel was already hanging his suit jacket over a kitchen chair, removing his cufflinks, and rolling up his shirtsleeves.

Kidston and Gabriel searched the lounge, emptying through the drawers of an old wall unit. Stark and Metcalfe started in the bedroom which was dominated by a large unmade double bed. Metcalfe pulled the duvet off. Stark flipped the mattress off the bed frame, revealing what lay underneath.

Stark saw the items first. 'Is that your steak knife, Alison?'

'Looks very much like it,' Metcalfe said, beaming at the discovery. 'And there's our Waterford wine glass. A proper little Aladdin's cave.'

'Boss, through here!' Metcalfe shouted, unable to disguise her glee in recovering two items that featured high on her most wanted *productions* list. Kidston brought Suzanne through and both items were photographed in situ from various angles. Metcalfe produced an evidence bag from her folder and carefully lifted the ebony-handled cutlery and gently dropped it in. 'The exquisite craftmanship of *Forge de Laguiole*, if I'm not mistaken,' she said, remembering the blurb provided by the company.

Gabriel shouted the others back through to the lounge where he was pointing out two articles in a drawer under the TV unit. 'Brown envelope with the name "Audrey" written on it, no doubt in Ryan Ferrier's handwriting. Money's gone though. I also found a logbook for a blue Bedford van, so we'll get the reg number circulated and get this guy pulled over before he causes us any more grief.' Suzanne snapped some shots of the latest items before Metcalfe gathered them into evidence bags.

Kidston clapped his hands. 'Brilliant work, cracking result. Well done, everybody. Bit of a false start with the DNA but it led us to the right guy, now all we need–' He was interrupted by the buzz of his pager. 'It's Mork. Let's hear what he's got to say.'

Kidston crossed the landing to the next-door neighbour's flat and showed his warrant card to the young mother who answered the door. She was happy to allow him to call his young detective. 'You still taking that statement?'

'No worries on that score, boss. I sent out for a McDonald's. He's having a wee smoke break, but the duty officer was looking for you. Urgent call to the control room from councillor Matthew Brodie reporting a suspicious man hanging around outside his house in a blue van. I got the division to despatch a panda, but Brodie was asking to speak to you or DI Gabriel.'

'Good thinking, Mork.'

'But, boss, a guy called Marc Monaghan's been phoning your old Gorbals office number asking for you personally. The desk sergeant passed me his message, says to tell you "The guy Nicky has been hanging around outside his flat.'

'Which call came first?' Kidston asked.

'The Monaghan call was around five minutes ago; the Brodie call was thirty-five minutes ago.'

'Good man, Mork. We're on Michael Nicolson's trail now; he's our man, he's Nicky. Contact Partick police office, get them to send officers to Monaghan's home address asap. Keep Richard talking for a while longer and we'll cover both these calls as backup. Our boy Nicky's on the move.'

Kidston explained the details of Mork's call and prepared a hasty plan. He and Stark would head west and check on Marc 'Dusty' Monaghan. Metcalfe would sit tight; hold the house as a crime scene, allowing Suzanne to take more photographs, and summon a full forensic search. There may be other treasures to unearth and there was a chance Michael Nicolson would come back. Kidston's plan included an element of calculated risk. Gabriel would attend Brodie's home; hopefully to reassure the chair of the police board, rather than find him dead.

CHAPTER THIRTY-SIX

Hello darkness, my old foe.

Grace felt her fear of darkness engulf her. Dread rushed through her veins; it filled her throat, chilled her heart, and touched the pit of her stomach. Fear laid its cold menacing finger on her unborn child. Although her captors would have no way of knowing it, Grace had spent much of her life scared of the dark. Terrified. Regardless of how irrational it might seem for a woman approaching forty, her childhood had been scarred by the fear of darkness.

They'd left her alone for a couple of hours in her pitch-black subterranean prison. She'd used a mix of chewing, blowing, and spitting and managed to push some of the cotton material out of her mouth and was breathing without difficulty. She picked and pulled at the bindings on her wrists but wasn't making any progress on that front.

Where am I?

She estimated that the van had travelled for around twenty minutes, so she wasn't too far from home. *What is it all about?* Her mind raced with the possibilities. *Are they responsible for the attack on Luc's car? Are they going to get Luc to testify a certain way in a criminal trial?*

Are these men going to kill me?

She fretted about Florrie and Tallulah; her daughter would be missing her mum. She'd heard Tallulah howling after the van and was concerned what might have happened to her. Florrie was safe at Veronica's, but she would be missing Tallulah too; her green-eyed, red-haired toddler daughter had taken her first steps at ten months old by holding on to the husky's collar. Florrie's first words weren't 'Mummy' or 'Daddy' – it was 'Lula'; a decent stab at 'Tallulah' for a tot. Those two were inseparable. Grace was overcome by dread; what if she was never to see her daughter again?

Grace was determined to think warm and happy thoughts to combat her phobia. The time had allowed her to examine the roots of her fear. Her mind floated back to the summer of 1962. It had been five years since Luc had survived being thrown from a third storey tenement widow. He'd rescued her from the same fate. Back then she'd regarded him as her saviour, or at least some kind of guardian angel. She still thought about him in those terms.

He will save me again.

How can he if he doesn't know where I am?

One afternoon the neighbourhood kids were playing hide and seek when she and Luc decided to conceal themselves in a large unused coalbunker. It was a good hiding place; too good. No one could find them, and they'd stayed hidden longer than they wanted to. It was pitch dark inside the big wooden box and they were crouched together, shoulder to shoulder, listening to the rhythm of their breathing. After some time, she'd became fearful of the dark and thought they might be trapped. 'It's okay, I'm here,' Luc had whispered as he held her hand. She remembered her fear subsiding as she squeezed his hand tightly.

Luc threw off the lid, peered into the sunlight and burst out laughing. They were both manky; the bunker was filthy with coal dust. Spying one of their 'chasers', they made a run for it and headed through the back courts, through a tenement close where Luc took Grace's hand. They stopped in the back close and stared, misty eyed, at each other. Grace was trembling with anticipation. There were no words exchanged as the two twelve-year-olds shared their first awkward kiss. Stylistically, it didn't quite match what they'd seen in the movies, but lips, teeth, saliva, and coal dust all combined to create something magical. Grace felt her stomach lurch and her knees wobble. Time had stood still, and the world seemed to spin around them, breathless, dizzying. Twenty-eight years later, she still experienced a similar warm sensation in her tummy, when Luc kissed her or held her hand.

The memory of her first kiss provided the motivation to hide in that same coal bunker a second time. This time unaccompanied as the boys were all playing football. But that meant more space. Grace had become uncomfortable within minutes. Her fear and anxiety rose quickly. The darkness was terrifying without Luc. She felt her pulse racing, her heart pounding in her chest and she pushed on the bunker lid to let the light back in. It was jammed stuck. One of the other girls had spied Grace's hiding place and slipped a sturdy tree branch into the old hasp.

She was trapped in the darkness, her panic rising and overcome by a petrifying stomach-churning fear. At first, she was unable to catch any breath, then she'd screamed for help at the top of her lungs, her heart seemingly jumping out of her chest. When her friends opened the bunker top, they laughed at her obvious distress.

Grace's humiliation was complete. She'd wet herself.

Ten minutes of terror. Enough to make her sleep with a bed light into adulthood.

It was different now. She was a mother and a wife. Florence and Luc needed her to survive this; whatever *this* was. And there was a new baby to think of. *Luc will find me.* She couldn't be a victim. She *wouldn't* be a victim. *Luc will find me.*

She'd lost him once when they'd split up aged twenty and it had taken seventeen years to get back together. She couldn't bear the thought of losing him again. *Luc will find me.* She recited her mantra of hope. *Luc will find me.*

Grace shuddered. Despite her warm thoughts and reminiscences, and her unshakable belief in Luc, she was a pregnant woman, tied and bound in a pitch-black subterranean bunker. Grace began to sob. Her tears fell like drops of sorrow. She was separated from her husband and daughter, and no one knew where she was. Frightened and alone; swallowed by the darkness. She felt fear's cold, merciless hands caress the unborn child in her belly.

CHAPTER THIRTY-SEVEN

Marc 'Dusty' Monaghan had seen the blue van tailing him when he walked back from the shops in Dumbarton Road. It was a day off and he'd spent some time in the impressive Partick Library with its vast skylight and tall windows. It was one of his favourite places in the city. He'd flicked through a copy of Stephen King's *The Stand* and become engrossed in the book's plot about a lethal flu pandemic. He checked it out on his library card to read at home. He stopped at his favourite bakery and bought two croissants for lunch. Then he picked up a bottle of Irn-Bru from the café. As he walked home, he'd seen the van. He recognised Nicky, peering through the driver's window, and wondered if he'd been at his door while he was at the library.

Dusty felt the fear rise in his chest; his heart pounded in his throat. Nicky could only be after him. He juked down a side street and quickened his pace, all the time looking around to check for the blue van. When he was sure he'd lost it, he doubled back around and took a longer route back to his house. He would phone DI Kidston and let him know about the sighting. Bennets had been crawling with plain-clothes and

CID the last few nights. Photofit pictures were being shown but nobody had come up with any information and Nicky hadn't been back to the club since the detectives first called.

————

Back in the flat, Dusty flicked on the kettle, emptied his washing machine, hung some clothes on the dryer and sat by the kitchen table. He spread strawberry jam on his croissants and looked out DI Kidston's card for the phone number he needed. After two unsuccessful calls, Dusty's hands were trembling. He knew the police were looking for Nicky and maybe it would be best if he called 999. On the third attempt, he got through to the desk sergeant who explained that Kidston had moved to a different station, and he passed on the number. Fourth time lucky; a DC Williams answered and explained that Mr Kidston was out on enquiries but given the urgency of the situation he would page him and get him to call back. Dusty felt a wave of relief wash over him.

He took the first bite of his strawberry croissant and set down his mug of coffee.

'Dusty! Dusty!' a voice boomed from the landing as the front door crashed in. 'You little bastard, you fired me into the polis.' Michael 'Nicky' Nicolson crossed the hallway in huge strides and was at Dusty's throat in no time, causing him to choke and splutter on a half-swallowed piece of jammy croissant. 'What the fuck's going on?'

'I'm sorry, Nicky,' Dusty spluttered, raising his arms to protect his face. 'The CID asked a lot of questions about you.'

'You should have said fuck all.' Nicky stared down at him. He grabbed Dusty by the collar and hauled him up out of the chair. 'You know how these things go.'

'Don't hurt me,' Dusty pleaded. 'Please don't hurt me.' It

was the first time Dusty had seen those eyes close-up and in daylight. They were extraordinary: the darkest grey, the iris almost merging with the pupil, as near black as he could imagine human eyes. The darkness terrified him.

'I'm not going to jail for you, ya wee scrote.' Nicky pulled a silver spandex dress from the clothes-horse. 'Is this one of your Dusty dresses? Maybe I should get you to put it on and get you to blow me. How much would you pay me for that?'

'My wallet's on the table, Nicky. There's thirty quid in it. Take it all.'

'For a blow job?'

'Anything, Nicky. Please don't hurt me.' Dusty cowered in fear as Nicky swung the silver dress around the neck of his latest prey.

Nicky spun around behind him and formed the dress into a garrotte and pulled the material tight around Dusty's neck. 'You're not singing now, ya wee scrote.' Dusty clawed desperately at the silvery cloth ligature as Nicky pulled tighter and tighter, dragging him back, lowering him down to the floor. Dusty looked up, Nicky's face directly above him now, and saw the fearful darkness in those murderous eyes.

Darkness and fear.

He felt himself passing out.

CHAPTER THIRTY-EIGHT

S tark bombed the car towards Partick. Kidston used the car radio to direct the control room to confirm a local response had been despatched. They took the Clydeside Expressway, crossing the Clyde alongside the landmark Finnieston Crane, a sleeping cantilever giant, that once loaded steam locomotives onto ships for export around the world. This iconic behemoth now stood sentinel beside the river, silent and still, an enduring symbol of the city's engineering heritage. Stark exceeded the speed limits and ran a number of red lights, but without *blues and twos*, he had to rely on banging the horn to safely navigate the busier stretches.

'Let's make sure we get there in one piece, Gregor,' Kidston said with a mocking smile as his young DS lost the back wheels of the Ford Escort taking a corner as they neared Monaghan's Stewartville Street flat.

Kidston spotted the blue Bedford van parked at the close and saw the police panda pull in behind them as their CID car came to an abrupt halt. The DCI won the foot race, through the common close and up two flights of stairs. The splintered keeper of a damaged Yale lock was the obvious sign that Monaghan's front door had been breached.

'You're not singing now, ya wee scrote.' Kidston heard the exchange as he ran through the hallway. Nicky had his back to the kitchen entrance and was in the act of dropping Dusty face down to the floor. His hands gripped a shiny silver band of clothing material around Dusty's neck.

As Kidston swept into the room, he picked up the Irn-Bru by the neck and in a flowing movement smacked Nicky on the back of the head. The glass bottle remained intact but Nicky went down like a felled tree.

'Thank God you're here,' Dusty spluttered as he pulled the spandex dress from his throat. 'I thought I was a goner.' He burst into tears as Kidston and Stark aided him back to his feet. A badly shaken Dusty wobbled and clung to Kidston's arm. 'Thank you... thank you.'

'I'll need to take that, please...' Stark reached for the spandex garment. 'The dress... as evidence,' he said, responding to the quizzical look from Dusty.

'Of course... here, take it. I won't be wearing it again.'

'Looks like the Lycra stretch material could have saved your life,' Stark said.

'Oh my God, you're right.' Dusty pulled on the cloth's elasticity as he handed the garment to Stark. 'What did you hit him with?'

Ignoring the foaming bottle of Irn-Bru that was now back on the kitchen table, Stark went inside his jacket and fished his police-issue baton from its holder. 'Good old polis baton saves the day, again.' He gave his boss a sly smile that suggested there would be no mention of *Scotland's other national drink* in the official statements.

Kidston returned Stark's smile with a small nod of the head. His young DS was coming along nicely.

Nicky gasped back to consciousness to discover he'd been handcuffed by two uniformed constables who were kneeling either side of him. Kidston did a cursory examination of their prisoner's scalp, a dirty big lump but no broken skin. He could be processed back at the station without the need for a hospital visit. Kidston got his first proper look at Nicky. He was as all the witnesses had described him; tall, lean, and muscular. The eyes were different from Richard's. Kidston saw how the darkness in Michael's dead black eyes would unsettle people. Recalling the wedding photo, he wondered how anyone could believe the two boys in the picture were not twins.

'Michael Nicolson, I'm arresting you for the attempted murder of Marc Monaghan and detaining you as a suspect for the murders of Adrian Harrison and Ryan Ferrier.' Nicolson looked shocked when he heard the names of his two murder victims. Kidston continued with the common law caution.

When invited to respond, Nicolson made the strangest reply:

'I'm no murderer, I've just got a problem controlling my temper. And don't tell them I'm gay.'

Kidston felt a tidal wave of relief; one of the biggest cases of his career, and his first as a DCI – a high profile double murder investigation solved, and a potential serial killer halted. A highly challenging case that he'd started to believe was running away from him, the complexities of dealing with DNA, but the police evidence was irrefutable. Michael Nicolson would be interviewed in the presence of his solicitor – *how much would he tell them?*

CHAPTER THIRTY-NINE

'Do you think he's a serial killer?' Stark asked Kidston as they finalised preparations to interview Michael Nicolson and waited for his solicitor.

'I'm not sure, Gregor,' Kidston replied. 'I think there's gangsters and criminals out there who've killed more victims than Michael Nicolson, but nobody uses that term for them.'

'But if you hadn't rattled Nicky's skull with that Irn-Bru bottle Nicolson's tally would be three. That's serial killer territory.'

'Nicolson seems too mundane to be classed that way,' Kidston began. 'Not flashy, no big media splash or prolonged manhunt. He's a killer, no doubt, but maybe I'm just uncomfortable with the term.'

'If the tabloids had splashed "*Gay Strangler*" or "*Gay Ripper*" headlines – would that have convinced you?'

'Nobody wants to work in that spotlight with that pressure, so no.' Kidston ran a hand through his unruly mop of hair. 'You'll learn, Gregor. Sometimes it's better to work under the radar.'

Adam Sharkey, the solicitor representing Michael Nicolson, arrived at the office. As a former detective sergeant and procurator fiscal, he was a familiar face and remained popular with his old colleagues even though, as a defence lawyer, he was working for the opposition. Already waiting was Dr Finola Donnelly, who'd been invited to listen in on the interview by Kidston. She would observe the session on a remote monitor. The pathologist and the solicitor listened intently, while Kidston related the story of the DNA mix-up, the attempted strangulation of Marc Monaghan and the dramatic arrest of Michael Nicolson.

Nicolson had an air of detached nonchalance as he adjusted his lanky frame into the chair. Adam Sharkey sat alongside his client. Stark explained the preamble to the taping procedure and switched on the recording device, then conducted a quick roll-call and a date and time check. Kidston reread the common law caution, reminding the prisoner that he was detained on two counts of murder and the attempted murder of Marc Monaghan. The DCI checked Nicolson's understanding of the reasons for his detention and his right to remain silent. Hearing the names of his victims snapped Michael Nicolson from his nonchalance.

'Adrian Harrison and Ryan Ferrier,' Kidston began, 'you seemed shocked when I read out the grounds for detention earlier, Michael. Those names a surprise to you?'

'Dusty Monaghan, obviously I'm caught in the act. No surprise there.' Nicolson's dark eyes stared intently at Kidston. 'Who are the other men?'

'Come on, Michael. Do you think I'd be detaining you for murdering two men that you don't know? I think you know them both well enough.'

'I don't know who you're talking about.'

'Adrian Harrison and Ryan Ferrier were close friends and were both seen by witnesses in your company, clubbing at Bennets and Goodnights and playing tennis at Titwood.' Kidston eyed his suspect closely. 'What do you say to that, Michael?'

'No comment.'

'You can do the "no comment" bit if you like, Michael, but, trust me, and your lawyer will confirm this, it will go much better for you at court if you answer my questions.'

Nicolson glanced at Adam Sharkey, who nodded in agreement.

'I wouldn't have killed Dusty,' Nicolson said. 'That was just an argument.'

'Looked to my colleague and I that you were strangling the life out of him.' It was Stark's turn to nod in support of his DCI.

Kidston gestured to Stark, who reached down to retrieve a brown paper bag from the floor. Stark took over commentary. 'For the benefit of the tape, I am showing Michael Nicolson items of evidence that were recovered from his flat earlier today under search warrant: one black wood-handled steak knife, a Waterford crystal wine glass and a brown envelope, inscribed "Audrey" in Ryan Ferrier's handwriting.' Stark held up the knife which was now sheathed in a transparent plastic tube.

'What have you got to say now, Michael?' Kidston's pale eyes were fixed on his suspect, who was now shifting uncomfortably in his seat. 'How did these items come to be in your flat?'

'No comment.' Nicolson looked deflated.

'Come on, Michael. That's the steak knife that killed Ryan

Ferrier. What happened that night to make you slash his throat?'

Silence.

Kidston let the silence linger a short time and then asked his next question. 'Did you go there to kill him?'

No answer.

'Did Ryan Ferrier provoke you, Michael?'

'He did, aye.' Nicolson spoke in a flat, monotone, matter-of-fact voice. A detached manner about him. 'There was an argument. Ferrier got a bit amorous and made a move on me, offered fifty pounds for sex. I offered to take a blow job from him for that and that's how it started. He took the blow job initially, but then he came on too strong... wanted full sex but I warned him.'

'You never went to Ryan Ferrier's house with the intention of murdering him or attacking him?'

'No.'

'What then?'

'I was looking for some money... some work,' Nicolson said. 'I'd done a good job on Adrian's garden; he'd told Ryan and he mentioned that he'd like some work done. I went to look at a job.'

'Was there a chance of some extra money for sex?'

'I was up for that but not intercourse.'

'You killed him, what, because you lost your temper?'

'I lost it totally, but I warned him not to push it.'

'How did it escalate into violence?'

'He was sucking my cock, through my zip like, but he got too excited and started to make moves on me, demanding sex, offering more money. He tried to pull my trousers down and I warned him not to do it. Then Ryan loosened his own belt and started to pull his trousers down, started to wank himself off. I warned him again, but he wasn't taking any notice.'

Kidston observed a vacant nothingness in those dark dead eyes. It was rather disconcerting, but his suspect was talking freely about his crimes. Maybe he was unburdening himself or perhaps it was the irrefutability of the evidence. The police productions laid out on the table in front of him made a very convincing case. Kidston pressed on with his questioning, keen to direct the interview, gather the evidence he needed. 'You hacked off the man's penis and stuffed it in his mouth. Why?'

'He pushed it when I warned him not to... twice I warned him.' Nicolson was more animated now. 'It was mental, I was raging. It was his fault... I warned him to back off. The knife was on his table, and I grabbed it.'

'All that blood, Michael. Did you slash his throat first?'

'Aye, that came first. I ripped his throat. It was mental. The blood spewed out his neck.'

'Then you stabbed his chest. More blood. You were still angry, furious?'

'I'd never known fury like it, I was stabbing at Ferrier's chest, blood gushing out everywhere.'

'But you kept going, Michael, even with all the blood, you hacked off Ryan Ferrier's penis. All that bloodlust. What was going on with that?'

'I was still raging... I got carried away. I've never seen blood like that before, never stabbed or slashed anyone before.' Nicolson's vacant expression intensified, seemingly lost in the memory of his bloodlust. He shook his head. 'So much fuckin' blood, man.'

Kidston saw his opportunity. 'Why didn't you just strangle him like you did with Adrian Harrison?'

Nicolson smiled at his questioner. 'Strangling's a lot easier... a lot less messy. All that blood was fascinating but way too much mess. You weren't convinced by my suicide set-up?'

'It took us a while to work it out, Michael, but I know you

strangled Adrian Harrison with the dressing-gown cord. Same as you tried to strangle Dusty.'

'I think I prefer strangling. How did you work that out?'

'We found your DNA on the dressing gown and Adrian's DNA on the cord.'

'How do you know it's my DNA? How does that work?'

'Turns out, your DNA is on file with Blackpool police from an investigation when your cousin Richard was assaulted in a pub. His DNA led us to you.'

'What, because we're cousins?'

'More or less.' Despite the strong temptation to inform his suspect that he and Richard were twin brothers, Kidston feared it might overwhelm him and become the focus of the interview. For the moment, he could keep it vague. 'Michael, suffice to say, you and Richard share the same familial DNA.'

'Like genetics?'

'Exactly.' The young man would learn more about genetics in the coming days, but Kidston had more questions. 'You say you prefer strangling; we know about Adrian Harrison and Dusty, how many other people have you strangled?'

'Those two and way back, long ago, there was Darren Spence from my class at high school. I suppose he was my first ever victim.'

'Tell us about that.'

'Darren and I were in the same second-year class. He was fourteen and had just discovered wanking. I was showing him how to do it properly.'

'Were you touching each other?' Kidston asked.

'Yes. We were sucking each other off. Darren got very excited.'

'What made you so good at it, Michael?'

'I was taught by my parish priest when I was an altar boy.'

'Tell us about that, Michael. What age were you when this started?'

'I was twelve when it started, and it went on for over a year. When we did the Mass Father Giacomo would ask one of the boys to stay behind to help clean up, put away vestments and all that. If you did a good job, he'd give you fifty pence or a pound. I think the money came from the plate. He taught me how to masturbate. I did it to him and he did it to me and would give me two pounds if I promised not to tell. After a while Father Giacomo asked me to choke him with his cincture – a bit like the dressing-gown cord that I strangled Adrian Harrison with. Back then I knew all the names for the vestments; the cassock, the stole, the chasuble, the amice, and the cincture.'

Kidston remembered a long-forgotten school lesson on priests' vestments and could have sworn that the cincture was supposed to signify chastity and purity. He felt the tectonic plates of his lapsed Catholicism shift, further exposing the giant chasm where his childhood beliefs once dwelled. The chilling irony of what he was hearing made him sick to his stomach. His mind began to wander to a beach at St Monans; walking hand in hand with Grace in the breezy Fife sunshine, Florrie sitting atop his shoulders and Tallulah frolicking in the North Sea surf. But Michael Nicolson's words jarred him back to the here and now. The young man was confessing to another murder and Kidston needed to let him talk.

'What did he do when you were choking him, Michael?'

'He wanked himself off and would shout, tighter, tighter until he came, or the rope was too tight.'

'Did you ever tell anyone?' Kidston asked.

'Never.'

'And what happened to Father Giacomo?'

'He moved away the next year to a different parish.'

'Did any other boys tell you it happened to them?'

'No, but I'm sure it must have.'

'And is this what happened between you and Darren Spence?'

'Yeah. We were dodging school at his house one afternoon. Everyone was at work, and we were hanging around his bedroom. I told Darren about the rope trick, and he wanted to try it, so we used his school tie. He was enjoying it, but the tie was too tight, and he passed out. I realised he was dead.'

'What did you do?' Kidston asked.

'I made it look like he hung himself from his wardrobe door with his tie.'

'So it would be treated as suicide?'

'Yeah, but it kind of was... he asked me to tighten the tie.'

'Did it excite you to watch Darren choke?'

Nicolson paused before answering, his dark eyes giving nothing away. 'It must have because I sometimes dreamed about it later... even years later.'

And there it was, Kidston thought. He'd wondered about the type of mind that – in the throes of murder, and in its frantic aftermath – could coolly stage a crime scene. It was clear now; Nicolson had staged a murder scene before. There could be no rearranging the Ryan Ferrier scene – it was too much of a bloody mess.

'Okay, Michael, we'll be making further enquiries and fresh investigations based on what you've admitted in relation to Darren Spence. Given that you were fourteen when the incident happened it will be up to the procurator fiscal as to whether an additional charge is added to the three cases you're already facing.' Kidston looked at Adam Sharkey, who nodded his agreement. 'In a similar vein, Michael, Strathclyde Police is re-examining any murders on our books with a similar profile to these cases, and I reserve the right to interview you again in the future. It might help your case if you tell us about any other murders or attacks that you're responsible for.'

Michael Nicolson looked blank and shook his head. Kidston couldn't find a flicker of emotion; those dead eyes had gone to some very dark place. 'That's everything, there'll be no need to bother me again.'

Kidston gave Stark the nod and the young DS read the common law caution and recited the full set of charges against Michael Nicolson. When invited to reply he stared intently at Kidston and said, 'No doubt I'll be found guilty, but I was a victim too.'

———

With Nicolson returned to his police cell, Finola Donnelly joined Adam Sharkey and the two detectives in the interview room.

'Congratulations, Finola,' Kidston said, 'your profile of Nicky was pretty spot on.'

'A very strange young man,' Sharkey said. 'Definitely a cold fish.'

'Dead behind the eyes,' Kidston said. 'Hardly a flicker of emotion. The kid's damaged goods. What do you think, Finola? Is Nicolson a psychopath?'

'Hmm,' Finola mused. 'More sociopath than psychopath, based on that session. Sociopaths tend to be more self-centred, hot-headed and less likely to worry about other people. Remember most of my views are based on studies with very limited actual experience in the field but the way he blamed everyone else for his actions and offered up excuses – those are the traits of a sociopath. Michael Nicolson's not interested in anyone but himself.'

'And the sex?' Kidston asked.

'Nicolson's youth was marked by shocking levels of child abuse,' Donnelly replied. 'Sex has been a transactional event in his life since childhood. I could argue that the frenzied attack on Ryan Ferrier was a manifestation of the rage he carries against his parish priest.'

'He's not insane then?' Kidston was thinking of pleas in bar of trial.

'Not in my opinion,' Finola said. 'Maybe one for Adam.'

'The court will ask for a psychiatric assessment,' Sharkey said. 'They always do in these cases, but I think he's well aware of his actions.'

'Thank you for my first sociopath, up close and personal,' Finola said. 'It was important given that I'd seen his handiwork on Ryan Ferrier. And your first ever serial killer.'

'I suppose so,' Kidston said inattentively as he felt his pager go off. 'I didn't really think of him as a serial killer. I saw a complex, very troubled young man, a victim of his own life circumstances.'

Kidston felt his pager pulsing again and noticed, in all the excitement of the arrest and interview of Michael Nicolson, he'd missed several notifications. 'Excuse me please, this might be something important.' Kidston's face formed into a worried frown. While Stark escorted the two visitors out of the station, Kidston returned to his office to call the number.

He was still talking on the phone when Stark returned. Kidston held the phone away from his ear, an incredulous look on his face as if he couldn't quite believe the information he'd been given.

'What is it?' Stark asked, concerned by his boss's expression.

'Grace is missing.'

CHAPTER FORTY

'I 'll be over as soon as I can, Veronica,' Kidston said. It was a fraught call.

'Please come quickly,' Veronica said. 'I'm getting very worried.'

His sister-in-law had raised the alarm when Grace hadn't returned after walking Tallulah earlier in the morning. Most worryingly, she was now missing for over six hours. A further pressing concern was the report from Julie Gray, the local vet, who'd contacted Veronica to report that Tallulah had been brought in, having been badly injured in a traffic accident in Kilmarnock Road.

With Michael Nicolson processed, cautioned, and charged and placed in a police cell, Kidston and Stark raced to Giffnock. Michael Nicolson's paperwork would have to wait. Kidston was fearful that Grace may have popped home and had an accident. How else could he explain Tallulah running free on the main roads?

The first telltale clue was the half-empty bag of dried dog food lying on the pavement beside his garden gate. Dozens of pieces of food were strewn all over. Kidston checked the house's interior, no sign of Grace. There was a flashing answerphone message; it was from Julie at the vet's about Tallulah's road accident. Stark checked the gardens. No trace. Nothing suspicious. They did a hasty door-to-door with the neighbours; most were at work. Nobody had witnessed anything untoward.

They headed the short drive to Veronica's house.

'Thoughts?' asked Stark, concerned by his boss's worried expression. 'Tied to the attack on your car the other night?'

Kidston nodded. 'It might be. My initial reaction to Jimmy was that Ronnie Miller had smashed up my Beamer after that debacle at the briefing but then I remembered if Ronnie wanted a fight he'd just come and kick your door in. That's just not his style.'

'Who then?' Stark asked.

'I'm working my way through a list of my enemies but I'm struggling to think of anyone crazy enough to abduct my wife in broad daylight.' Kidston looked intently at his young neighbour. 'Thoughts?'

'Phil Canavan.'

'No hesitation. Why?' Kidston was intrigued by his sergeant's certainty.

'Did you see the way he looked at you on Saturday night when you threatened him with Barlinnie? I've never seen a look of hatred to match that. We're pretty sure that the twenty thousand pounds we lifted in that drugs seizure was Canavan's cash. Word is that was his last bit of product and we've messed up his pension plan. You know he blames you for his hand.'

'But that's madness.' Kidston looked bemused. 'Everyone knows what happened.'

Stark absentmindedly traced a finger over the small scar on his forehead; a souvenir of his joust with the Gorbals Samurai. 'Think about it, boss. His criminal compensation was turned down flat. Word is he was expecting a massive payment. Polis blocked that when we gave the official version of what went down.'

'Truthful version.'

'Then his lawyer sues the force for failing in our duty of care. He's looking for a big payout. They get a letter back from the chief constable quoting the sheriff's comments about your heroic efforts. That's got to have stuck in Canavan's craw. Remember, losing his hand forced him out of the heroin business. He's managing his sister's nightclub; that's quite a climb-down.'

'Okay, Gregor. Very persuasive. Phil Canavan moves to the top of my list of suspects. You think there's a ransom demand coming?'

'I imagine that's how it will play out,' Stark said, 'but Canavan might want to punish you, let things stew for a day or two.'

'I swear to God if he harms Grace I will swing for the bastard.'

'And Johnny Boy's likely to be involved. Phil's down to one hand.'

'He'll still do some damage with that steel claw,' Kidston said.

———

'It looks like Grace popped home for more dog food,' Kidston said. 'That's when they snatched her.' Kidston had paid a brief visit to the small lounge that Veronica used as a playroom and bounced Florrie on his knee for a few minutes. His toddler daughter was oblivious to his concerns and happy to play with her cousins and the family's two cats on the giant activity mat laid out on the floor. Florrie was safe. Her mother was his number one priority.

A worried-looking Veronica outlined the events of her morning to the two detectives. She'd become increasingly concerned when Grace had not returned from walking Tallulah. The two houses were only a fifteen-minute walk between them, and she knew Grace wouldn't go to the supermarket with Tallulah in tow. She thought perhaps they'd gone to Rouken Glen Park as it was such a nice day but that was a long shot.

When Julie Gray telephoned to say that Tallulah had been brought to her surgery, badly banged up after a road accident, Veronica knew something serious had happened, especially since it wasn't Grace who brought the dog in. Julie knew Tallulah and knew that Grace and Veronica were sisters, having looked after Veronica's two cats, Ziggy and Marley. Veronica related the story provided by Julie:

'About 10.30am, a woman motorist, who happened to be a dog owner, was driving south on Kilmarnock Road, and had to brake suddenly when a white Transit van travelling in the opposite direction knocked Tallulah down. The strange part was that the woman had said the husky appeared to be chasing the van and that the vehicle had veered deliberately towards the dog.'

'Deliberately?' Kidston's blood ran cold.

'Yes,' Veronica continued. 'She didn't get the number as it took all her concentration to come to a stop to avoid running over the stricken husky. The woman had flicked on her hazard warning lights and scooped Tallulah into a dog blanket and headed straight to the vet's. Julie says it's touch and go for Tallulah.'

'There was a similar message on our answerphone when I checked the house on the way here,' Kidston said. 'But no mention of a white Transit, that's good, that might be our first clue.'

Stark nodded his agreement.

'I'll get the details of the good Samaritan motorist from Julie at the vet's,' Kidston said, biting his lip. 'Sounds like she's gone the extra mile.'

'I need a quick word before you head off, Luc.' Veronica beckoned him into the hallway and closed the lounge door behind them.

'What is it?' Kidston asked, concerned by his sister-in-law's expression.

'I shouldn't be the one telling you this, but Grace got confirmation from your GP this morning... she's expecting. She was so looking forward to telling you tonight. She's absolutely delighted at the news.'

'I had no idea... how far gone is she?' A jumble of emotions competed for Kidston's attention; joy, anxiety and fear.

'Around three months.'

'You did the right thing telling me. I'm sorry you were put in that position but given what we're facing you were right to let me know.'

'I know you can't tell me everything, but whatever's happened... whatever danger your family is facing... that's the reason Grace and Florrie have been staying with me?'

'It was just a hunch... a niggle that wouldn't go away but I still couldn't protect her.'

'You've always protected her, Luc.' Veronica was fighting back a sob. 'Since you were kids. Now go and find Gracie.' She gave him a massive hug and he held her tightly. Veronica had succinctly defined his mission.

After a final hug for Florrie, Kidston headed to see Julie Gray en route back to the police office. When he saw the vet's grim expression, Kidston feared the worst.

'Fractured radius, which I've set and given her anti-inflammatories. She's heavily sedated I'm afraid,' Julie said as Kidston made his way into the treatment room at the rear of the surgery. 'Tallulah's one badly banged-up girl. We'll know more tomorrow.'

Kidston grimaced when he saw the full-length plaster cast on Tallulah's right foreleg. The bright yellow bandaging didn't ease his anxiety. He leaned over the sleeping husky and ruffled her neck. 'Come on, girl, you can pull through. I'm going to need my running partner on four legs again soon.'

'I think the lady who stopped her car and brought her straight here prevented a much worse outcome,' Julie said.

'If you can pass on her details, please, I'll make sure I thank her properly.'

As he left the surgery, Kidston wiped a discreet tear from his eye.

CHAPTER FORTY-ONE

The creaking hatch and the slim shaft of welcome daylight that flooded her bunker announced the return of her captors. Right up to the moment that she'd heard Canavan and Johnny Boy's hushed voices, she'd entertained a sliver of hope that Luc was coming to rescue her. As the hatch closed, the darkness was illuminated by two torches as both men descended the wooden stairs, Johnny Boy shining a cone of light directly in her face. The smell of fish and chips permeated the damp air of the cellar and won the battle against her fear and nausea. Grace realised she was hungry.

Johnny Boy lit the lamp and loosened Grace's bindings. She shook her arms in front of herself and wrung her hands to restore circulation. He removed the gag from her mouth, tearing off the gaffer tape in surprisingly gentle fashion, and shone the torch in her eyes. 'How you doing, missus?'

'I'm a bit stiff, sitting for hours in one position. Is it okay if I stand up and have a quick stretch?' She'd decided to play nice with her captors. Her jaw still smarted from the earlier exchanges.

'Aye, go on then,' Johnny Boy said. 'I hope you like fish and chips.'

'Yes, thanks, I'm starving.' Grace stood up and stretched out her full height, pulling on her shoulders and elbows to get some blood flowing. With her hands free, she was able to sneak a first look at her wristwatch and was surprised to see that it was 5pm. She marched on the spot and felt her leg muscles awaken to the movement. Even wearing flat training shoes, she towered above Johnny Boy. She momentarily imagined smashing the chair over his head and taking her chances with the one-handed Canavan. It was a folly. There might be opportunities to escape but this wasn't one. They'd probably be armed, and she had an unborn child to think about as well as Florrie and Luc.

As she sat down, Johnny Boy dropped the newspaper-wrapped parcel of battered cod and chips onto her lap. He handed her a plastic bottle of water, which she placed on the floor after a refreshing first slug.

She ate quickly with her hands. The way she always enjoyed a fish supper. Her fingers scraping at greasy paper, devouring the thick battered cod and well-fried chips. 'Do you want a bit?'

'Naw thanks,' Johnny Boy replied. 'I just done a sausage supper and a tin of Irn-Bru.'

'What about your friend?' She was concerned that Canavan was sitting back in the semi-darkness not saying much.

'Same for him, the boss had a fish supper.'

As Grace licked the salty and vinegary remnants of the unexpected feast from her fingers, she thought about what she was witnessing. They still weren't using first names; it was always 'boss' and 'wee man'. They were banking on her not knowing them; all she'd seen was the little and large silhouettes cast between the half-light of the lamp and torches. She'd not seen their faces or been able to make out their features, although

221

Canavan's steel hand was a bit of a giveaway. *Were they stupid as well as dangerous?* 'Thanks for this, I was famished.'

'Nae bother, we need to look after you,' Johnny Boy said.

An interesting comment, Grace thought. Did that mean that she would ultimately be released unharmed? She gulped down more water and decided to probe a bit further. 'Will I be getting let go?'

'Aye, at some stage,' Johnny Boy said. 'That's the plan.'

'What about going to the toilet?'

Johnny Boy flashed his torch into the corner of the room. 'That bucket's your toilet. Mind and put the lid back on or you'll stink the place out. And only when we're here, mind, because you'll be tied up.'

'How long are you going to hold me?' Grace chanced her luck. 'I've been here all day.'

'That depends–' Johnny Boy started to say but was interrupted by a voice in the darkness.

'How long will it take for your man to get his hands on twenty grand?' Canavan spoke calmly, in a matter-of-fact manner.

'Twenty thousand pounds! Are you crazy? We don't have money like that lying around.'

'But he could get it,' Canavan said. 'He could sell that nice red Beamer of his. Or he could just get the money out of the office safe.'

Grace bit her tongue just in time. Was this confirmation on who'd smashed up Luc's car? He'd been right to trust his instincts; something bad was about to go down and now she was right in the middle of it.

'Look, guys, I'm three months pregnant.' It was a spur-of-the-moment announcement – her own survival instincts kicking in. She'd been thinking about one of Luc's old negotiator stories; the one where one of the three female hostages lied to her two male captors that she was pregnant and received better treatment than the other two women. *Surely, they wouldn't hurt a pregnant woman?* 'I'm not sure if you know how that works but I need to go for medical checks and I can't be sitting in this chair for hours at a time. How long are you intending to keep me here?'

'As long as it takes to get my money,' Canavan said from the semi-darkness. 'And don't you worry your pretty little head, you'll be well looked after... if you behave yourself.' Canavan flicked his torch on and flung the beam over his right shoulder, illuminating the far corner of the room clearly enough to reveal Grace's longer-term accommodation. An old iron camp bed with an ugly blue-and-white-striped mattress half covered by a dark quilt which looked like a sleeping bag.

'Your money?' Grace directed her question at the man in the shadows.

'Your husband cost me a lot of money, Mrs Kidston,' Canavan began. 'He forced me into early retirement, and I'm owed payback for my losses.'

'My husband might not agree with your logic. What if Luc can't pay or won't pay?'

'He's a family man, right?' Canavan said. 'He'll pay.'

'Have you sent a message asking for the money yet?'

'You're asking too many questions, Mrs Kidston,' Canavan said. 'Time for you to be gagged again.'

'Wait... wait. Can I go to the toilet first?'

'Help yourself.' Johnny Boy flashed his torch on the blue bucket in the corner and handed her the torch. Grace was grateful for the flashlight as she cautiously navigated her way through the darkness. As she squatted down over the makeshift toilet, she had to endure the humiliation of two grown men laughing at the sound of her pissing into a bucket.

As Grace returned to her chair quietly bemoaning the basic

lack of hygiene, her mind wondered again to how this might play out. She tried hard to block out the various Hollywood scenarios that raced through her mind; particularly the ones where the victim is murdered. Surely, Luc would get the cash or at least start negotiations on the pretext that the cash was coming. She knew that her value to her kidnappers was as ransom; that value would only be good if they believed the money was forthcoming. Would she compromise her safe release if they thought she knew their identities? No money would be handed over unless she was being released at the same time – right? They must know that money or no money the police would be hunting them. This was personal for Luc. He wouldn't let this rest – surely, they must realise he'll be coming after them.

Grace was jarred from her thoughts by Canavan. 'We might not be back tonight, Mrs Kidston, so if you want to be more comfortable, you should probably lie down on the bed. That's where you'll be sleeping tonight.' Canavan nodded at Johnny Boy who shone his torch towards the bed she'd glimpsed earlier.

'This way, madam, our finest suite.' Johnny Boy chuckled at his own joke. He beckoned Grace to follow the cone of torchlight, which gave her a better view of the bed. One bracelet from a pair of police handcuffs dangled from the metal headboard rail.

Grace leaned over the bed and tested the mattress; it was damp and smelly but seemed reasonably firm. The sleeping bag would work as a top sheet and a cover. 'Thanks, I'll definitely be more comfortable here. Can you leave me a torch, please? I don't really like the dark.'

Johnny Boy looked at Canavan, who shook his head and gave him the answer. 'I'll leave the lamp on,' Johnny Boy said, 'but it'll probably run low on paraffin.'

'What about the toilet?' Grace asked.

'If you want it, carry it over.' Johnny Boy pointed his torch to the other corner of the room.

Grace shuttled back through the gloom and emptied the bucket into the compacted soil floor before carrying it to her bedside. *All the home comforts*, she thought. *Where the hell am I and how will Luc ever find me?*

CHAPTER FORTY-TWO

Back at the station, Kidston ran through his priorities with a hastily convened enquiry team. Anticipating a ransom demand, DCs Zorba Quinn and Mork Williams were despatched to Kidston's home to monitor his landline and prevent any attacks on his property. He wouldn't be going home anytime soon. DC Paul Kennedy would monitor Kidston's office extension. Police office receptions across the division were instructed that any visitor attending with mail addressed to Kidston was to be detained for interview.

The remaining group of Gabriel, Stark, and Metcalfe discussed next steps. They'd checked the home addresses of both Canavan and Johnny Boy without success. Stark placed a 'lookout request' on PNC for Canavan's Mercedes. It would be broadcast regularly over the police radio network with a direction to 'stop and detain' driver and occupants. The white Ford Transit clue was a limited lead. Without a registration number, there was just too many of them in the greater Glasgow area to provide a meaningful clue.

'If we find Canavan, we find Grace,' Kidston said. 'Their next move might be the ransom demand and instructions for a money drop.' As a trained negotiator, Kidston was familiar with the operational plan for such cases. But, as yet, there was no confirmation that anyone was holding Grace. Until he had that *proof of life*, he couldn't be sure that Grace wasn't already dead. He couldn't shake the dread feeling that Grace may not survive a confrontation with one of his sworn enemies. The purest form of vengeance for Canavan may just be to murder Grace, dispose of her body and delight in the suffering and loss he would cause. Gregor Stark's theory on the money aspect had offered some reassurance. Canavan had lost a formidable amount of money in the last two years added to the recent seizure of his twenty thousand pounds. Grace had a value. If Canavan was behind this, he was making the biggest mistake of his criminal career. If he'd hurt Grace or caused any harm to their unborn child, Kidston would take the law into his own hands.

Kidston had put the word out. All the touts in his network of criminal informants had been alerted to the case of a missing woman and a possible kidnap and extortion scheme. He'd not revealed the identity of the woman in question; there was no need at this stage. He would see what came back. His team had followed suit. Major cash inducements and big favours were on offer to anyone with information that could assist the police investigation.

'Thoughts on how our money drop goes down?' Kidston posed the question to the group.

'We've covered your main phones,' Gabriel said. 'Are they daft enough to post a letter?'

'They could hand a letter into the station,' Metcalfe said. 'Maybe use a proxy; a pensioner or a child.'

'I may have found something, boss.' Gregor Stark looked up from the computer terminal he'd been interrogating. 'I've been searching all the incidents on the *command-and-control* system. Just on a hunch. Someone posted a hit-and-run accident in

Newlands at 10.10 hours this morning. A white Transit hit a large Alsatian or husky-type dog in Kilmarnock Road and made off. The reporter gave a registered number. Time fits and location's right for what we've got.'

'Who's the registered keeper?' Kidston asked.

'Already on it, boss,' Stark said. 'An Alexander Young with an address in Seath Street, Govanhill. A bit of a strange one, really, because you very rarely see incidents like this posted on *command-and-control*, especially after the event.'

'What do you mean?' Kidston asked.

'Police weren't called to the scene at the time,' Stark said. 'The reporter attended en route to his work because he caught the number plate and thought police might be looking for the van. Somebody public spirited enough to make the report, probably a dog lover. Most bar officers wouldn't bother to log it.'

'What station took the report?'

'Here. The guy works at Matthew Algie, the coffee supplier at Lawmoor Street industrial estate but it was Chrissie McCartney who posted the incident onto the computer.'

Kidston was already ringing the community policing extension to be told they were out on patrol. Stark put a radio call out with an urgent request for them to attend the CID office.

'What can we help you with?' Costello asked the assembled CID team when he and McCartney attended a few minutes later. He knew the request was for his neighbour, but his default tendency was to act as a buffer for Chrissie.

'Chrissie, you logged a hit-and-run from Kilmarnock Road this morning,' Kidston said. 'A white Ford Transit versus a dog?'

'Yes.' McCartney shot a quizzical glance at her big neighbour. 'An Alsatian or a husky in Newlands. I was filling in for the bar officer at the front desk. Is everything okay?'

'Absolutely it is. That was my dog. Her name's Tallulah.

She's a Siberian husky. She's at the vet's now in a bad way. A broken leg may be the least of her worries.'

'Oh no, I'm so sorry,' McCartney said. 'I hope she pulls through. I put the registration plate on the incident in case it was reported somewhere else.'

'It's more than that, Chrissie, a lot more,' Kidston said grimly. 'Whoever ran over Tallulah probably abducted my wife. I'm anticipating a ransom demand, imminently.'

'Oh my God! I hope Mrs Kidston's okay.'

'I'm hoping the very same thing, Chrissie. My wife's name is Grace, and you may have provided the first clue, at the moment our one and only clue, in me being able to get her back.'

'I'm so glad I posted that.' McCartney looked at Costello. 'Peter always taught me to put information into the system, every chance I got.'

'Let me guess.' Kidston smiled. 'If only Strathclyde Police knew what Strathclyde Police knew, they would be formidable. Something along those lines?'

'Word for word. More or less.' McCartney looked at her big neighbour who was nodding his head sagely.

'Same as he taught me back in the day. We were both mentored by one of the best, Chrissie.'

'I told you I taught Mr Kidston everything he knows.' Costello was grinning, the briefest distraction from the grave matter in hand. 'Can we help you look for the Transit?'

'That would be great.' Peter Costello had been by his side when Kidston was a young probationary constable, fresh out of police college. The big man had guided him through many sticky moments in his younger career. He'd been at his side again at the conclusion of the Gorbals Samurai investigation and had probably saved his life. After twenty-five years in the job, Costello had maintained his scrupulous standards for policing. Especially regarding intelligence sharing. For Kidston, policing wasn't as complicated as some tried to make it out. It was always frustrating that cops and detectives were so unwilling to pool the criminal intelligence they possessed. *Knowledge is power*, went the old adage; *and if I share my knowledge with you, I weaken my position and strengthen yours.* Kidston had no time for that kind of short-sighted thinking. If only everyone adhered to Costello's standards, the force would be *truly* formidable. Chrissie McCartney was learning good habits in her policing career – she would be a strong candidate for the CID.

Thanks to the diligence of PC McCartney and her attention to detail, a team of four detectives and two community cops set off for Seath Street, Govanhill to speak to a man about a white Transit van.

CHAPTER FORTY-THREE

Grace had made herself relatively comfortable on the camp bed. Her left hand was cuffed to the metal headboard frame so she could slide off that side of the bed and make use of her portable toilet. She'd slipped herself half inside the sleeping bag; it covered her bare legs, but she wished she'd worn more substantial clothes when she'd left home. The bunker was feeling noticeably cooler.

Grace realised that, while she was alone in the bunker, she was entirely inside her own head – she could decide how frightening or how hopeful that space would be. She went for hopeful. She'd continued her routine of positive thinking and happy hopeful thoughts and repeated her new mantra. *Luc will find me. Luc will find me.* Her thoughts swam back to the memorable honeymoon they'd enjoyed in Nashville, Tennessee. It had been a lifetime ambition to visit Music City and it got even better when Luc had persuaded the staff at Tootsie's Orchid Lounge to allow her to play a short set with a borrowed acoustic guitar. The small, narrow honky-tonk bar located just behind the Ryman Auditorium was a Nashville institution.

With a three-piece 'backing band' playing on a tiny, cramped stage in one of the inside window spaces, Grace stood atop the bar counter and played three songs, finishing with the Jim Reeves classic, 'He'll Have to Go', which, as always, she dedicated to Luc. She'd been blown away by the reception she received and was embarrassed when the bucket was passed around and part filled with generous tips. One of the greatest moments of her life. She vowed right then that they'd return one day with their children.

She was roused from her reverie when she heard footsteps on top of the trapdoor. *One set rather than two?* The hatch creaked and a furtive shaft of daylight crept its way into the bunker. Could it be Luc? Had he paid the money and been told where to find her? Had he come to rescue her? Grace's heart slumped when the lamplight revealed her visitor was Johnny Boy. As he arced his torchlight towards her, she saw that he was carrying a litre container of paraffin and a bottle of water.

'Are you sleeping? I'm sorry if I woke you up,' Johnny Boy said softly.

'No, I don't think I'm likely to sleep much... too anxious.'

'I'm sure it'll all go okay... once the boss man gets his cash. I see your wee lamp's doing okay. I brought some more paraffin in case we need it.' He sat on the edge of the bed.

'Are we going to need it?' Grace asked, a note of alarm in her voice. She glanced at her watch and saw that the time was 6.15pm. 'How much longer do you intend to hold me here?' She shifted slightly across the bed to allow him more space.

'Boss man doesn't want you to be here any longer than necessary. He wants his money then you'll be released.'

'Does he not think the police will be looking for you both for this?' Grace was taking a chance, but she was sensing the slimmest of opportunities. 'You know my husband's very good at his job.'

'I know but the boss man has lost the plot. He hates Mr Kidston with a vengeance. He's been doing a lot of coke and I think he's losing touch with reality. All he can see is his money but I'm not sure his plan will work.'

'Why not?'

'I think the polis will come hunting us for this and I don't want to go back to Barlinnie.'

'You don't need to... think about it... You can let me go... I'll let the police know that you rescued me.' Grace hesitated. How far could she push this line? 'Remember, I'm pregnant. You'll be in credit with my husband. He'll make sure you don't go back to jail.' She could make out Johnny Boy's features in the half light. She'd taught English to many younger versions of boys just like him – it was as if the wheels were spinning in his head. He looked to be giving her proposition some serious consideration.

'What would you be willing to do for me?' Johnny Boy ran a hand along the neckline of her dress and traced his fingers down towards her cleavage.

Grace stiffened in terror and then pulled the sleeping bag tightly around her hips, unsure of what level of protection it would offer. 'I'm a pregnant woman. Doctor says no hanky-panky until after the baby comes. Too dangerous.' It was an outright lie but she was banking that his knowledge of gynaecology wouldn't be enough to call her on it.

'I understand that, no problem,' Johnny Boy said in a surprisingly tender voice. 'How about just a wee snog... a wee play wi' your lovely tits and a hand job? Then I'll let you go.'

'Please stop.' Grace grabbed his wrist with her free hand. 'I won't enjoy that... please stop... please don't.' She felt the nausea rise in her chest and resisted the urge to vomit. 'I'm pregnant, I'm handcuffed, and I love my husband and this... this is no way to seduce a woman.' She'd been fortunate not to experience morning sickness when expecting Florence; the same, so far, with this pregnancy but her stomach was roiling now. There was a strong chance she was going to bring up her fish supper. She curled her knees into her midriff to avoid retching, pulling the sleeping bag up above her chest for some protection. 'Please, just let me go. I promise the police will know that you rescued me... please.'

'I'm sorry, doll. I just fancied a wee romantic moment with you. I think you're gorgeous. You cannae blame a man for trying. How about a hand job while I get to look at your tits?'

'No staring at my tits. Absolutely no kissing, no fondling or feeling me up. No touching at all except for me wanking you off?' Grace could hardly believe the words she was speaking but if this pervy negotiation was what was required for her to avoid her being a victim of something worse, she'd be able to live with it. 'I give you a hand job, you let me go right away, and you get to avoid Barlinnie. But you must take this handcuff off, so I can do it right.' In the dim lamplight she could see him fumbling in his jeans pocket for the key and noticed his erection bursting out of his pants. Her nausea was making her head spin now, a bitter, metallic taste rising in her throat.

Johnny Boy was undoing his belt and unzipping his jeans when the trapdoor opened suddenly, the bunker filling momentarily with light, before slamming shut and returning the room to semi-darkness and the light from the lamp and Canavan's torch. 'Hey, wee man. Did you get the extra paraffin?'

A startled Johnny Boy straightened up and sorted out his belt and flies in quick order. He placed a surreptitious forefinger over his lips. 'Shh, not a word,' he whispered as the light from Canavan's torch illuminated their corner of the room. 'I got a litre of paraffin, boss man, and some water for our guest.' He handed Grace a plastic bottle of water.

Grace sat up in bed and sipped the water, not knowing whether she'd avoided a sickening and perverted sexual encounter only to be faced by a fate worse than death.

CHAPTER FORTY-FOUR

Seath Street was in the shabbier quarter of Govanhill, bordering Aikenhead Road on the very edge of Polmadie and adjacent to the giant Alcan manufacturing plant that made tin foil containers and chewing gum wrappers. Alexander Young's close in a two-storey tenement block was grubby and graffitied with the sharp stink of stewed piss. His name was on the door of a ground-floor flat.

Costello and McCartney searched the area and surrounding streets for any trace of the van. Gabriel and Metcalfe took up a position in the back court, while Kidston and Stark rattled the letter box.

'Okay. Okay,' a voiced boomed down the hallway. 'No need to waken the fuckin' dead.' Young opened his door to be met by two grim-faced detectives. He was late forties with thinning brown hair and a pot belly protruding through a fully unbuttoned blue denim shirt and hanging over his trouser belt.

'CID,' Kidston said. 'Did we wake you up?'

'Nah, you're all right.' Young's voice had dropped a few decibels. The CID 'uniform' clearly familiar.

Kidston and Stark strode through the hall and into the living room of the four-apartment flat without waiting for an invite. 'We've got some urgent business, Mr Young. What do I call you... Alex or Sandy?'

'Aye, Sandy's fine. What can I do for you?'

'You're the owner of a "W"-plated Ford Transit van?' Kidston read the full registration number from his notebook.

'I used to be.'

'What do you mean?' Kidston reacted angrily. 'You're showing as the registered keeper at Swansea.'

'Somebody stole the van,' Young said in a voice lacking confidence.

'Really?' Kidston asked sarcastically. 'That's unfortunate.' Young's announcement was so unconvincing that Kidston wasn't buying his story for one second. 'You'll have reported the theft to the police, yes?'

'No... not yet,' said a very hesitant Young.

'When was it stolen?' Kidston asked.

Stark flipped open his folder. Kidston spoke. 'My colleague is about to note a theft report for your van. Think carefully, Sandy. If you get this information wrong or make a false statement to the police, then I guarantee you're going to do time in Barlinnie.'

'Was the van involved in something?' Young's nervous gaze shifted between the two detectives – looking for a clue.

'Stop dicking around, Sandy, before I really lose my temper.' Kidston glared at Young. 'This is an urgent police investigation. When did you last see your Transit van?'

'Er... er, I'm not sure.'

Stark made a show of flicking his jacket open and removing his handcuffs from their pouch on his belt. 'Wrong answer, Sandy. Too bad. You were well warned.' Stark began reciting the common law caution. 'You are not obliged to say anything–'

'No wait... wait. I lost the van after getting a loan for a

gambling debt.'

'Lost?' Kidston shot a quizzical look.

'I owed a bit of cash to a moneylender. He took the van as payment. It's ten years old but it covered my debt, saved me getting a beating.'

'Which moneylender?' Kidston knew the answer before he heard it.

'Phil Canavan,' Young said. 'I gave the van and the logbook to Johnny Boy McManus last Friday. I've not driven it for over a week.'

'We need to be crystal clear here,' Kidston said. 'You gave Phil Canavan your Transit van to clear off a loan. Johnny Boy drove it away last week. Were you driving it this morning?'

'I've not seen the van for a week,' Young said meekly.

Stark spoke while noting Young's statement in his pad. 'We can still do you for failing to inform Swansea of a change of registered keeper. But believe me, if you're lying to us, it will be much worse than that if we have to come back.'

The group of six met up in the close mouth. Costello and McCartney confirmed that there was no trace of the Transit anywhere in the area. Costello radioed the control room to place an urgent lookout request for broadcasting force wide.

'It's now virtually certain that Phil Canavan and Johnny Boy abducted Grace and ran down my dog,' Kidston announced as he swept a wave of raven locks from his forehead. 'This is personal for me now – as personal as it gets. I'm going to catch these two fuckers and it's not going to be pretty. Anyone who needs to opt out of the next stage of this investigation should speak up before things get too ugly.'

Five faces looked back at him. Five heads shaking in the negative. Firm in their collective resolve.

'We're all in?' Kidston offered one final chance.

'All in.' Five voices in unison.

CHAPTER FORTY-FIVE

Kidston and his team headed straight for *Canavan's Castle*; the detached villa in the city's Myrtle Park area paid for by Phil Canavan's profits from his long spell as the principal heroin dealer in Glasgow's south side. They forced Canavan's door but there was no trace of either suspect or their captive. The *Castle* was given a good turn, including the expansive basement which had been fitted out as a games room with snooker, darts, and table football. Kidston paused while looking through Canavan's collection of VHS tapes as the chilling thought of a hostage video slipped into his mind, but they were all old cowboy movies taped off the television: *The Man Who Shot Liberty Valance* and *The Magnificent Seven* were top of the stack.

Next up was Johnny Boy McManus's flat on the top floor of the Queen Elizabeth Square multi-storey tower block, which three years earlier had been the scene of a dramatic showdown in the Gorbals Samurai case. Kidston wandered out to the veranda balcony and took in one of the best views of Glasgow. That familiar giddy lurch of vertigo; so slight now, even this high off the ground. Following that incident, Kidston had sought professional help for his acrophobia. Max Van Zandt, the forensic hypnotist, who'd assisted with the Ellie Hunter case, had recommended a brilliant young Paisley-based behavioural psychologist, Lynsey Weir, who successfully treated Kidston's condition with neurolinguistic programming. NLP proved to be very sympathetic to the tools and techniques that Kidston had learned and taught as a hostage negotiator: mental rehearsal, mirroring, and anchoring. With some hypnosis sessions and his own NLP toolkit, Kidston had changed the way he thought about his phobia. The triggers still occurred from time to time, but Kidston now had a technique to control them.

The search team met with the same negative result. On another day the searchers could have made more of some of the stuff they found; a consignment of malt whisky in Canavan's basement looked dodgy as did a stash of video recorders and contraband cigarettes in Johnny Boy's flat. These items were handed over to uniformed colleagues – further enquiries could wait for another time. Grace Kidston was their priority and, worryingly, there was nothing in either suspect's home that linked to her abduction. Kidston and his team returned to the office to discuss next steps.

———

Back in the main CID office, Kidston put a call in to DC Zorba Quinn, who confirmed that there had been no contact made on his boss's home phone line. DC Paul Kennedy, covering Kidston's office extension, confirmed that no ransom calls were received but handed him a pile of messages.

'The one on top might be the most important, sir.' Kennedy peeled off the top message. 'I was just going to page you as the guy phoned a second time around five minutes ago. Mr Cooper, he said it was important.'

'Thanks, Paul. Go and grab a tea break with the others.'

Kidston smiled at the name. *Henry Cooper* was a nom de plume used by his former father-in-law, Eddie 'Banjo' Bridges. Eddie, a former boxer and carpet fitter who had, back in the day, provided muscle for Phil Canavan's late father Big Davie, never used his real name when he was touting for Luc. Eddie had been a brilliant informant for Luc during his rise through the CID. Used sparingly, never compromised, Eddie's tips tended towards assisting major investigations – big cases.

'Eddie, it's Luc. I'm just picking up my messages. What have you got for me?'

'Hi, son. It might be nothing, but it might be something. Couple of years back, a wee pal of mine, Malky Henderson, was in hock to Canavan for two thousand pounds. They snatched him off the street and held him hostage until his family raised the cash.'

'How does that help me, Eddie?'

'Malky says he was held underground for three days. Big bunker, down a flight of stairs he says, nae lights just lamps and torches, handcuffed to a camp bed. They let him go when his missus handed over the money.'

'Where was the bunker?'

'He's no sure but it was close to Canavan's house.'

'How could he know that?'

'They took him out blindfolded in the boot of Canavan's Merc. Johnny Boy driving but he heard Canavan say that he'd walk back to the house. Malky told us the car stopped at *Canavan's Castle* and waited for Phil to come back out. It was near. Very close.'

'When was this?' Kidston asked.

'Two years ago. What do you think?'

'Definitely worth checking out. Can you bring Malky in?'

'He'll no come in. He's a doo fleer and you'll no get him away from his doocot the night. He's waiting for one of his birds to come back.'

'A pigeon fancier?'

'Aye, Malky's a keen doo man. His doocot is over on a patch of waste ground in Dalmarnock. I've got my taxi. If you need to see him, I'll take you over and back. I can pick you up in ten minutes.'

'Just tell the bar officer to ring up the CID extension – taxi for Kidston.'

———

Kidston used the time he had to flick through the half-dozen messages that Kennedy had passed. Fairly routine, nothing that couldn't wait. One from Colquhoun; probably in relation to the arrest in the Ferrier and Harrison case. It would have to wait; he hadn't informed any of the bosses about Grace's abduction. Q would want to establish a full *Red Centre* for a kidnap and extortion operation and impose a detective superintendent from headquarters to run it. He knew his ACC would remove him from the case for being too closely involved. As the victim's spouse, he shouldn't be anywhere near the investigation. He knew that; he'd completed Red Centre training. Maybe if they hadn't got the Canavan lead, he would call in headquarters, but this wasn't the right time. For the moment Grace's fate was in his hands. Tomorrow. Maybe.

He had time to call Finola Donnelly. She answered after three rings. 'Apologies for having to rush away, Finola,' Kidston said. 'I had to deal with something urgent.'

'No worries, Luc. I realised something important had come up.'

'The final word on Nicolson and the DNA, for the moment. My colleagues have established that he was separated at birth from his twin brother.'

Gabriel had confirmed Martin Reynolds' extended family theory and had sat with the two distraught mothers; natural and adopted, who admitted their separation scheme. With five young daughters already, the twins' natural parents had been content to raise one of the boys and gift the other to close family. There was a loosely agreed plan in place to tell the boys when they turned twenty-one. For Michael Nicolson, that anniversary would be in prison.

The back story had captured Finola's attention. 'In criminology, twin studies are a fascinating topic – family or environment?'

'Nature or nurture?' Kidston posed Finola's question in different terms. 'I don't know, but what happened to him is as evil as any of his own deeds. But I'm phoning for your advice on the other, more urgent matter.'

Donnelly listened intently as Kidston outlined his thoughts and fears around Grace's abduction and his suspicions of who was behind it. 'I'm terrified Grace may already be dead. Gregor's just about persuaded me that this is about money but Canavan's a vengeful bastard. The best way to take revenge on someone is to hurt the thing they love most. If he really wants to get even with me, he injures or kills Grace... tell me I'm wrong.'

'It's early in the abduction, Luc,' Donnelly began. 'Go with Gregor's theory about the money. That's a strong motivation for a criminal like Canavan. From what you're telling me, Grace has been gone around ten hours. Canavan will want his money.'

'But there's been no ransom demand, Finola and that's what's eating away at me.'

'Stay strong, Luc, keep your focus on the money as Canavan's main motivation. Getting one over on a senior cop will be enough to satisfy his thirst for revenge. I'm sure there'll be a ransom demand coming.'

'One question I specifically wanted to ask you, Finola. These abduction cases. I'm sure I've read that the victim is usually held somewhere close to the perpetrator's base.'

'That's normally the case. It's about control and access. Less common for the victim to be held at their kidnapper's home but not to be ruled out completely.'

'We've been through the house, including the basement,' Kidston said.

'She'll be close, Luc. I'm confident you'll find her. Be careful and good luck. You're in my prayers.'

'Thanks, Fi.' He realised he'd used her pet name from when they went out.

Kidston slumped forward in his chair, elbows on the desk, head in hands, rubbing his temples. Adrenaline was competing with exhaustion. He and his team had just captured a potential serial killer but he'd never experienced pressure like this. He'd never expected that his personal and professional lives could fuse in such a terrifying way. He pushed his hands back through his hair and exhaled a long deep sigh. He thought about some of the NLP techniques he'd learned to combat his acrophobia. Some positive mental rehearsal might help his current situation. He would need to maintain a confident front for his crew, even though his dread was engulfing him like a waking nightmare. He closed his eyes and twirled his wedding band, the way he'd been taught. He thought about Grace, the love of his life, the mother of his child with another baby on the way. She always said that he had saved her but, in reality, she had saved him. His life lacked any real meaning until they reconnected as a couple.

Kidston pressed his wedding band between his thumb and forefinger, applying more pressure and, with a series of short twists, rehearsed a mental list of his career successes. His instincts told him that he was close to tracking his wife's kidnappers and he had to believe that Grace was alive. Canavan was doing this for money. Revenge was a secondary motivation, but Kidston would be more convinced of that when he got a ransom demand. *Why no ransom demand?* With the niggling negativity of that thought threatening his positive mental rehearsal routine, Kidston shook his head vigorously to clear his mind and focus on the lead that Eddie Bridges had just given him. He felt sure he was getting closer to finding Grace.

'Half a mile to a one-mile radius around Canavan's house.' Kidston addressed his team in front of the large street map of Southern Division on the squad-room wall. 'For kidnap and abduction cases, a likely location would be close to the culprit's home, for ease of access and greater control of events. Think possible underground locations in this immediate area.' Kidston made a sweeping circle with his forefinger. 'Gregor and I will be back in around thirty minutes once we've spoken directly to the source of the information.'

'Boss,' Gabriel began, 'I'm duty-bound to point out that we need to think about involving headquarters at some stage.'

'Thanks, Jimmy. I'm aware but not quite yet until we firm up on this latest lead. If this doesn't play out, I'll do a full briefing for Q and hand over the whole operation.'

One of the office phone extensions rang. Metcalfe was nearest and picked it up.

'Taxi for Kidston.'

Kidston and Stark made their way downstairs to their waiting transport. Kidston thought about the number of times his former father-in-law had come through for him in big cases. This was the biggest, most important case of Luc's life and he was hoping Eddie could offer a glimmer of hope to help find Grace.

CHAPTER FORTY-SIX

'Tell me a bit more about Malky,' Kidston said once he'd introduced Stark to Eddie without revealing his former father-in-law's back story. Eddie was driving a black Hackney cab. The two detectives sat in the back, looking to all the world like customers.

'A big doo man,' Eddie said. 'Those pigeons are his life. Widower a good while back and lost his job as a French polisher. Too fond of the bevvy.'

'I don't understand pigeon fanciers,' Stark announced. 'The birds are like flying rats.'

'Ooft! Don't let Malky hear you talking like that, son.' Eddie laughed. 'You'll not get anything out of him if you take that line. Those birds are his life, racing them, catching-in other doos, looking after them. Man's devastated when he loses a doo.'

'This is a way of life for these men, DS Stark,' Kidston said with a wry smile. 'There's been stabbings and slashings over fallouts between doo fleers.'

'Your boss is right,' Eddie said. 'It's a serious business if you steal another man's birds.'

'What was his run-in with Canavan?' Kidston asked.

'The wee man borrowed a few hundred quid to help out with his daughter's wedding. He defaulted and with Canavan's interest rates it was up to two thousand after two weeks. That vicious bastard Canavan burned down his doocot, killed all his birds. Malky swore that was the debt paid but Canavan scooped him off the street and held him hostage for three days. Malky's missus paid the debt, but the stress nearly killed her. She died no long after that.'

'No love lost then?' Kidston asked.

'There's a queue of people lining up to celebrate when Phil Canavan finally gets his just desserts. Malky Henderson will be right at the front of it. Phil's father was a vicious gangster, but old school, treated people with a bit of respect. Canavan Junior doesn't have an ounce of his old man's class.' Kidston would baulk at any notion of Davie Canavan being a gentleman gangster, but he wouldn't be contradicting Eddie on this occasion.

———

The taxi route had taken them through Govanhill, Polmadie and Oatlands and crossed the Clyde at Richmond Park. Eddie had taken just over ten minutes to reach their destination. Dalmarnock was a neighbourhood in decline. Once home to Sir William Arrol's vast Dalmarnock Works, his civil engineering empire had given the world the Forth Bridge, Tower Bridge, and the colossal Titan Crane. The deindustrialisation of the 1960s and 1970s had robbed the area of much of its once thriving community. Streets of fine Victorian red sandstone tenements contrasted with inferior grey stone maisonettes and mixed with modern industrial units, small factories, and shops. Eddie pulled up alongside a large area of brownfield scrubland that Kidston recognised as the site of the former Dalmarnock

Power Station that had been demolished around ten years earlier.

Eddie pointed out a small-framed man in a crumpled suit and a tartan bunnet: Malky Henderson, who was standing by his doocot looking to the skies through a pair of binoculars. Eddie waited in his taxi as the two detectives strode towards the doo man. Kidston noticed that the large area of ground was swathed in an incongruous mix of colourful wildflowers, birch scrub and other shrubs. It occurred to Kidston that any of the old Glasgow housing schemes undergoing urban demolition saw a rise in doocot construction on any patch of spare ground.

'Remember to be impressed by Malky's birds,' Kidston said. 'Whatever else we talk about, there'll be no criticism of pigeons or doo men.'

'I got the gist of that from the earlier comments.' Stark had laughter in his voice. 'What a lovely-looking bird.' The young DS grimaced. 'Just don't expect me to touch one.'

'I'm the same. Dirtiest search I ever did was a tenement loft in Govan, where the householder had converted the full attic space into pigeon pens. The smell would knock you on your back.' Kidston grimaced at the memory. 'I'm getting nauseous just thinking about it. We did find the sawn-off shotgun though.'

As they closed in on the doocot, Kidston watched Malky, who had set his binoculars aside and was engaged in some secret communication with a distant pigeon flying overhead. Malky was nodding and making a peculiar pecking motion with his head. He made a strange soft cooing sound, clearly designed to attract the bird to his loft. Kidston stopped, reluctant to disturb the doo man or interrupt what was going on.

'Naw, yer awright, chief. Yon wee blue hen isnae wan o' mine.' He spoke in a gruff voice. 'I was hoping she was gettin' lured in by ma big silver doo but he's away chasing a wee blonde.'

'A familiar story, eh?' Kidston laughed. 'Chasing a bit of blonde tail. Are you Malky Henderson?'

'Aye, that's me, chief. Fur ma sins.'

'That's some doocot you've built yourself.' Kidston appraised the twenty feet tall monolithic structure, mainly constructed of old wooden doors. The six-feet-by-six-feet tower was reinforced with corrugated sheet metal, painted a dark green and protected by barbed wire on the top. There was an entry door at the base, triple padlocked and secured by full width iron bar hasps. Kidston knew the inner sanctum of the doocot would contain two or even three storeys of bird cages and an internal ladder would give access to the skylight on top which was protected by a felt-covered single pitched roof. He was able to work out the basic mechanics of the doocot; a landing board protruded from the top in front of a trapdoor shaped like a pram hood. Malky would spring the trap with a long wire that ran the full height of the doocot. The pigeons wouldn't see it coming. 'Heavy security, Malky. You need to protect your birds?'

'Aye, a lot of thieves about wi' the doo fleein'.' Malky looked as if he needed a good feed. His scrawny frame didn't fit the suit he was wearing, and his frayed shirt collar and soup-stained tie hung wide and loose around his neck. Under the tartan bunnet and straggly grey hair, Malky had darting, beady eyes and a face like a half-chewed caramel. He sucked on the dying embers of a fag end as if his life depended on it.

'I hear Phil Canavan took out one of your doocots and some of your pigeons,' Kidston said. 'Was it over a debt?'

'Burned it doon, the bastard. Thon poor doos... terrible, terrible thing.' Malky's face crumpled and melted into a pained expression.

'Then he held you in an underground bunker?'

'He did, aye. Three days and two nights. Ma poor missus thought I was deid.'

'Definitely underground?'

'Aye.'

'Did you see much down there, Malky?'

'I had a sack on ma heid at first, but they took it aff an I saw a wee bit.' Malky took another deep draw of his fag end. 'There wis a couple of wee paraffin lamps. Him and Johnny Boy had torches. There was a bed... they handcuffed me to the bed. That's where I slept until they let me go.'

Kidston's thoughts turned to Grace and the hellish ordeal she might be facing. His wife's fear of the dark meant that she would be terrified by the underground bunker Malky was describing. 'Did they feed you okay? Were there blankets? Was there any toilet?'

'Bottles o' ginger, fish suppers and that but they wurnae about a lot. There was a sleeping bag. The toilet was a bucket.'

'How did they approach your family about the money they were looking for?'

'That shamefaced wee bastard Johnny Boy chapped ma door and told ma wife to her face. The poor wummin pawned everything she had to raise the money, borrowed from family and friends... it near broke her.'

'Did you know where you were?'

Malky took a final draw, inhaling the last dregs of nicotine from his cigarette end. Then he stubbed it out against the corrugated metal of the doocot wall, sending a shower of glowing red sparks onto the ground, before stamping the dout underfoot. 'I was underground. Down a set of wooden stairs... nae lights. It was only when they took me oot that I got a clue to where I was. I knew we were close to Canavan's bit because after a few minutes I heard them talking outside his hoose.'

'Did you see the house?' Kidston asked. 'How did you know it was close?'

'Naw, I was locked in the boot of Canavan's big motor, but I heard them talking and Canavan saying he needed to stop at his place on the way out.'

'What size was the room they kept you in?' Kidston asked. 'Can you remember?'

'Aye, it wis a big basement room.' Malky stared up at the roof of his loft. 'This doocot's about twenty feet high and the room was a fair bit bigger... say about thirty-six feet square.'

Close to half a tennis court. Kidston made a mental note. 'How did you get in and out?'

'There was just the wan way in and out. Through a big hatch and a flight o' stairs.'

'Did you see much of the room when you weren't blindfolded?'

'A wee bit. They maistly left the sack off ma heid apart frae goin' in and oot.'

'What did you see?'

'A bed in wan corner, an auld settee, couple o' chairs, a bit o' shelving and a couple o' auld wooden chests lying around. Wan o' the chests wis used as a table.'

Gregor Stark, who'd been writing busily in his folder, posed a question. 'Malky, anything down there that would give you an idea what the room was used for?'

Malky's beady eyes viewed Stark as if he was just noticing him for the first time. After a long, thoughtful pause, the doo man spoke. 'There wis wan o' they wee line marker machines they use fur fitba pitches and such. Thing looks like a wee lawnmower, but it's got a box of that white chalky lime stuff they use fur the lines. It was knackered like; aw the white stuff was well dried out.'

'So an old bit of marking equipment?' Kidston asked. 'The

Holyrood School playing fields are in that neighbourhood. Maybe an old groundsman's store?'

'Aye, mibbes, but I dinnae really know that bit o' the south side.'

'Anything else that might help us pin it down, Malky?' Kidston asked.

'Canny remember anything else that might help.' Malky bent over a wicker panier at the base of the doocot and delicately extracted a large pigeon. It was the colour of wet cement with iridescent oily green markings on its neck. The doo man cradled the bird gently in his rough hands and ruffled its nape. It cooed softly. 'I want to put this big boy up.' Malky released the bird with a flourish and the two detectives watched it flutter skyward and soar towards the far horizon.

Kidston folded up a ten-pound note and handed it to Malky.

'Nah, you're awright, chief. I'm no' a polis grass. I just want Canavan to get his comeuppance.'

'Take it, Malky. What you've just told me could be worth a lot more than that.' Kidston pushed the money into his hand. 'Buy some birdseed for your pigeons. I can see how much they mean to you.'

'Thanks, chief.' Malky accepted the note, his right hand raised to his bunnet in a little salute. 'I like to watch them coming home.'

Coming home, Kidston thought. The old man's words had struck a chord with the detective. Malky hadn't given them any concrete information, but this sliver of intelligence might well prove to be a vital piece of the jigsaw that Kidston was puzzling with. His hopes of being reunited with Grace and their unborn child lifted ever so slightly.

CHAPTER FORTY-SEVEN

'What have we come up with?' Kidston asked. The big street map on the squad-room wall was covered in yellow Post-it notes.

Gabriel took the lead. 'Assuming that it's not the basement of one of those big villas in Myrtle Park like Canavan's, we've tagged four decent possibles in that one-mile radius circled area. We've got Crosshill railway station to the west of Canavan's home. Some fourth-year Holyrood pupils were caught using a basement chair store as a den in the old part of the school in Albert Road. There's also the Holyrood School playing fields; football, tennis, and hockey. Quite a large area, although they did give up a couple of their football pitches when the school was extended in the early to mid-seventies.'

'Does anyone remember or know of a groundsman's hut for the school playing fields? I certainly don't and I went to that school. What about you, Peter?' Costello was a former Holyrood boy and knew the area better than anyone.

'What's your thinking, boss?' Costello asked.

Kidston related Malky, the doo man's description of his

underground prison and the line-marking tool he'd remembered from his captivity.

Gabriel looked at Costello. 'Peter, you've got a theory about Cathkin Park.'

Cathkin Park football stadium was the former home of Third Lanark, a team that had played in the topflight of Scottish football until their sudden and untimely demise in 1967. The club, one of the founders of the Scottish Football League, vanished from the game amid allegations of asset stripping, corruption, and a Board of Trade investigation. The ground was only saved from being sold off for redevelopment when the old Glasgow Corporation compulsorily purchased it and designated Cathkin Park as open space.

Costello stood up his full six feet five height and crossed to the wall map. 'Can I cover this bit, Inspector?' he asked Gabriel.

'Of course, Peter.' It made sense. Gabriel had no interest and limited knowledge about football teams. Kidston and Metcalfe would be similar. Stark and McCartney would have been children when Third Lanark went bust. 'What can you tell us?'

Costello's massive build made the map seem suddenly smaller as he picked the Post-it note off the section marked as a football stadium. 'What most people don't realise is that there's still a football ground on this site. While it would be a stretch to call it a stadium, there is still an arena and an oval football pitch surrounded by terracing – the original terracing survived on three sides of the pitch. Mother nature's reclaimed vast swathes of it but the old terracing steps are still in place. It's sheltered by high trees and well-hidden but it's there.'

'Is there a groundsman's hut?' Kidston asked.

'There was a grandstand on the north aspect of the pitch. Built in the early sixties, so the club only got limited time out of it. I have a vague childhood memory of a large area underneath the stand being fenced off behind railings. I think that's where the ground staff kept the mowers and tools, but I think there was an underground storeroom at that part of the grandstand.'

The big cop had their interest. 'The grandstand today, how much is left of it?' Kidston asked.

'None,' Costello replied. 'By the late sixties the grandstand had been vandalised and set on fire, bits of it destroyed. The council had it demolished in the early eighties. The whole area is like parkland now, a haven for dog walkers, still a bit of recreational football played on it.'

'The storeroom?' Kidston asked.

'That side of the stadium is all trees and shrubs,' Costello said. 'What if the demolition work never filled in the basement and it's still there under all those bushes and stuff?'

'It's definitely worth checking.' Kidston looked around the group who were nodding their collective approval. 'Let's rule out Crosshill railway station. Malky never mentioned anything about train noise. Peter's Cathkin Park theory fits closest to his description. Make that priority one. If that's a non-starter, we'll rouse the school jannie and get a check of the playing fields and their basement chair store.'

'Boss, we need to think about a POLSA with search teams and firearms officers,' Gabriel said. 'Even as backup. You know Canavan's a blade merchant and both he and Johnny Boy have used firearms before.'

Kidston sighed. But his new Gorbals DI was right. Recent developments in using POLSAs – police search advisors – trained in search techniques, had worked for him in the past. But in this case, he had already mapped out his search ground and wouldn't be needing their help. The firearms aspect was more pressing. Kidston's mind drifted momentarily back to a storm-swept evening three years earlier when he'd confronted an armed Phil Canavan on the high balcony of a Gorbals tower block. 'I know, Jimmy, but I'm thinking of the time factors involved. If we call out the three-ring circus it could take hours.' Kidston was referring to a term senior officers used for the scaled up major incident response the force used for firearms operations. 'Grace might not have hours.'

'There's six of us,' Costello said. 'That's enough to search the old Cathkin site. We'll soon know if there's a hatch or not. If we need to extend it to the school and the playing fields, we can call in the support unit search teams and the dog branch.'

'That's a good compromise, Peter,' Kidston said as he picked up a telephone. 'I'll call the duty officer and get the Armed Response Vehicles readied as backup.'

The group saw Kidston's frown as he listened to the duty officer's end of the conversation. He replaced the receiver, a grave look on his face.

'Problems?' Gabriel asked.

'Duty officer confirms that both ARVs are tied up in a firearms operation in south Ayrshire. Expects them to be operationally unavailable for the next two or three hours, given the geography and the nature of the incident... apparently a young farmer has turned a shotgun on two of his friends. The Tactical Firearms Unit has been called out and is en route to assist. Could be hours.'

'No TFU or ARVs. Other options?' Gabriel asked.

'We can arm up any divisional AFOs to assist the operation, but we'll need the usual superintendent level authorisation.' Kidston looked across the group. 'Who's got an up-to-date AFO card? I've kept my card in date.' He was referring to the force's card system for maintaining its specially trained volunteer cohort of Authorised Firearms Officers. To remain valid, cards were updated four times per year on training and requalification shoots, known as *requals*.

'I'm up to date, requalified a few weeks back,' Gabriel said.

'Firearms training days were always a good way to get out of headquarters for a while. Plus, I didn't like missing out on special branch operations when they're looking for additional close protection officers.'

'That's two out of six,' Kidston said. 'We could do with two more for an effective containment. Gregor, pop down to the control room and ask the controller how many AFOs are on duty tonight and let the duty inspector know to prepare for a firearms issue.'

'He'll ask for an authorising officer,' Stark said. 'Who shall I say?'

'Tell him Detective Superintendent Sawyers is authorising. I'll phone him right now.'

Kidston returned to his office and phoned his long-time boss, who was still at his temporary office in Edinburgh. It was the first chance he'd had to update Joe Sawyers on the arrest of Michael Nicolson. There was little time to savour Sawyers' praise and congratulatory comments before Kidston revealed the primary purpose of his call and his grave concerns for Grace's fate.

'Good grief! How are you bearing up?' Sawyers asked. 'Especially on top of all the hours you're working on the double murder investigation.'

'I'm shattered but adrenaline is edging out exhaustion right now. I need to find Grace and I need to find her alive.'

'Given what you've outlined, Luc, authorisation is a given, but if this is the location that they're holding Grace, please don't do anything hasty or reckless. Wait for the TFU to arrive, they're the experts but you and your crew can contain the scene until they arrive.'

'Thanks, Joe. I appreciate it.'

'You realise I'll need to brief Q on the issue. I know he's running the Ayrshire incident so he'll be busy, but his advice would be the same as mine. Containment, Luc; wait it out. Given that Grace is involved there will be serious questions about you running this operation but given the pace of developments and the urgency of your enquiry, I'm sure we can justify that. I'll turn out to support you and make my way from Edinburgh. If this is a no go tonight, we'll have to mount a full manhunt for Canavan and Johnny Boy tomorrow and a co-ordinated search for Grace. Seriously, Luc, this is no time to go maverick.'

'I hear you, Joe.'

Stark was waiting in the main office when Kidston came off the phone. 'How's it looking, Gregor?'

'I thought we had two but it's down to one. PC Freddie Goodman's been snaffled by the TFU for the incident in Ayrshire.'

'Who's left?'

'John Wylie's on late shift with the community policing team.'

'John's a brilliant shot,' Kidston said. 'Always scoops up all the cash in the kitty at the requals. While I'm scraping through on a bare eighty per cent, he's got every shot on target, mostly around the bullseye. It's always embarrassing doing the same requal shoots as John.'

'He's going to join us at the uniform bar,' Stark said. 'The duty officer is prepping out the weapons and armour. We should get moving.'

When the group arrived at the uniform bar, the duty inspector had cleared the area. Prisoners awaiting processing were held in detention rooms while the serious business of issuing police firearms was conducted. Kidston managed to grab a few minutes to brief Wylie. His former DS asked the same question that had been running through Kidston's head for most of the afternoon. 'Where's the ransom demand, Luc?'

'Exactly, John. That's the missing link that's causing me most concern. If it is Canavan, I'd have expected something a bit slicker... more professional.' Kidston's deep frown betrayed his emotions. 'I'm worried Canavan has killed her as revenge... pure and simple, to get back at me.'

'You can't afford to think like that, Luc.' Wylie placed a reassuring hand on his colleague's shoulder. 'Canavan's lost a lot of earnings since you forced him out of the heroin trade. It'll be about money... that's what you need to focus on.'

The duty officer was a keen young inspector, clearly familiar with force standing orders. Three AFO cards were inspected to ensure they were current. He'd logged the serial numbers of the three .38 Smith and Wesson revolvers to be issued and these were recorded against the registered number of the recipients. Six bullets per gun.

'Can I ask all three of you to read the reminder on the reverse of the card and confirm to me that you fully understand the message.'

Kidston turned his card over and read:

You May open fire against a person only if he/she is committing or is about to commit an act likely to endanger life, and there is no other way to prevent the danger, that is the law, remember your training.

The carefully worded notice rammed home the gravity of the duty he and his colleagues were about to undertake and offered a timely reminder of the legal limitations on police use of firearms. Kidston inhaled a deep breath. 'Confirmed.'

Only when all three officers had given a verbal confirmation did the inspector hand over the weapons and ammunition, which were supplied with belt-clip holsters.

'Thank you, Inspector,' Kidston said.

'Unusual circumstances, sir,' the inspector said.

'Issuing firearms?' Kidston queried. 'Fairly uncommon practice.'

'Issuing firearms to three senior officers,' the inspector said.

'That's what happens when the TFU and all the AFO cops and sergeants are in south Ayrshire,' Kidston said.

'Very true, sir. But you're all "in card" and trained for the job. I hope your investigation can be resolved without recourse to firearms. I've logged your incident with force control. When the TFU are clear in Ayrshire, I'll divert them to your location.'

'Thanks, Inspector,' Kidston said. 'Trust me, no one will be more thankful than me if we hand you back eighteen bullets this evening.'

'I've sent DS Stark and PC Costello to the equipment store for seven sets of body armour and four ballistic shields,' the inspector said. 'That's everything we've got protection wise, but I've suggested they borrow the two big Dragon lights that we keep on charge. Gregor's described the locus of your inquiry, and it sounds like you might need them. Our guys use them for nighttime missing persons searches in the Queen's Park and they're invaluable. You'll be running out of daylight soon.'

'Thanks, Inspector,' Kidston said. 'I really appreciate all your support.'

Kidston, Gabriel, and Wylie loaded their revolvers in the casualty surgeon's office away from the uniform bar area and the curious glances of colleagues. Kidston felt a peculiar anxiety as he fumbled several attempts at loading his revolver. A task he'd completed dozens of times before with minimal fuss was now presenting an unfamiliar challenge, dropping two bullets onto the floor. 'I hope you're still scooping the kitty at the requals, John, because I'm having difficulty even loading my rounds.'

'My scores have actually dropped dramatically since I swore off the hard stuff,' Wylie said with a wry smile.

'I hope you're joking, John,' Kidston said as he finally managed to insert the last bullet into its chamber.

'I'm just kidding.' Wylie laughed. 'Don't worry. I can still hit the target better than you.'

'Thank goodness,' Kidston said. 'We don't want to rely on my shooting to hit the bad guys. What about you, Jimmy? What's your requal average?'

'I tend to shoot in the low ninety per cent.' Gabriel clipped his holster onto his trouser belt and smoothed out the line of his suit jacket while checking his reflection in the office mirror.

'I'm clearly in the bronze medal position with you two.' Kidston laughed along with his two colleagues. Their humorous exchange had lessened the tension. They all understood the enormity of the task facing them.

The three armed officers stepped out of the office to be met by their colleagues. Peter Costello was wearing an oversized navy-blue ballistic vest and carrying six more heavy sets of body armour: three slung over each arm. Gregor Stark and Alison Metcalfe were each carrying two full-length ballistic shields, all equipped with armoured glass viewing ports. Chrissie McCartney carried two massive Dragon lights: one across each arm, secured by shoulder straps.

'One set each,' Costello said as the group relieved him, one by one, of the ballistic vests. The big cop had kept the largest one for himself.

'I hope you got a specially tailored one for DI Gabriel, Peter.' Kidston was keen not to let his crew see his anxiety.

'I've held on to the extra-extra-large.' Costello laughed.

Both Kidston and Gabriel discarded their jackets to don the armour, Wylie did the same with his tunic. Stark slipped his armour on over his suit. Metcalfe was able to do likewise and retain good ease of movement over her outer layer of clothes. McCartney, the shapelier of the two women, had some difficulty adjusting her chest under the armour. 'Definitely not designed for us girls,' she remarked to Metcalfe with an air of resignation.

'I'm fortunate not to have your disadvantage,' Metcalfe said with a smile as she patted her vest to emphasise her flat chest.

The seven police officers stepped out to the two unmarked CID cars, loaded their kit into the boots and checked that all their radios were set to the same talk-through channel. This ensured a dedicated frequency would be reserved for use by Kidston's firearms operation and avoided working cops across the division listening in for entertainment. Once the radio checks were completed, they set off on the short drive to Cathkin Park. Kidston considered his *Magnificent Seven*, a motley crew and a mix of CID and uniform with a wide range of experience. Five males, two females, three handguns, four ballistic shields and two portable spotlights. He had no doubts about any of his crew – every one of them had proven themselves capable. If Grace was being held where he now believed she was, he had the right people around him to rescue her.

CHAPTER FORTY-EIGHT

Grace didn't raise any great expectations when she heard the voices of her captors returning and watched the late evening light filter through the open hatch. Her watch showed 9.30pm – surely her ordeal would be over soon. The two men's conversation was heated as they descended the steps before slamming the hatch shut.

'The letter made it clear where the money was to be dropped,' Canavan said. 'You said the letter was handed in but how do we know it got to Kidston?'

'I watched the boy hand it in and I waited for him to come out,' Johnny Boy said. 'He told me he handed it to the desk sergeant. I paid him a tenner.'

'I might have known you'd make a cunt of it.' Canavan was making no effort to conceal his anger.

'I told you to phone it in!' Johnny Boy raised his voice. 'A letter was taking too many chances for it to go wrong.'

'Pipe down, ya wee wanker. Do you want somebody to hear us and phone the polis?'

Two torches turned on her. Grace was lying inside the sleeping bag with the zip fastened right up to her neck and pretending to be asleep. Johnny Boy's amorous advances had left her wary of a repeat.

'Right, missy, sit up.' Canavan shone his torch beam directly in Grace's face. 'Something's gone wrong with the money drop – you're going to be with us for a while yet.'

Grace rubbed her eyes to feign waking up. 'What happened?' She shielded her eyes from the torchlight. She sat upright and rested her back on the metal headboard and pulled the sleeping bag back up above her chest.

'It's all turned to rat shit,' Canavan said. 'The cash wasn't where your husband was supposed to leave it. Maybe he doesn't want you to be released. Cheaper than a divorce.'

'Maybe he couldn't raise the money in time – it's not been that long really.'

'We happen to know that there's twenty thousand pounds of drugs money in the office safe,' Canavan said. 'That's the money I was expecting him to drop.'

Grace had a vague memory of Luc telling her that sizeable cash seizures were transferred and held at a central storage facility tied to the Sheriff Court, but it wouldn't be to her advantage to share that with her captors. 'Let me try and help... please. I want to go home to my daughter, and you want me out of your hair. Let me help try and get you the drugs cash.' Grace took a slug of water. 'Walk me through your plan and I'll see if I can help you find where it might have gone wrong.' Grace heard herself sounding as if she was speaking to a couple of errant fifth years, whose exam project was going off the rails.

'The wee man handed a letter... a typed letter mind you... into Gorbals police office, addressed to DI Kidston. He got a young kid to do it, in case there was any questions... just a messenger. The letter said to put twenty thousand pounds, wrapped up in a black bin bag and put it in the cistern of the gents' toilet cubicle in a Gorbals pub at 7pm. It would be busy then and we sent an associate in to check but it hadn't been delivered. Our guy waited for over an hour but your hubby's not playing ball.'

'Okay,' Grace began. 'That sounds like a good plan, but the glitch might be that DI Kidston doesn't work at the Gorbals anymore. He's moved to Craigie Street station, and he's a DCI now.'

'When did this all happen?' Canavan asked with a defeated tone.

'Monday,' Grace said. 'Your letter would go into a mailbox and then it gets posted through internal police mail. There's a very good chance my husband's not even seen it yet and that's why you've not got your money.'

'Aw fuck!' Johnny Boy let his feelings known. 'I told you to phone it in, boss.'

'Pipe down,' Canavan remonstrated. 'So your husband's the big boss now. Easier to get control of my money.'

'If he knew about it, you'd have your money by now.'

'What makes you so sure he'll pay up.' Canavan shone his torch at Grace's face.

'He has no choice,' Grace replied. 'This will be driving him crazy.' She'd been missing now for almost twelve hours and if she knew Luc, he'd be out of his mind with worry.

'He'll get your drugs money to you if you leave clear instructions.' Grace saw Canavan's eyes glisten in the lamplight. 'Try again... try the phone this time. I want to get back to my daughter and my husband.'

'Don't fuckin' tell me what to do, missy.' Canavan rose from the sofa, tucked his lit torch into his waistband and walked over to Grace. The torch beam illuminated his face at an odd angle, and she saw him properly for the first time; large, dilated pupils in bloodshot eyes, blinking in the bright torchlight. *Was Canavan high?* He grabbed her hair with his good hand, jerking her neck back, and ran the jagged forefinger of his steel claw across her exposed neck. 'I've told you before about being a mouthy cow. I'm calling the fuckin' shots here – not you! You'll be lucky to see your family again if you don't pipe the fuck down.'

Grace ran her free hand across her neck and felt the blood trickle from the wound.

Canavan switched off his torch and returned to the sofa. She could see the blood on her hand from the light of the lamp. So much for keeping her safe – it had started. With their plan unravelling so spectacularly, she'd be fortunate to see out the night. Maybe they'd allow more time for the ransom note to get to Luc and she'd be forced to spend the night imprisoned in the terrifying darkness. A more frightening thought occurred to her; Canavan had let her see his face and made no attempt to hide his metal hand and she reckoned that could only be bad news. If her captors no longer cared about her knowing their identity, then the stakes had changed – Grace's odds of survival had just reduced dramatically.

CHAPTER FORTY-NINE

It was 9.30pm when they parked the CID cars in Myrtle Park and approached the old football stadium from its northern aspect. The light was fading fast, and it would be dark soon. The last of the gloaming would allow some time to search without flashlights or torches. Costello was right; the old ground was largely concealed behind the well-established line of trees, and it was three quarters complete. No grandstands or coverings remained and most of the terracing was overgrown with moss and weeds but remained intact on three sides of the pitch, which still looked to have a decent grass-playing surface. Someone had attempted to renovate many of the old metal crush barriers which were painted a bright scarlet; Third Lanark's team colours. Kidston marvelled at how much of the arena had survived as he took in the natural amphitheatre formed by the banked terracing, its low retaining wall and narrow running track. Amidst the dense shrubbery, the moss, and the tall trees, the old football ground terracing rose up like a gladiatorial arena.

Costello pointed out the gap in the stadium – the obvious area where the old grandstand had once stood. It was now dominated by dense thickets of nettle bushes, wild azalea, and rhododendron. The blooms were gone but the shrubbery was green and abundant with thick branches and high leafy bushes growing well above the big cop's head. The sun had long set in the evening sky, and Kidston wanted to make best use of the rapidly diminishing light. Rather than split into teams and divide up the search, Kidston asked Costello to lead them to the area closest to what he remembered as the old grandstand and its storage areas.

Costello struggled to get his massive frame under the canopy of dense shrubbery. He raised a thick tangle of branches higher and allowed the diminutive McCartney to duck underneath. The little policewoman worked quietly and tenaciously to clear a path through the undergrowth, undeterred by the jaggy nettles, dog shit and broken glass. It didn't take her too long to find what looked like a track into the centre of the thicket. The soil looked to have been disturbed by foot traffic and bushes had been cut away on either side, leading to a man-made clearing right in the heart of the thicket. Further inspection revealed a wooden hatch measuring six feet by four feet. It was painted a muddy brown to match the adjacent ground, but it was clearly a trapdoor entrance to whatever lay below. She double flashed a high-powered beam from her Dragon light; the prearranged signal to confirm a 'find'.

Kidston summoned McCartney back to the main group to discuss her findings. They spoke in low, whispered tones. 'I think someone's down there, sir,' McCartney announced. 'If they'd left, there would be dirt lying on top of the hatch but there isn't any.'

'Okay,' Kidston began. 'We need to assume that there's people down there. Probably Grace, Canavan, and Johnny Boy. We know those two are likely to be armed with knives or guns or both. That means the threat to Grace's life is real and potentially imminent. But it also means the same threat presents to each of us, individually and as a collective group. I can't ask anyone who's unarmed to go any further forward at this stage.'

'Boss, I'm happy to stay up front with the rest of you,' said a crestfallen McCartney.

'It's not just you, Chrissie, it's Peter too. You both did a brilliant job of finding this hideout and I've a feeling I'm going to be forever grateful but don't take my word. Your inspector's here. John?'

'The DCI's right,' Wylie said. 'You've both done fantastic to get us to this point, but I'm armed and you're not. I'm going to ask you to secure access from the street, the way we came in. Peter, I'll leave you to decide if you need to cordon it off, but that sometimes attracts more rubberneckers. We're expecting Detective Superintendent Sawyers and the TFU but nobody else to be allowed past the cordon.'

'C'mon, wee yin.' Costello placed an arm around his neighbour's shoulder. 'The bosses are right; we need to step back now.' The look on his disappointed colleague's face told the entire group her true feelings on the matter. She handed her Dragon light to Alison Metcalfe and followed Costello to establish a cordon.

'My instructions are to set up armed containment and wait on the TFU, who we know have an ongoing incident and it might be a considerable time before they get here. Time might not be on my side with this one; that's probably my wife down there. Now, there's no way we know what we're dealing with until I rap on that hatch and see if anyone's willing to speak to me. I'm not going to be hanging about here containing an empty cellar. That could turn out to be a really bad joke. Once I've made contact and someone confirms we've got people down there, in my view, the incident is live. Does anyone disagree?'

Kidston looked each of the group in the eye. No dissenting voices.

'Gregor, Alison, you're both unarmed and I'd like you to be safe, well back behind the ballistic shields. Alison, I'd like you to oversee communications. We'll put all calls through you. Gregor, I'd like you to be closer to the hatch, help control the lighting down there. It's likely to be darkness. Our source says it's a couple of paraffin lamps... if that.'

'I'm good with that, boss.' Stark flicked the switch of his Dragon light off and on to demonstrate the powerful searchlight. 'Two hundred thousand candlepower, it's like having my own bat signal.'

'John, Jimmy.' Kidston ran a hand over the rubber grip handle of his revolver, patted it snug into the holster, reassured by its presence. 'I'll be opening that hatch and at some stage I may have to go down the stairs. I'm not asking either of you to follow me until we know what we're facing but, in all conscience, I'm not waiting for the TFU.'

'Luc,' Wylie began. 'We're with you. If there's an imminent risk to Grace's life, then we're all clear what we have to do.'

'Totally agree.' Gabriel nodded.

The group lined up in their designated positions. Alison Metcalfe wedged her ballistic shield under a high branch, which allowed it to stand unsupported and offered her the hard cover she needed a safe distance back at the edge of the clearing. Kidston directed Stark to remain with Metcalfe until the hatch was open and a fuller threat assessment was known.

Kidston, Wylie, and Gabriel lined their ballistic shields up at the mouth of the hatch.

Kidston's stomach was churning, and he felt his heart pounding in his throat. He gulped a huge, long breath, knelt behind his shield, and gave the hatch a heavy rap.

CHAPTER FIFTY

G race wiped more blood from her neck. 'Please don't hurt me. Please... I'm a pregnant woman. I can help you get your money.' She gathered up the sleeping bag tight around her neck.

'You're a lying cow. I'm not even convinced you're pregnant.' Canavan grabbed Grace's hand away from her neck and inspected the cut. 'I think you've just made that up so we would go easy on you. And that's just a flesh wound.' Canavan tugged roughly at the sleeping bag, pulling it down and ran the jagged forefinger of his steel claw along the line of her cleavage. 'We can do a lot worse than that.'

'Shush!' It was Johnny Boy who brought the bedside drama between Grace and Canavan to an abrupt halt. 'I can hear some cunt.'

Canavan placed his good hand over Grace's mouth. He spoke in a low menacing whisper. 'Not a word or I'll rip your throat wide open.'

Johnny Boy turned off the lamp and moved quickly to replace the gag in Grace's mouth. Both torches were switched off, plunging the room back into darkness.

The basement echoed with the sound of heavy rapping on the hatch door.

———

Kidston, revolver readied in his right hand, lifted the hatch up with his left to a height of around sixteen inches and yelled through the opening. 'Armed police! Armed police!' Gabriel swung the powerful Dragon light beam into the gap. Wylie lined his weapon up through a narrow space between his shield and Gabriel's. 'Armed police!' Kidston repeated. 'Identify yourselves and come out with your hands up.'

Resounding silence.

Kidston lay prostrate at the side of the hatch and peered into the underground blackness. The hatch opening allowed enough fading evening light to reveal the wooden staircase descending into the bunker, but he relied on Gabriel's Dragon light to search out the dark corners of the room.

'Luc! Luc!' A muffled shout from the darkness lifted Kidston's heart but chilled his soul. Grace was alive but surely in grave peril. Gabriel pointed his searchlight in the direction of the shouts, enough for Kidston to make out Grace and her two captors, sitting together, huddled on a bed in a corner of the bunker.

'Hold the light there, Jimmy,' Kidston directed. 'I can see them.' Kidston opened the trapdoor further – slowly, cautiously: fully. The late evening twilight flooded through the hatch, revealing the wooden staircase, and offering the first proper look at Grace's prison. Kidston craned his neck to get a fuller view. Malky Henderson's description was accurate. The bed, the sofa, and the chest were as described. Kidston couldn't see any weapons, so he called Stark forward with the other searchlight. They were needed to illuminate the far corners of the room.

Grace was sitting up on the bed, with a sleeping bag wrapped around her legs, squeezed between Canavan and Johnny Boy. The angle of her right shoulder told him that her left hand was probably cuffed to the headboard. When the beam revealed the marks on Grace's face and neck, Kidston's anger flared, and he battled his instinct to rush forward and rescue his wife.

'Canavan! McManus! Keep your hands up where I can see them!' Kidston roared his instructions. 'Remove that gag from her mouth, immediately!' A compliant Johnny Boy leaned across to assist Grace, but she was able to remove it unaided with her free hand. 'We're all armed. No false moves or I'll shoot. Step away from the woman and come out with your hands up. Grace! Are you okay? Have they harmed you?'

'I'm fine!' Grace shouted. 'I'm okay, don't worry about me.'

Canavan and Johnny Boy raised their hands in front of their bodies. The beam from a Dragon light shimmered and glanced off Canavan's steel hand like a flash of lightning. Neither man made any attempt to move off the bed.

Kidston used the handle of his shield to right himself and crouched behind his ballistic screen, peering through the bulletproof glass viewing window. His gaze fixed on the bed in the left-hand corner of the bunker, now illuminated by two portable searchlights.

'I hope you've brought the twenty thousand pounds, Kidston.' Canavan's bravado had no limits.

'What twenty thousand pounds would that be?' Kidston fought to conceal his scorn. He was in hostage negotiator mode now. Nobody was going to take on a shot with Grace sandwiched tightly between her two captors. Similarly, Canavan's steel prosthetic looked like it could do some damage. Rushing them carried too big a risk for Grace.

'Did you not get my note? I was looking to get back the money that the polis stole from me a couple of weeks ago.'

'The drugs seizure?' Kidston sought clarity. 'That's what this is about?'

'That, plus a few other things,' Canavan began. 'You really fucked up my life, Kidston. My hand; that's on you. My criminal compen: you blocked that. My lawyer filed a lawsuit: the polis blocked that. We got a letter saying you were a hero. Is that how you got DCI? Some fuckin' hero. My fuckin' life is destroyed.'

'What have you been smoking, Phil? You must be seriously deranged to think that the police are going to pay up on any of those. It's time to walk away from this, Phil.' The use of Canavan's first name was deliberate. 'Come on, you and Johnny Boy need to walk away from this before it gets any worse for you. The police never got any note. So technically we can rule out kidnap and extortion. We can plead it away as an abduction case, simple false imprisonment. That will go better for you.'

'You think I'm fuckin' stupid, Kidston.' Canavan gave a menacing smile. 'I've got a suspended jail sentence and I've no intention of going back to Barlinnie. Not sure how a one-handed version of me would cope. Too many enemies in *the big hoose*.'

'There's a firearms team coming our way, Phil.' Kidston spoke slowly and deliberately. 'You know how it works with the tactical guys – they don't take any prisoners. Walk away now with me before this thing gets out of hand. Let my wife go.'

'No can do, Mr Kidston,' Canavan said. 'I'm not going anywhere. The minute I stand up from this bed, you're going to shoot me. I can sense it... I can hear it in your voice. I want my lawyer here to make sure you and your team don't take any liberties.'

'I've had enough.' Johnny Boy McManus suddenly and without any warning stood up off the bed and raised his hands in the air. 'Don't shoot! Don't shoot! I surrender. This had fuck all to do with me. This nutter has completely lost the fuckin' plot since he started snorting coke. I warned the crazy motherfucker not to try this. I'm not going back to the Bar L for this one.'

'Walk this way, Johnny Boy.' It was Kidston issuing the arrest instructions. 'Keep your hands in the air. No sudden moves.'

'What the fuck?!' Canavan screamed at his long-time friend and enforcer. 'What the fuck are you doing, you fuckin' shitebag?' Canavan was screaming so loud it brought on a nosebleed and he dabbed the red droplets onto the back of his good hand before wiping them with his shirt cuff. 'You're fuckin' finished, McManus. And get that fuckin' spotlight out of my face.'

Two ballistic shields suddenly opened like a sliding door, and Kidston stepped through the gap covering the suspect with his revolver. 'Keep your hands up and move slowly,' Kidston commanded as he watched the little man known as the *Tasmanian Devil*, head bowed, a vividly lit figure bathed in brilliant spotlight, make his slow, surrendered ascent of the staircase. Johnny Boy's capitulation provided the ideal window to move the shield detail farther into the bunker and once their prisoner was in the safe custody of DS Stark, Kidston took the opportunity to descend the staircase. Three shields in unison descended the ten wooden steps and formed up at the foot of the stairs. Canavan and his hostage were now less than thirty feet away.

Kidston could hardly believe what he'd just seen. Johnny Boy McManus had been by Phil Canavan's side for over fifteen years; friend, driver, chief enforcer, and bodyguard. *How far must Canavan have strayed for his previously loyal lieutenant to desert him?* And Canavan, screaming like a maniac? That was never his style. Not one to get excitable or over-emotional; he was known for meting out his singular brand of violence with a detached cool. Canavan was always a formidable opponent; if his cocaine habit was making him this erratic and excitable, he would be a far more dangerous one.

Canavan was howling like a wounded animal. Johnny Boy's desertion had sent him over the edge. 'Get back!' He grabbed Grace by her hair and pulled her violently towards him. 'Get back! Get those fuckin' shields back up those stairs or I'll end this bitch right now.'

Kidston watched through the viewing widow of his shield, trembling with anger, and gripping his revolver tightly. Target and hostage too closely hunched. In his heart, at that moment, he knew just one thing for certain; Canavan would regret his treatment of Grace.

CHAPTER FIFTY-ONE

Stark and Metcalfe led Johnny Boy away from the hatch to conduct a quick interrogation and debrief of their prisoner. Wylie and Gabriel maintained their positions behind the shields, either side of Kidston, whose eyes never left Grace and her captor. Canavan was still screaming abuse at his betrayal. Three revolvers and two Dragon lights remained trained on the unravelling gangster.

With Johnny Boy handed over to Costello and McCartney, and secured in a CID car, Gregor Stark returned to the hatch and briefed Kidston, who kept his eyes trained on Canavan.

'First up, boss,' Stark announced, 'there's a handgun in there.' The young DS crouched down behind the bulletproof barrier held solid by his three armed colleagues and spoke in a low whisper. 'McManus says it's an old Beretta M9 semi-automatic pistol, but they've only got six rounds of ammo left. They started with a full clip of fifteen rounds, but Canavan was practising his shooting in the park. The gun's a black colour and was in the old chest, but Johnny Boy says Canavan went in the chest when the lights went out.'

'Can he shoot it left-handed?' Kidston asked.

'I asked that specifically,' Stark began. 'Says Canavan's been practising but he's struggling for accuracy; very erratic.'

'All the more reason for you and Alison to stay well back, behind hard cover. Any knives in there?'

'Johnny Boy says none. Since he told us about the gun, I tend to believe him but who knows what else is in the chest the gun came out of.'

'There's been no sign or mention of a gun as yet,' Kidston said. 'Clearly McManus bailed because he doesn't want to go back to Barlinnie. What else is going on with those two?'

'He was fearful that Canavan was going to kill Grace because she'd worked out who they were,' Stark said. 'Be careful, boss. Johnny Boy says Canavan's been doing way too much coke.'

'What was the plan?' Kidston asked. 'Was there any plan?'

'Johnny Boy handed in a ransom note to Gorbals office at midday, the instruction was to return the seized twenty K drugs money by wrapping it in a bin bag and placing it in the gents' toilet cistern in The Pig and Whistle pub at 7pm tonight. Grace was to be released once they had the money, but McManus thought Canavan was going to kill her anyway.'

'Johnny Boy's right,' Kidston said. 'Canavan has totally lost the plot. Anything else, Gregor?'

'I searched him and here's the key for the handcuffs.' Stark slipped the small key into Kidston's back trouser pocket. 'Grace is cuffed to the iron bed frame by her left hand, but you've probably seen that for yourself. And, one more thing, those two had nothing to do with the attack on your car. Johnny Boy had no idea what I was talking about and he's co-operating fully on everything else.'

'Thanks, Gregor. Very thorough. John, Jimmy, all noted? Any more questions for Gregor?'

'All noted.' Two voices in unison. 'No questions.'

'Right, Gregor,' Kidston began. 'Get back to Alison's position and get her to radio the control room; handgun confirmed, one armed suspect at locus, one female hostage confirmed, one suspect in custody. Ask if there's an update on the TFU's arrival and request an ambulance to standby at the outer cordon in Myrtle Park.'

'All noted, boss.' Stark scurried back to join Metcalfe, mindful to avoid the low branches that hindered his path.

———

Kidston considered the wisdom of mentioning the Beretta at this stage of negotiations. Canavan was apoplectic about Johnny Boy's betrayal, and this had the potential to heighten tensions further. Kidston wanted to keep things as calm as possible. He tried a different tack. 'Johnny Boy made the right decision, Phil. You should follow his example. Walk out now and we'll deal with it. You'd rather deal with me than a tactical team. Once they're here, Phil, I'll be pushed into the background, and they'll take over. I can guarantee your safe passage if you step out now.'

'I'm going nowhere. And as long as I have the lovely Mrs Kidston here, I'm safe.' Canavan wrapped his good arm around Grace and pulled her closer. A manic grin on his face, staring into the spotlight beam, he pressed his metal hand against her neck. 'Don't do anything silly, Kidston, or I'll slit her pretty throat.'

'Don't threaten Grace. That's a pregnant woman you're manhandling.' Kidston tried to maintain a calm register, but it was impossible; he was far too emotionally invested in this negotiation but there was no way he could trust it to anyone else. Every fibre in his body urged him to rush forward and shoot Canavan dead but the risk to Grace was too grave. 'You better not harm my unborn child or–' Kidston stopped himself mid-sentence. Here he was threatening his subject, something he'd never done in ten years as a hostage negotiator. But he'd never negotiated for the life of his wife and unborn child before.

'I want my money and my lawyer and then I'll think about letting Mrs Kidston go, once I've got safe passage out of here.'

'That drugs money is safely locked up in the Sheriff Court. It's not going anywhere, even if I'd be happy to hand it over for Grace.' Kidston rested his forefinger outside his trigger guard; it was a long time to hold a revolver and he couldn't risk an accidental discharge; not with Grace in the firing line. 'You need to get real, Phil. I can bring your lawyer as far as the cordon. He's a civilian, so he can't come into the middle of an armed police operation, but I guarantee he'll be there to meet you when you're getting put in the police car. I promise no one will manhandle you.'

'I want my lawyer here,' Canavan said. 'You three cowboys are desperate to fire holes into me. I'm not moving until my lawyer's in this basement.'

'Our procedures won't allow that, Phil. I've explained to you we can get him to the cordon, and you can see him there. I promise.'

'Fuck your procedures!' Canavan shouted. 'I'm sick of your fuckin' procedures. I'm going to do one last wee snort before your tactical guys come for me.' Canavan fished into his shirt pocket and produced a small poly bag with white powder. He expertly made two generous lines on the back of his steel prosthetic and fished out a short silver pipe from the same pocket.

Kidston saw the look of abject terror on his wife's face. 'Come on, Phil. No drugs. This is a time for clear heads not for snorting cocaine. It can't help our current predicament. Come on, put it away.'

'You don't understand the pain I've been in since I lost my

hand. This is the only thing that gives me relief. You can't deny a man a chance to relieve his pain.'

As Canavan leaned forward to snort the first line, Wylie whispered to Kidston. 'I've got a head shot. When he leans forward for that second line of coke, I can put one in his skull.'

'Too risky and hard to justify a kill shot,' Kidston replied softly.

'What about you, Grace?' Canavan asked. 'You fancy a wee line? No?' Grace recoiled in horror as he dived in for the second line of white powder, which vanished like a rat up a drainpipe.

'Bad decision, Phil,' Kidston said. 'We need to keep a clear head here.'

'Wow! That's fuckin' excellent coke. Nothing like a bit of top quality ching when you need a wee lift.' Canavan sniffed and snorted loudly, vigorously shaking his head from side to side. 'Wo... ow!' He thumbed some residual powder back into his nostrils.

Kidston watched Canavan blink violently into the searchlight beam as the cocaine started to take hold of his nervous system. Kidston blew a long slow exhale to steady his breathing. He was already facing the most difficult negotiation he'd ever encountered; bartering for the safety of his wife and unborn child was a nerve-shredding experience and Canavan had just added cocaine to the equation.

It was a bad mix.

'Come ahead, ya bastards!' Canavan screamed, a maniacal grin on his face. He was the fearless gang leader of his youth again. 'I'll fuckin' take you all on.'

Kidston regretted not letting Wylie take the head shot.

CHAPTER FIFTY-TWO

K idston wiped his sweaty palms on the fabric of his body armour and gripped tightly on the handle of the ballistic shield as he recognised his fear. That familiar sense of dread rising in his chest as his heart raced ahead of the danger. Rapid breathing that felt like all the oxygen was being sucked out of the air. *Gut-wrenching fear.* The deep-seated instinct warning him of the obvious threat confronting him and Grace. Kidston slowed his breathing to bring his fears under control. He imagined the frightening ordeal his wife would have gone through. Abduction was a horrifying prospect, for anyone, but Grace's fear of darkness meant that her underground captivity would be a truly terrifying experience.

'How about you let me take Grace's place, Phil?' Kidston was breaking every rule in his hostage negotiator handbook. Negotiation 101: *never offer a hostage exchange.* It looks good in a Hollywood movie, but Kidston had threatened to throw students off training courses for making such basic errors in exercise scenarios. But this was no training exercise; this was his pregnant wife; at the mercy of a cruel gangster who was under the influence of stimulants and likely armed. Normal rules did not apply.

'You'll throw down your weapon?' Canavan's interest was piqued. 'What about the other two cowboys?'

'They'll cover me while we do the exchange. Me for Grace.' Kidston laid out his offer.

'Don't do it, Luc!' Grace shouted. 'It's way too dangerous. Don't trust him.'

Canavan laughed at her. His two lines of coke taking further effect.

'I know what I'm doing, Gracie. I want you out of here safe.' Kidston raised his voice. 'Phil, you'd need to throw down any guns or knives you have in there with you.'

Wylie leaned in behind his ballistic shield and spoke to Kidston in a low whisper. 'It's too risky, Luc, unless he throws out his gun.'

Kidston spoke in the same low tone. 'If he goes for it, Jimmy, tuck your gun into my back waistband, just below my vest. John will cover me. I fancy my chances with a one-handed cokehead, but I've got to get Grace away from him.'

'What's your answer, Phil?' Kidston asked. 'You can trust me. I'll wait with you until the firearms team come. I'll walk you out.'

'The last time I trusted you, Kidston, I lost my fuckin' hand. Here's my answer.' Canavan pulled the Beretta out from behind his back and started shooting. Kidston focused on the muzzle flash as the first shot thudded against the middle ballistic shield. The next two bullets went high, over the shields and exited the hatch. Three armed officers crouched lower behind their bulletproof wall, thankful of the protection it offered. But Kidston had a duty to protect the others.

'Shots fired! Shots fired!' Kidston alerted Stark and Metcalfe. 'Alison, Gregor – hard cover now!' Kidston watched their assailant through the armoured glass window in his shield. He was shooting indiscriminately in the general direction of the black wall of shields bookended by two spotlights. Grace was too close to Canavan for any return of fire.

The next bullet took out one of the Dragon lights with a startling crack, as the glass of the portable searchlight exploded, reducing the lighting in the bunker by half. Kidston made a mental count of the rounds used. *That's four.*

'Fuckin' bullseye!' Canavan seemed pleased with his marksmanship. 'I told you to get that fuckin' light out of my eyes.'

'Luc! Luc!' Grace yelled. 'Are you okay?'

'We're all okay, Grace. These shields will protect us... we're all safe.'

'Please get back, Luc... be careful!' Grace shouted.

Canavan violently pulled her in tight with his prosthetic hand and pointed the gun at her temple. 'Fuckin' behave, missy.'

Kidston's heart leapt into his throat.

Canavan's survival instinct was kicking in; the closer to Grace the better, and the less likely that the police would take on a shot.

'Four rounds,' Wylie whispered to Kidston.

'I'm counting,' Kidston replied. 'I'm waiting for the click.'

Kidston watched through the spy window of his shield as Canavan lined up his next shot. Still sat on the bed, his aim looked awkward; the stance of a right-hander shooting wrong-handed. He was aiming at the remaining light, which Gabriel had wedged into the base of his shield, held steady by the shoulder strap. It shone directly at Canavan. His first attempt fizzled harmlessly into the soft ground.

'Five,' whispered Kidston.

Canavan adjusted, raising his gun hand, aligning the weapon's sights. He closed his right eye and took careful aim.

The round struck close to the Dragon light beam but plugged the shield with a deadened thud that echoed through the cavernous basement.

'Six,' whispered Kidston.

'Six,' agreed Wylie.

'We've got him,' Kidston said. 'He's out of bullets. I'm going to make a move.'

'Steady, Luc.' Wylie placed a restraining hand on Kidston's shoulder. 'There might be one up the spout.'

Canavan took aim, again.

Click!

'Forward,' Kidston commanded, and the three shields shuttled forward in unison. Small steps but moving as a single column.

Click!

Click! 'Bastard!' Canavan held the Beretta to Grace's forehead. 'Stay back, ya bastards!' Snarling and screaming now. 'Stay fuckin' back! I will shoot this bitch.'

'Stop!' Kidston halted the column. He saw the look of sheer terror on Grace's face. His stomach lurched and his legs turned to jelly as he contemplated her fate. Momentarily, it seemed as if the planet had stopped spinning on its axis – time stood still. His entire world in freeze frame. His rational brain kicked in; after three clicks there were no bullets in Canavan's gun. 'Forward.' Kidston pushed the line ahead – a slow advance.

Click!

Breathe. Kidston's heart rate slowed.

No rogue round in the chamber. Canavan was out of ammo. Out of options.

'I warned you, Kidston.' Canavan tucked the Beretta into his waistband and scooped up the container of paraffin by its handle, removing the cap with his teeth. 'Come ahead, ya bastards!' He poured the paraffin over Grace, splashing the entire contents over her head, shoulders, and her body, which remained largely encased in the sleeping bag. She pulled frantically at her handcuffed wrist, but there would be no escape. Oblivious to Grace's shrieks, Canavan flung the empty container at the column of shields and watched it bounce off harmlessly. He pulled Grace closer and took a cigarette lighter from his pocket, holding it menacingly close to Grace's neck, and flicked the flame on. 'Keep back... or else.'

The column stopped, now only ten feet from their target.

Kidston lined up his shot, but his hand was shaking too much. He tried to slow his breathing, focus on the target but hesitated; Grace was still much too close to Canavan.

'Duck, Grace, Duck now!' It was Wylie. As Grace lunged forward, quickly dropping her head and shoulders down to the soft landing of the bed, a single shot ripped through Canavan's throat. As the wounded criminal slumped off the bed towards the floor, the lighter dropped from his hand. The bottom of the sleeping bag was instantly ablaze, the flames engulfing Grace's feet. She was cocooned in a fiery shroud, the flames rising quickly up her body – chained to a bed that had transformed into a blazing funeral pyre.

Grace's screams filled the bunker as she shrieked in terror, while trying to push the burning sleeping bag off with her free hand. Kidston tossed his shield aside and rushed forward. He grabbed the burning sleeping bag and dragged it off his wife's body while Gabriel grabbed her shoulders and pulled her clear of the flaming material. Wylie attended to his victim who was gurgling a strange death rattle. Canavan grinned maniacally, a peculiar look in his eyes, as Wylie removed the gangster's gun from his waistband.

'Watch that hand, John!' Kidston screamed at his colleague as he was freeing Grace's handcuff.

It was too late. Canavan brought his steel claw around in a

sweeping arc, the improvised finger blade slashing Wylie's throat which slit wide open. Blood billowed from the incision like a scarlet waterfall in miniature. Kidston rushed to his stricken colleague and knelt beside him, but he was fading fast. Kidston clasped Wylie's hand which still held his revolver, his dying colleague's finger still on the trigger. Kidston tightened his hand around Wylie's and applied the pressure needed to fire two rounds into Canavan's black heart.

Canavan's reign was over.

'Stay with me, John... stay with me.' Kidston couldn't find a pulse in Wylie's wrist. The blood was still pouring from his neck. 'Stay with me, John... stay with me.'

Grace crouched beside her kneeling husband and threw her arms around him. He held on to Wylie's hand, but pulled her in close, wrapped his free arm around her and held her tight. Grace wept on his shoulder.

'It's okay, I'm here. You're safe now.'

The awful, dreadful sound of John Wylie's death rattle.

'He's gone, Luca... he's gone.'

'I know, Gracie... I know.' He held her closer, pulled her tighter, finally releasing his grip on his dead colleague's hand.

CHAPTER FIFTY-THREE

'Gregor! Alison! Call that ambulance forward. One female casualty to be checked out. Two fatalities.' Kidston could hear Gabriel shouting the orders above ground. He'd given the couple some privacy. They knelt together on the soft ground, locked in a close embrace, and near to the bloodied remains of John Wylie and Phil Canavan. With the surviving Dragon light now above ground, Kidston was grateful that the tiny beam from his small torch spared Grace from viewing the ghastly scene alongside them. He felt the rise and fall of his wife's chest as she sobbed into his shoulder.

'Did you see Florrie?' Grace asked between sobs.

'Florrie's all good with her Auntie Veronica. Missing you but safe and sound. Veronica told me the baby news.'

'I guessed that much.' Grace wiped at her tears. 'Tallulah's missing.'

'Tallulah's at the vet's. Those bastards ran her over but that's the reason we found you. It's a long story but I'll tell you all the details later. I thought I'd lost you, Gracie.'

They hugged each other tight in a long, silent embrace.

'Let's get you out of here,' Kidston said eventually. He

helped Grace to her feet and assisted drying the paraffin out of her hair with his shirtsleeves. She used a corner of her dress to finish wiping her face. He picked up the container and emptied the last dregs of the paraffin onto his hands. The detective washed off John Wylie's blood and some gunpowder residue before discarding the container. Kidston put a supporting arm around Grace and they climbed the staircase together. The old stadium was in total darkness now and Gabriel shone his Dragon light to illuminate a pathway through the thicket. Kidston pulled, pushed, and lifted branches to allow Grace safe passage through the shrubbery. They were met by two paramedics who wrapped Grace in a foil blanket.

Gabriel asked the senior medic to confirm that nothing could be done for John Wylie or Phil Canavan and led him to the grisly scene in the basement. They emerged a few minutes later. 'Life pronounced extinct in both cases, Luc,' Gabriel began. 'We'll complete the formal pronouncement when the pathologist attends.'

Kidston pushed Grace's paraffin-soaked hair back and ran a gentle hand over his wife's face to examine the scratch on her neck and the bruising on her cheek.

'I'm okay, Luca, I promise.' Grace pulled the silver blanket tightly around herself.

'Just let the professionals check you out. I need to remain at the scene. There's very strict procedures for a police shooting.'

'I understand but look at your hand. You'll need to get that nasty burn checked out.'

Kidston raised his left hand for closer inspection. It was scorched and blackened with ugly red blisters on his palm, thumb, and forefinger. He hadn't noticed it.

'I promise I'll get it checked.' He embraced Grace, who leaned in and kissed him lightly on the cheek. 'I'll get you a run home once Gregor's got a brief statement from you and the medics are done. Remember to tell them that you're pregnant.'

The paramedics led Grace away.

Kidston wandered towards the north-east corner of the terracing and sat on the end of the low boundary wall. He rested with his head in his hands, absent, broken and utterly exhausted. The old stadium took on an eerie feel; the moon, a thin pale disc, hung in the dark night sky like a communion wafer. The warm evening air was turning to chill and Kidston shuddered at the events he'd just witnessed. Lost in his own thoughts, he allowed himself to reflect on John Wylie's heroism and his own actions. Grace was alive; John was dead, but it was dreadfully close to being the other way around. He was still there, ten minutes later, when Gregor Stark found him, elbows resting on his knees, staring into the darkness. Stark flashed his torch to signal his approach. 'There's a medic over at the cordon who wants to apply a dressing to your burnt hand. You okay, boss?'

'John Wylie's dead, Gregor.' Kidston's voice was flat.

'I know, Luc... I know, but we can't dwell on it.' Stark squatted down on the wall beside him.

'If it wasn't for John, Grace would have been burned alive. That madman was determined to kill us all... coked up, crazy... unbelievable.' Kidston looked at his young DS, a hazy, vacant look on his face. 'You should have seen the shot he took on to take Canavan out... unbelievable and in semi-darkness. I think he aimed a bit higher to make sure he missed Grace. John would normally have gone for the double tap.'

'I heard,' Stark replied. 'Jimmy told me. Quite an ordeal for all of you. Grace is checked out, she's fine. I've arranged Chrissie McCartney to run her home in a CID car. She told me to let you know that she'll pick up Florence at her sister's and they'll be sleeping in their own beds tonight.' Stark placed a gentle hand on his boss's shoulder. 'Are you going to be all right?'

'I need to be,' Kidston began. 'After we finish post-incident procedures here, we've got the small matter of writing up the case against Michael Nicolson. Have you forgotten about our serial killer?'

'Case is written,' Stark said. 'It's on tape for a typist,' Stark glanced at his watch to confirm it was just after midnight, 'first thing this morning it'll go to the fiscal ahead of the accused. It's all organised.'

'How?'

'Well, given what we were dealing with I asked Paul Kennedy if he fancied writing a case for a double murder and an attempted murder. He was sitting all day and all night waiting for your phone extension to ring, so I passed him my case notes and he's written up the police report.'

'Good thinking, Gregor.' There was enough torchlight for Kidston to see the huge grin on Stark's face.

'He was delighted to be able to contribute in a more meaningful way. Sam Brady has been briefed to expect an abstract report with full statements to follow in the next few days. Given that Ryan Ferrier is the victim, I think Sam would be happy to receive the case on the back of a Woodbine packet.'

'Gregor, I don't think I tell you this enough, but you're a superstar.' Kidston was surprised by the emotion in his voice. He inhaled a huge gulp of air, stood up and patted his young DS on the back.

The two detectives walked towards the cordon, Stark lighting the way by torchlight. They were met by Detective Superintendent Joe Sawyers and the inspector in charge of the firearms team. The rest of the TFU had been stood down. The cordon was reinforced, all police weapons were seized and within forty minutes the entire locus, including the underground bunker, was bathed in temporary lighting to allow forensic examiners and ballistic experts to do their thing. Crime-scene examiners would be collecting all the bullets and shell casings from the incident – the only three rounds that mattered would be found in Canavan's lifeless body. But Grace's temporary prison was both a murder locus and the scene of a police shooting. The site would be under tight control for some time.

The official verdict would never be challenged. Grace Kidston and DI Jimmy Gabriel saw Inspector John Wylie rush to disarm Phil Canavan after shooting him in the throat. The dying gangster slashed Wylie's throat and DCI Kidston rushed to his fatally wounded colleague's aid in time to witness Wylie shooting Canavan twice in the chest. John Wylie's heroism would be the focus of the inquiry – his quick, skilful action saved an innocent woman from being burned alive.

———

Grace had been unable to sleep until Luc joined her in bed, well into the wee small hours. It was hardly surprising; pumped full of adrenaline, the horror of her abduction and imprisonment and the shock of witnessing two killings. Back in her own bed, safe in her husband's arms, with their daughter slumbering soundly next door, Grace slept the sleep of angels. But an exhausted Kidston battled a fitful sleep. It was John Wylie's face and the events of the previous evening that plagued his slumber. He should have trusted John to take the head shot – Wylie could have made the shot. John's death would live with him forever – lurking in the shadowy corners of his mind, those dark places where guilt and conscience reside. Kidston knew; *it's the failures that are etched in your psyche forever.* In his dark night of the soul, there was no remorse for Canavan. There were no nightmares; none of the falling dreams that had plagued Kidston's childhood and returned to haunt him as an adult in times of severe stress. Canavan died by his own hand. Kidston had offered him several chances to walk out peacefully. Canavan had chosen violence. It was a righteous kill; no doubt, no regrets and zero compunction for the loss of a vicious gangster. In that respect, Kidston's conscience was clear.

CHAPTER FIFTY-FOUR

K idston went into the office at lunchtime.

He was struggling to shake off the events of the previous day. Grief floated in the air like an invisible mist. The pungent, oily smell of paraffin seemed to be caught in his nostrils as he looked over the case papers prepared by DC Paul Kennedy. All the officers involved in the shooting incident had been offered time off. All had declined. Joe Sawyers had tried to persuade Kidston to take a few days to allow his burned hand time to recover, spend some time with Grace but his wife was keen to quickly restore the normal family routines. All agreed a compromise; once he'd bottomed out the paperwork for the shooting incident and the Michael Nicolson case, he'd take a week off. They would borrow Veronica's little cottage in St Monans in the East Neuk of Fife. His first duty after a late breakfast had been to check on Tallulah. When he and Grace called in to see Julie Gray, the veterinarian had more hopeful news for them. Tallulah had had a good night and looked likely to survive her injuries, but there would be a lengthy period of recovery.

———

Kidston had agreed to do the formal identifications of John Wylie and Phil Canavan at the city mortuary. When he arrived both post-mortems had already been done. The familiar smell of death and all its unpleasant business assailed his olfactory senses. Both bodies were laid out on tables, fully covered by white cotton sheets. A mortuary attendant lowered the sheet so Kidston could confirm both identities and marked up his details in the mortuary book. His legal duty performed, Kidston didn't look past the white cotton sheet covering his dead colleague – he knew what lay underneath and had no desire to remember John Wylie as a cadaver. Canavan was easily identifiable by the ugly scar that ran off the left side of his mouth. He saw the hole that John Wylie had made in the gangster's throat – it was a helluva shot.

Kidston knocked on the door of the medical room, where Donnelly was alone, seated at her desk, writing up some notes. 'Can I have a quick word, Finola?'

'Ah, Luc, of course, come in, come in.'

'Did you do the PMs on John and Canavan this morning?'

Finola stood up from her desk and greeted him with a half hug. 'How is Grace? I read the police report. That's quite an ordeal you all went through last night.'

'I'm fortunate that my wife's not laid out on one of your tables next door, but it was a close-run thing.'

'Just awful. I was very saddened to see your colleague on the table... quite unsettling,' Finola said in her soft Irish lilt. She stood closer and laid a hand on Kidston's shoulder. 'What about the PMs?'

'Did you do them?'

'Yes, me and the Prof, two doctor post-mortems as per. What's troubling you?'

'John had a head shot on Canavan when he was snorting the coke. I talked him out of it... Grace was too close.' Kidston's voice was cracking – the sight of his dead colleague on a mortuary slab. 'If I hadn't talked him out of it, John would still be here.'

The pathologist hooked her arm through Kidston's. 'Here you, you can't be thinking like that. All those ifs and buts and maybes won't do you any good at all.'

'Could Canavan have survived being shot in the throat?' Kidston's pale-green eyes fixed Finola for a response.

'Wylie's first shot did a lot of damage; there's lots of vital structures in the neck; the carotid and vertebral arteries, cervical spine and spinal cord are all around that area. The velocity and trajectory of a nine millimetre round fired at relatively close quarters and the massive trauma it caused, Prof Cochrane and I agreed that the shot was likely fatal, but it was academic as the next two blew up Canavan's heart at close quarters.' Finola gave him a quizzical look. 'Why is it important?'

'That shot saved Grace's life, but Canavan lived long enough to murder John. I'm sure if Grace wasn't so close to Canavan in the bunker, he'd have double tapped him, but it was too risky... he was thinking about Grace.'

'What did I tell you about those ifs and buts and maybes. Your colleague saved your wife, and you couldn't save him... there you are, bluntly put and I don't mean to be cruel, but you need to give yourself a pass on this one, Luc, or it will consume you.'

'You're right, Fi. Thanks, I promise I won't dwell on it.'

'John Wylie's going to be viewed by relatives later,' Finola said. 'The technician will make sure he looks nice for the family.'

'I met John's partner, Joanne Simpson, this morning when I broke the news to her. A lovely lady and absolutely devasted.'

Prior to the dreadful task of identifying the bodies, the most difficult part of Kidston's morning had been informing Wylie's partner of his death. Joe Sawyers had excused him from the duty, but Kidston insisted that he should accompany him as he was in a position to tell Joanne exactly how John had died. A first-hand account would be better, and he'd be able to answer all her questions. It had been well after 3am when they roused Joanne Simpson from sleep. Wylie's partner had sensed what was coming but the details of his murder shocked her. Over mugs of tea, Kidston emphasised Wylie's bravery and had choked back his own tears as he explained the personal debt that he owed John for his heroic actions. They left Joanne in the care of her two daughters with both detectives reiterating that all the assets and resources of Strathclyde Police would be at the family's disposal. It was one of the toughest duties Kidston had ever performed but relaying the dreadful news in person had been the right thing to do.

'You're a good man, Lucas Kidston. There'll be some tough times ahead, but I know you well enough... you'll get through this.'

'Thanks, Fi.' The former lovers held a short embrace and Kidston made his way out, back through the chamber of horrors in the main examination room. Stepping out into the fresh air and blue skies of Saltmarket and Glasgow Green, he gulped a huge breath, glad to depart the macabre precincts of the city mortuary. For the moment, he'd had quite enough of this house of death.

———

Kidston looked up from his paperwork when he heard the soft knock on his open office door and wasn't too surprised to see a solemn-looking Sarah Canavan. 'Sorry to disturb you, Luc, but I was hoping for ten minutes of your time.'

'Of course, Sarah, come in.' Kidston ushered her in and offered one of the chairs in front of his desk. 'Please, take a seat.'

'Thanks.' Her sad and puffy eyes told of her emotional state and how little sleep she'd managed. She looked exhausted.

'I'm sorry that I couldn't break the news of Phil's death personally, but I was visiting my dead colleague's partner conveying the same news. Hopefully DI Gabriel and DS Metcalfe were able to break the shocking news without adding to your obvious distress.'

'They were very professional,' Sarah said, 'both of them, but they didn't go into too much detail. I was hoping you'd be able to tell me a little bit more.'

'Up to a point, how much do you know?'

'I understand he killed a police inspector who shot him but I'm a bit confused on the details.'

'Did you know he kidnapped my wife as ransom for twenty K of drugs money that we seized from one of his associates?'

'No.' Sarah Canavan looked genuinely shocked at the revelation. 'That's crazy, total madness, who comes up with a scheme like that?'

'Did they tell you that he set my wife on fire?'

'Oh my God!' Sarah Canavan shook her head in stunned disbelief. 'Is she okay?'

'My wife is fine, thanks, but it was one hell of an ordeal. Did you know that he fired off six rounds from a handgun and tried to kill me and my two colleagues?' Kidston was struggling to contain his anger over John Wylie's death. He would need to rein it in – it was hardly Sarah Canavan's fault.

'Did he shoot your colleague?'

'No, he ripped his throat with that steel contraption of a

hand. I'm sorry the facts are so distressing, Sarah, that's why my colleagues held some aspects back.'

'How did Phil die?' Sarah was choking back tears. 'Can I ask that?'

'He was shot three times by the inspector he killed,' Kidston explained. 'The first shot hit Phil in the throat and put him down, but he was able to slash Inspector Wylie's throat as he was checking on him. The next two shots were close range, through the heart, just before Inspector Wylie bled out.' Kidston grimaced as he remembered John Wylie's final act and his own role in it.

Sarah started to sob. 'I'm so sorry he put you and your wife and your colleagues through all of that. Phil's been doing a lot of coke lately.' She was weeping freely now. 'He was becoming paranoid that you were going to send him back to jail. I only became aware of his coke habit very recently and I was going to get him into rehab. I blame myself.'

'Don't upset yourself too much, Sarah. There's very little any of us could do when Phil embarked on that crazy kidnapping plan. Even Johnny Boy couldn't stomach it. You'll be able to visit him in Barlinnie and he'll give you his take on it. Phil was snorting lines of coke just before he started shooting at us.'

'Unbelievable. You know how much he hated you, Luc. He blamed you for everything that's gone wrong since his amputation. Despite my arguments to the contrary, he holds you responsible for the loss of his hand... sorry, *held* you.' Her tears were flowing freely now. 'Did you at least give him a chance to surrender?'

'I gave him several chances to give himself up, just the same as three years ago,' Kidston said. 'I told him repeatedly to give it up. He died by his own hand, Sarah.'

'I've taken up enough of your time, thanks.' Sarah stood up and dabbed her eyes with a paper tissue. 'I appreciate your honesty.'

Kidston placed a gentle arm on her shoulder and walked her to the door.

CHAPTER FIFTY-FIVE

FIVE DAYS LATER

Veronica's cottage was the perfect getaway. Grace seemed largely unaffected by her ordeal. Kidston watched her closely – her period of captivity had been mercifully short. As part of his hostage negotiator training with the Metropolitan Police, Kidston had spent time with a number of actual hostages, like PC Trevor Lock, the hero of the Iranian Embassy siege and remembered the quiet trauma that lingered years after the event. The longer the time held as a hostage the more likely it was to result in psychological issues. But their five nights at St Monans were idyllic. Breakfast as a family was one of the first markers of normality. There were long walks along the beach, Florrie sitting atop his shoulders, screaming, and giggling with delight as her daddy high-kicked and splashed through the foamy rollers. Tallulah hobbled in and out of the North Sea surf, her rehabilitation coming along nicely. There were family lunches in dog friendly St Andrews pubs, and they caught some brilliant sunny weather. Day trips to the old fishing villages of Elie, Anstruther, Pittenweem, and Crail allowed Luc and Grace to restore some much-needed equilibrium after what they'd been through. They talked about their unborn child and their hopes for their growing family.

During one walk along the beach at St Monans, with Florrie asleep in her buggy, they were discussing their ordeal. 'When Canavan held the gun to your head, it was as if I was momentarily paralysed by fear...' Kidston paused. 'I think I understand the triggers and emotional responses to fear much better from my acrophobia therapy sessions. The fear of falling and my aversion to heights is one thing, but this level of dread was off the scale.'

'I know what you're saying, Luca. I think my day in the bunker has cured my phobia of darkness forever. As a wee girl I fretted over the monsters and bogeymen that I thought lurked in dark places, but then I met two real-life monsters.'

'Those psychological fears can't compete with death staring you in the face.'

Grace offered a fresh insight to her captivity. 'Johnny Boy was about to release me if I agreed to give him a hand job.'

'Eh?' Luc recoiled in horror. 'How in hell's name did that come about?'

'He was negotiating sexual favours for my freedom.'

'I hope you didn't include that in the statement you gave to Gregor Stark.' Luc laughed. 'Seriously? How close did it come to that?'

'Let's see, I talked him down from intercourse, playing with my tits and snogging him.' Grace laughed. 'See, you're not the only negotiator in the family.'

'I'm glad you avoided that.' Luc pulled her closer and wrapped an arm around her shoulder. 'And I'm glad that pervy wee shite is going back to Barlinnie. I'm going to make sure he gets another two years added for those moves.'

Kidston was relieved to see his wife laugh again. John Wylie's murder had loomed large over the trip, but they seemed to be moving beyond it. They would be home in time for the funeral and that would help too.

In the big soft double bed in the master bedroom, Luc was reminded of how sexually voracious Grace was when she was pregnant. It had happened with Florrie and this time around it was even more intense – possibly connected to their joint brush with a violent death. They couldn't get enough of each other, Grace persuading Luc that the baby was perfectly safe during their energetic sex.

'I knew you'd find me and that you'd save me,' Grace whispered in the warm afterglow of their lovemaking.

Luc kissed her gently on the forehead. 'I think the fates were smiling on us again, Gracie. It's one of the strangest cases I've ever worked; a dog, a white van, a hit-and-run, a doo fleer, the diligence of a young policewoman, and her big neighbour's knowledge of an old football stadium. Can't stress how many pieces of the jigsaw needed to fit together but if Tallulah hadn't chased that van, then the other pieces would have been lost and I might have lost you.'

'I just love these decompression sessions, don't you?' Grace whispered as she pulled him closer.

She knew his answer when he gently pushed her thighs apart.

CHAPTER FIFTY-SIX

Kidston picked up Gregor Stark's expression. The young DS would never have seen anything like it. A phalanx of uniforms lined the long driveways on both the eastern and western approach roads to the large chapel at Linn Crematorium. A group of besuited detectives waited at the chapel entrance for the arrival of the cortège.

'Impressive,' Stark said. 'I hope I get a turnout like that for my funeral.'

'You don't actually,' Sawyers replied. 'A funeral like this means you've died too young. You want to go with only a small handful of mourners. That means you've outlived everyone else.'

'I never thought about it like that.' Stark looked awed by the sense of occasion.

Kidston nodded, a small thin smile on his lips. John Wylie had given his life to save Grace. Kidston would be forever indebted to his fallen comrade.

A sombre-faced Jimmy Gabriel looked like he'd emerged from a *L'Uomo Vogue* fashion shoot in a very expensive black three-piece, fit for the occasion. He was supporting Alison

Metcalfe, who, slightly overwhelmed by the event, had taken her new DI's arm to steady her.

The five detectives made their way along the line towards the chapel. As pall bearers, the four men needed to be in place ahead of the hearse. Kidston, his left hand still tender, was determined to bear the coffin into the service. It was a short distance, and he would be positioned on his good side. As he approached the CID mourners in the line, many former colleagues stepped forward to greet Kidston. Well-meaning handshakes and pats on the back didn't alleviate the guilt Kidston was feeling over John Wylie's death. As they reached the chapel entrance, Kidston spotted Grace, there as a mark of respect to the man who'd saved her from being burned alive. She was with Chrissie McCartney, Peter Costello, and the rest of the community policing team, who were all dressed in their finest parade uniforms. Wylie hadn't been their inspector long, but his team had turned out in full.

Kidston snaked through the crowd towards Grace. He kissed her lightly on the cheek and asked, 'How are you holding up?'

'I'm doing okay, thanks,' Grace replied. 'Chrissie's looking after me. It's quite the attendance, quite the occasion.'

'Wait until the piper starts up, that's when people normally start to lose it,' Kidston said. 'I need to go and get lined up. Are you all set, Peter?'

'Yes, sir,' Costello replied. The big cop fell in alongside Kidston as they made their way to join the pall bearer party. They passed the force's media officer who was shepherding a group of reporters a respectful distance back.

As the hearse led the cortège along the approach path, a police piper, in full Highland dress, started playing 'The Flowers of the Forest'. The uniforms snapped into a smart salute as the coffin passed. The other mourners bowed their heads in respect. The skirl of the bagpipes split the quiet solemnity – the stillness of the occasion now surrendered to the anguished funereal howl of the pibroch. As Kidston bit into the edge of his tongue to hold it all together, he saw that Gregor Stark was crying. The young detective sergeant bowed his head and did a good job of hiding his emotions. They watched as Wylie's partner, Joanne Simpson, supported by her two daughters, was helped from the funeral car. Recognising Kidston and Sawyers, she made her way towards the two men who'd delivered the dreaded death message on that fateful morning. They in turn introduced her to Gabriel, Metcalfe and Stark who'd been with John on the night he was killed.

With the chief mourners safely installed in the chapel, the pall bearers lined up under the direction of the undertakers and lifted their fallen colleague atop their shoulders for his final journey. To the skirl of the Highland bagpipes, Peter Costello, the senior member of Wylie's community policing team, slow marched to the head of the detail and saluted the light oak coffin. The giant cop did a smart about-turn and expertly slow marched ahead of the casket as a last escort into the chapel.

The bearers laid the coffin to rest on the catafalque, allowing the official decorative pall to be draped over the casket. Rich blue velvet plaited in gold tassels and featuring a large Strathclyde Police crest; the thistle, the crown, and the Latin motto *Semper Vigilo*. The pall was then topped with a bouquet of beautiful white lilies and a gold-braided police inspector's hat. The pall bearers took their place in the row behind Joanne and her daughters. The front pew on the other side of the aisle was full of senior officers, impressive in full uniform with all their braid and oak leaf sprigs on show. It made sense when Kidston thought about it – it was extremely rare for an officer to be killed on active duty. John Wylie died a hero. It was fitting that the top brass paid their full respects. Kidston would have preferred that Joe Sawyers had read the eulogy. ACC Farquhar Colquhoun did an okay job, but Kidston was certain he'd never met John Wylie.

As the service concluded the coffin slowly sank into the catafalque, as the hydraulics lowered it at a respectable pace, leaving just the blue velvet pall draped over the empty space. A dramatic departure, like a magician's trick, met with shrieks and loud sobbing. Wylie's final disappearing act. The mourners exited to the sound of Sammy Davis Jr's 'Mr Bojangles' in honour of the fallen detective's old nickname.

––––––

'What are you smiling about, Gregor?' Kidston asked his young colleague.

'I'm thinking about the last conversation I had with John, when he told me how he was punching above his weight with Joanne.' Stark grinned. 'He was right. You can see how John would have fallen for her.'

Kidston agreed. 'Helped him turn his life around. She'd have hoped to have him about for longer.' Kidston's voice cracked. 'That death message was one of the toughest things I've ever had to do in my entire service. Remarkably resilient woman.'

They were part of a sizeable group toasting Wylie's memory. A generous purvey had been laid on at the Busby Hotel. The deceased would have been impressed by the turnout. Soup and sandwiches, sausage rolls, pies and pakora were among the fare on offer, as Joanne Simpson and her daughters mingled among her late partner's friends and colleagues.

Kidston spent some time chatting with Wylie's community policing team. Costello and McCartney were sipping soft drinks. Costello's giant hand gripped a sausage roll that disappeared in two bites. 'Nice purvey.' The big cop wiped his mouth with a napkin. 'Have you tried the pakora?'

'It was very nice,' Kidston replied. 'Chrissie, can I have a quick word, please?' He led the little policewoman to a quieter area of the room.

'Yes, sir, what can I help you with?'

'It's not an ideal setting but it is the right time to discuss this,' Kidston began. 'Have you given much thought to your future in the job?'

'How do you mean, sir?'

'Well, this Canavan case would have turned out very differently without your input. It was your instincts with the Transit van that led us on the path to finding Grace. You've got a bright future ahead of you. That can continue to be in community policing if that's what you want. You'll be a strong candidate for a promotion to sergeant or you might fancy CID. What's next for Chrissie McCartney?'

The young policewoman smiled. 'Do you think I've got the makings of a good detective, sir?'

'CID is crying out for strong female appointments. There's a DC's post here for you at the South if you want it. Have a chat with Peter, talk to Alison Metcalfe, they won't sugar-coat it and you might be in the running for uniform sergeant, but I'd advise you to give some serious thought to it.'

McCartney's smile widened. 'I appreciate you saying that, Mr Kidston. I've always enjoyed working with the CID, especially the big cases.'

'Let me know what you decide, Chrissie. I'll put a good word in for you. You deserve it.'

Kidston moved around the reception meeting old friends and former colleagues. It only took ten minutes for Stark to circle back to his boss, the young DS eager to share something. 'I hear Chrissie McCartney's being considered for CID.'

'My, my.' Kidston smiled. 'Doesn't take you long, Gregor. I hope you're giving her good advice.'

The baby-faced DS looked flustered. 'Well... the thing is–'

'Spit it out, Gregor.'

Stark's cheeks flushed. 'Would it make a difference if Chrissie and I were going out?'

'Is that a thing? Are you and Marianne finished?'

'Marianne ended it. Chrissie and I are having our first date at the weekend, and I didn't want to keep that from you,' Stark began. 'Full disclosure and all that, I know you're not a great fan of office romances.'

'If Chrissie's appointed, she'll be at Gorbals and you're working from DHQ, so there's no obvious problem. I'll even roster you on the same rota for shift work to give the two of you a chance.'

'So no problem then?'

'No problem. Good luck.' Kidston smiled as the young DS scurried off to tell his new romantic interest that they had a green light.

The formal eulogy was forgotten as Wylie's friends exchanged anecdotes about their departed colleague. Polis yarns and war stories flowed. A former crime squad colleague related a tale about an armed turn, where Wylie had the hotel concierge open a drug dealer's room door only to discover that colleagues had provided the wrong room number. The honeymoon couple writhing naked in bed got more excitement than they'd bargained for with two armed detectives rousing them at gunpoint. Kidston smiled as Gregor Stark told the company about a hospital interview, with a sword attack victim of the Gorbals Samurai. The wounded drug dealer, who'd been drunk at the time of the assault, told the officers that he couldn't provide any details of his assailant as he was 'half cut' when the incident occurred. John Wylie had managed to hold in the laughter until the two detectives returned to their car. Stark struggled to remember Wylie's infamous soliloquy about the ragman's trumpet. Kidston could have recounted it word for word, but it was another former colleague who was able to complete the recitation. 'I've been used, abused, and penalised. I've been fucked with the blunt end of the ragman's trumpet.' The peal of laughter across the group and number of nodding heads told of the catchphrase's familiarity. Kidston wasn't surprised – Wylie had been delivering his rant against the bosses for over twenty years.

The man was a bona fide legend.

The man who shot Phil Canavan.

CHAPTER FIFTY-SEVEN

TWO DAYS LATER

K idston and Gabriel had been summoned to headquarters to see Colquhoun. Joe Sawyers was still based in Edinburgh. Gabriel parked the CID car in a tight space in the labyrinthian multi-storey car park built onto the back of the seventies extension to police headquarters. Walking towards the main offices and the basement home of the force's executive suite, they encountered Ronnie Miller making his way back to his car.

'Here's the golden boys.' Miller had more than a note of sarcasm in his voice.

Kidston was in no mood for his insults. Miller had avoided him at John Wylie's funeral. 'Have you had your discipline disposal yet?'

'I've just left the deputy chief's office.' Miller had that big stupid grin on his face. 'Severe reprimand, some equality training programme but no other punishment. I'll be working at HQ for a while though.'

Cockroach, Kidston thought but he was in no mood for a fight. It appeared Gabriel was.

'Did you smash up Luc's Beamer, you shitebag?' Gabriel roared at his fellow DI.

'Who are you calling a shitebag?' Miller's posture altered as he sped up his approach. 'Fuckin' gay boy.' Miller balled his fists and leaned into a fighting stance. 'You're the boxer, Gabriel, come ahead.'

Kidston placed a hand on Gabriel's shoulder. 'Come on, Jimmy, the car attack could just be random... leave it.' But Gabriel was already closing down the space between them.

Miller put his dukes up, rolling his shoulders. Waiting for his opponent.

Gabriel stopped a safe distance back, sprang onto the balls of his feet and started to throw a flurry of left and right hooks, jabs, and uppercuts into empty air. He taunted his rival. 'What's this, Ronnie, Queensberry Rules?' Gabriel threw in a dazzling *Ali Shuffle*, Miller unable to take his eyes off his opponent's dancing footwork.

'Behave you two,' Kidston pleaded but was intrigued as to how the match would play out. He didn't have to wait long.

Miller dropped his hands and closed in on Gabriel, leading with his head. Going for the long, drawn-out, hardman's head-butt, where two opponents rub brows like rutting stags in a dance. That was Gabriel's cue. Expertly executed, the 'Glasgow Kiss' can be a thing of true, violent beauty. Gabriel struck swiftly and decisively; a single blow, using the bony protrusions of his forehead, smashed hard and down onto Miller's nose which erupted in warm, scarlet blood. The bout was over in one strike; Miller, dazed and defeated was rendered helpless to fight back. His black eyes would fade in a week, but he'd probably require a rhinoplasty or otherwise be left with an ugly lifetime reminder of the attack. Jimmy Gabriel had just demonstrated the true art of the Glasgow kiss: the swiftness of the strike; like a mongoose killing a cobra.

They left Miller pulling his shirt tails out to stem the flow of blood from his broken nose and made their way to meet Colquhoun.

'Not the Queensberry Rules then, Jimmy?' Kidston had laughter in his voice. 'Ronnie's been asking for that a long time.'

'Not bad for a gay boy.' Gabriel rubbed his forehead and smiled at his boss.

————

The two detectives sat in Colquhoun's grand office as he outlined the purpose of the meeting. 'John Wylie is being recommended for the Strathclyde Regional Medal for Bravery.' The ACC shuffled some papers on his desk. 'I think the posthumous award will recognise his courage and it will be a fitting tribute for his partner and the family.'

'I think Joanne would prefer a widow's pension to a medal,' Kidston said.

'Come on, Luc,' Colquhoun began. 'It's not the force's fault that they never married.'

Kidston shook his head. 'We need to change the rules, sir. Joanne Simpson was a full-time partner to John, a wife in all but name. It's just unfair.'

Colquhoun looked unimpressed that Kidston was taking the gloss from his medal news. 'And you'll both be put forward for the highest commendations.'

'Well, sir,' Kidston replied, 'I hope that list includes Gregor Stark, Alison Metcalfe, Peter Costello, and Chrissie McCartney. It was very much a team effort and without the group Grace wouldn't have been traced and rescued.'

'Of course, of course,' Colquhoun said. 'I'll make sure all the paperwork goes through you and Joe Sawyers for confirmation. We wouldn't want to miss anyone out.'

CHAPTER FIFTY-EIGHT

THE NEXT DAY

Tam Baillie, the desk sergeant at Gorbals police office clutched the envelope and the letter, staring disbelievingly at its contents. He ushered the mother and son into the small side room in the foyer. The woman's claims had seemed nonsensical, but he thought there may just be a grain of truth in what she was describing.

'Mrs McAnespie, you said, and this is your boy?' Baillie asked. 'How old is he?'

'Aye, this is Elvis,' Mrs McAnespie said. 'He's twelve. Looks older, everybody says.'

The boy was big for his age, and he had a look that Baillie recognised. His face, hunched shoulders and anxious disposition told Baillie that young Elvis McAnespie had been given a serious chastisement by his mother. There was no way the kid was attending the police station without his mammy dragging him there. 'Tell me, son, how did you come into possession of this letter?'

Elvis shot an anxious glance at his mother.

'Tell the sergeant what you told me, Elvis.'

'A man gave me ten quid to hand the letter into the station for the detective.'

'What detective?' Baillie asked. 'It says *Detective Inspector Kidston* on the letter, is that who you asked for?'

'Aye,' Elvis replied sheepishly.

'But you never gave it to him,' Baillie said. 'What happened?'

'I asked the guy on the desk... no' you, the other desk guy but he says DI Kidston disnae work here anymore.'

'What did you do then, son?'

'I'll tell you what he did, Sergeant.' Mrs McAnespie gave her son a dirty look. 'He stuffed the letter back into his pocket and told the man he'd delivered it, so he could keep the tenner. I just found the damn thing in his jeans this morning when I was doing a washing.'

'You've read the contents, Mrs McAnespie?' Baillie asked.

'Aye, when I saw the bit about the twenty thousand pounds I thought it must be one of his daft pals on the wind-up.' Mrs McAnespie was wringing her hands; a deep frown wrinkled her brow. 'But I saw all the stuff about ransom and killing an' that, and it worried me that it could be important. That's just helluva...'

'Helluva,' Baillie agreed. The woman had sounded the word 'helluva' as if it had two 'f's rather than a 'v' but the sergeant had heard many Glasgow women use the term, and understood its application, even if it lacked a degree of specificity. 'Has anyone else touched it other than you two?'

'Naw, Sergeant. Just us two.'

'Have you told anyone else about it?' Baillie asked.

'Naw, I came straight here, Sergeant. It's been in his pocket for over a week.'

'When did you get this, young Elvis?' Baillie reached into a bank of drawers and produced a poly bag, dropping the letter and envelope inside and smoothing it out on the desk.

'It was lunchtime, no' last Thursday but the Thursday before,' Elvis said. 'I was just going to a football training thingy at St Francis' boys' club.'

'Who gave you this?' Baillie held up the poly bag.

'A guy in a big Merc.' Elvis avoided the sergeant's gaze and looked to his mother.

'You told me who it was, now tell the sergeant,' Mrs McAnespie scolded her son.

'Er... it was Johnny Boy McManus.'

———

Baillie phoned upstairs and arranged for full statements to be taken from the McAnespies by CID. He rang the DCI's extension at divisional headquarters.

'DCI Kidston.'

'Boss, it's Tam Baillie at the Gorbals. Canavan's typed ransom note for your wife has just been handed into the office.' He relayed what the McAnespies had reported and read the note over the phone:

'Detective Inspector Kidston,

    We have your wife.

    You have our money.

No harm will come to your wife if you return our £20k that you seized from Arthur Penman on 1st August 1990 at the Lawmoor Industrial Estate. That money is rightly ours. Wrap the money in a black bin liner and place it in the cistern of the gents' toilet at The Pig and Whistle pub by 7pm tonight. Once we have our ransom money your wife will be released. Do not try and double-cross us or she will be killed.

We know where you live.'

'Chilling to hear that, Tam,' Kidston said after a long pause. 'Even if it is two weeks after the event. Johnny Boy was certain that Canavan was going to kill Grace, that's one of the reasons he bailed out. I thought so too.' Hearing Canavan's name made him think about John Wylie; those two names would be forever linked; Grace's too, like some unholy trinity.

'How's your good lady doing now?' Baillie asked.

'She's fine, thanks. Not something she'd ever want to experience again.'

'I can only imagine,' Baillie said. 'I've arranged full statements.'

'Thanks, Tam.' Kidston's thoughts turned to his late nemesis. 'Canavan really thought he was going to get that drugs seizure money back from the office safe. Incredibly stupid plan.'

'Definitely kidnap and extortion,' Baillie said. 'Johnny Boy won't be able to blame it all on his dead boss now. He was the one that got the wee boy to hand it in.'

'Hard to believe Phil Canavan ran a fearsome criminal empire for all that time,' Kidston said.

'Too much cocaine really fucked up his head,' Baillie said. 'All that hate, and paranoia took him to a dark place in the end.'

'Too true, Tam,' Kidston mused. 'I think that investigation took us all to some very dark places.'

THE END

ACKNOWLEDGEMENTS

Huge thanks to Betsy Reavley and her team at Bloodhound Books for the continuing support and for believing in my writing. Thanks to Abbie Rutherford for ensuring that the production process went smoothly. Once again, I'm indebted to my editor Ian Skewis, for applying his considerable talents to my manuscript and for all his advice, support, and encouragement. I worked with Ian on my first novel and had no hesitation in enlisting his expertise for this second book.

I'd also like to place on record my sincere gratitude to my former police colleagues John Weir and Peter McLaughlin for their initial thoughts and constructive feedback on the first draft. John, as a former DCI, keeps Luc Kidston on the right investigatory path. He also floated the idea of 'DNA twins' as a plot device, based on one of his past cases. I had to make some major adjustments to fit it to my plot due to the timeline of the book. DNA was a very new and shiny thing back in 1990. Big thank you to Andrew Sweeney and Lara Lee for not allowing me to stretch my poetic licence too far in relation to the DNA and forensic aspects of the story. To my other police readers and advisors, who prefer to remain in the shadows, I'm truly grateful for your time and feedback. Any remaining police procedural errors in the text are the fault of the author.

Thanks also to all my beta readers, Nick Edmunds, Elizabeth Coby, Isabel Flynn, and Joyce Bingham for their valuable and constructive feedback on the early draft of the novel. We all met through our Open University, Start Writing

Fiction group and it's wonderful to have the support and friendship of so many creative writers.

Cathkin Park still stands as a viable football venue at the time of writing. I was unable to establish beyond doubt that there was a storeroom below the old main stand, but these were a feature of other old stadiums of that era. Other liberties may have been taken in respect of Bennets nightclub. My research suggests that drag nights were held at other venues in Glasgow, but I wove them into my version of Bennets to fit my plot.

Finally, I'm very grateful to my family. As 'first reader', my wife Jacqueline has the early say on what I've produced, and her initial feedback is always invaluable. Huge thanks to Ross, Julie, and Dexter and to my wider family for all their continuing encouragement.

ABOUT THE AUTHOR

John Harkin is a former shipbuilder, police officer and company director. He was born in Glasgow, Scotland, where he still resides. He is married with an adult son. Apart from writing, his passions are music, cinema, books, and football. He is a season ticket holder at Celtic FC.

This is his second novel.

John's books can be found on Amazon, via the link below:

https://amzn.to/3xNyZ9r

Social Media

Twitter: @LuboLarsson

Facebook: www.facebook.com/john.harkin.50

LinkedIn: linkedin.com/in/john-harkin-5b8858l4

A NOTE FROM THE PUBLISHER

Thank you for reading this book. If you enjoyed it please do consider leaving a review on Amazon to help others find it too.

We hate typos. All of our books have been rigorously edited and proofread, but sometimes mistakes do slip through. If you have spotted a typo, please do let us know and we can get it amended within hours.

info@bloodhoundbooks.com

Printed in Great Britain
by Amazon